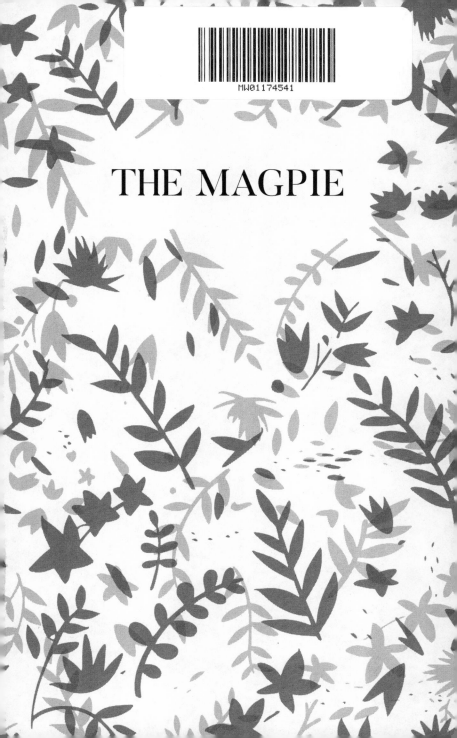

THE MAGPIE

THE MAGPIE

DOUGLAS DURKIN

with a new introduction
by Bart Vautour

Throwback | Invisible Publishing
Halifax & Picton

Durkin, Douglas, author
     The magpie / Douglas Durkin ; introduction by Bart Vautour.

Originally published: Toronto: Hodder and Stoughton, 1923.
Issued in print and electronic formats.
ISBN 978-1-988784-13-7 (softcover).--ISBN 978-1-988784-17-5 (EPUB)

     I. Vautour, Bart, 1981-, writer of introduction II. Title.

PS8507.U76M3 2018   C813'.52   C2018-905205-8
                                             C2018-905206-6

Cover and interior design by Megan Fildes
Typeset in Laurentian & Slate
With thanks to type designer Rod McDonald

Printed and bound in Canada

Invisible Publishing | Halifax & Picton
www.invisiblepublishing.com

We acknowledge the support of the Canada Council for the Arts, which last year invested $20.1 million in writing and publishing throughout Canada.

To the Memory
of
My Father

INTRODUCTION

by Throwback Books editor Bart Vautour

THE MAGPIE is about many things: it's about struggling First World War veterans, it's about politics, it's about economics, it's about labour movements, it's about Winnipeg and the prairies, it's about romance, love, and betrayal, it's about class and generational divides, and it's about the struggle to articulate the complexities of living in an increasingly fragmented world. And as if that's not enough to keep us turning the pages of his novel, Douglas Durkin skilfully provides additional depth by utilizing art to think through all of these issues of post-war, modern society. Whether it's literature, painting, or sculpture, Durkin asks us to use art (and his characters' reactions to, and deployment of, art) in order to attend to the world—both his and ours—as clearly and as precisely as possible. For me it's this lens—this interpretive framework—that keeps this historical novel undeniably current after nearly a hundred years.

Durkin's novel opens in July of 1919 with the protagonist, Craig Forrester, writing a journal entry on the eve of his thirtieth birthday. In this short excerpt, the protagonist—ironically nicknamed "The Magpie" due to his reluctance to voice his opinions—sets the scene of the cultural, social, and political climate that persists throughout the book: the post-war world is "shaking" and caught between hope that the war was fought in order to usher in a better world and the conflicting efforts of the capitalist class to reconstruct pre-war social, political, and economic stratification (9). As a result, class antagonisms become increasingly pronounced throughout the novel. Having come to the city from a rural farm childhood to take a job at the Winnipeg Grain Exchange shortly before his deployment to Europe, Craig is seemingly able to travel across class lines. But the first thing the reader learns about Craig (other than his impending birthday) is his discomfort with effusive talk:

> Yesterday I picked up young Dick Nason and drove him home. Dick is just twenty. I confess I felt a little uncomfortable with Dick. I always do. Dick doesn't know there has been a war. He insists that life is pretty rotten and that nothing really counts. Dickie says that we need a few Oscar Wildes and a few Shelleys to bring the world back to form. He thinks the world ought to be psychoanalysed. [...] Dickie talks a great deal about—mostly about talk... (9)

The awkwardness of Craig's interactions with Dick Nason stems from the latter's disengagement from social and political matters through an approach to life as artistic performance—that is, an art for art's sake performance. By beginning the book with this focus on Dick Nason's aestheticism, Durkin is signalling that readers will be asked to think about the role of art in social engagement, a persistent issue as relevant in the twenty-first century as it was in the 1920s. Through his protagonist, Durkin comes down squarely on the side of socially engaged art, but is also clear that art doesn't solve any problems by itself.

One of the many uses Durkin makes of a sustained metaphor of artistic production is to undermine strict divisions between urban and rural identity in common representations of Canadian masculinity. For example, Durkin offers us a sense of his protagonist through a sort of slideshow of clichéd characterizations: "If traditions were followed to the letter, Craig Forrester should be painted as a man in shirt sleeves, guiding a plow across a field at the other end of which a blood-red sun sinks in a sky of pale amber" (14). Instead of representing Craig as the archetypical masculine settler-Canadian, Durkin presents Craig Forrester as a modern amalgam of the urban and the rural. Durkin suggests that it was "old man Forrester, Craig's father, who had ordained that his son should don a suit of business grey instead of the toggery of romance" (15). Importantly here, the decision made by Craig's father was not made out of a desire for his son's upward mobility, but as an idealistic extension of his own work on the farm: he told his son to go to the city "and learn the business of bringing the wheat to the people of other lands that can't grow it the way we can" (15). In positioning Craig as a cosmopolitan practitioner of both rural and urban life, Durkin undermines the nostalgic tendencies of early-twentieth-century Canadian writing to plant masculine identity firmly in country soil. Craig is painted into a complex characterization of modern settler-Canadian society, accompanied by the contradictions and anxieties that such a position implies.

The Magpie offers neither a totalizing anti-modern, nostalgic portrait of rural Canada nor a comfortable identification with the artistic solipsism embodied by the performative urbanity of Dick, the bourgeois young man who attempts to shock and spurn his family by adopting the role of an aesthete. The book's opening pages foreshadow a continued search for an artistic mode of production to match Craig's growing social and political convictions in response to both global political instability and localized social and political crises.

Craig's continued search for an adequate means of representing his personal values takes on a more prominent role as the book continues. He comes to identify the sinister character of the compulsive drive towards progress and efficiency as the "Machine." He searches for a way to articulate the "Something-or-other that was opposed to the Machine. He thought of calling it by various names. The Soul. Humanity. The Spirit. Perhaps it was the Ideal. Perhaps there was no word for it in the language" (159). Craig begins to develop a better understanding of the "Something-or-other" through the figure of Martha Lane, his childhood sweetheart.

Craig encounters transformation with Martha's sculptures and finds a mode of expression in Martha's modernist practice that matches an epiphanic experience he had in Flanders, which helps characterize the "Something-or-other" he sought to articulate in opposition to the "Machine." This moment of insight in Martha's studio signals Craig's increasing ability to express his own principles and values, to find his own voice.

Readers won't be surprised to learn that the social and political strife of post-war Canada isn't magically resolved in the novel. *The Magpie* remains a realist novel from start to finish. For me, it's the way Durkin focuses not on resolution in the text, but on the necessity of finding articulation, that keeps me returning to this novel. Durkin allows a sub-plot about artistic experimentation embedded within the realist narrative to consolidate the values of the novel's protagonist. For Craig, aestheticism is too detached from society, nostalgic romanticization thwarts modern realties by mythologizing the Canadian past, and corporate appropriation of art aestheticizes a capitalist logic that espouses inequitable social relations. In placing a figural modernist production in the background of his own realist narrative framework, Durkin articulates ways in which multiple artistic practices might arise in the settler-Canadian context to help articulate a social and political understanding of his contemporary moment. This new edition of *The Magpie* serves as a timely reminder of the necessity of clearly articulating current social and political conditions as a prerequisite to affecting change, and how crucial art is to finding that critical voice.

PART ONE | MARION

CHAPTER I.

One

ON AN EVENING in the last week of July, 1919, The Magpie wrote in his book:

"To-morrow I shall be thirty years old. I wonder if there ever was a time in the history of the world when it meant so much to be thirty... Yesterday I picked up young Dick Nason and drove him home. Dick is just twenty. I confess I felt a little uncomfortable with Dick. I always do. Dick doesn't know there has been a war. He insists that life is pretty rotten and that nothing really counts. Dickie says that we need a few Oscar Wildes and a few Shelleys to bring the world back to form. He thinks the world ought to be psychoanalyzed. He is just finishing his second reading of the memoirs of someone he calls by the name of Casanova. He says I ought to read them now that I have gained a reading knowledge of French. Dickie talks a great deal about— mostly about talk... Old Dad Robinson, the janitor, thinks the world is lost and that civilization is crumbling. At least he says the world is shaking. The war was a blight and peace, he says, is a disease. He looks for an act of God to restore the world to its happy condition of five years ago. I think Dad's chief concern is the fact that he hasn't been able to buy a couple of favourite varieties of tulip that he used to get from England. When he can get the tulips he will be in a fair way to admit that God's in His heaven again and the world set right... For my part I think I like old Dad's view-point pretty well. Dad's past fifty—perhaps that's why I like him. A man of fifty may be wrong in what he thinks about the world, but he's probably right in what he feels. There's something wrong in the way Dickie feels, though perhaps he thinks a little more clearly on some things than I did when I was twenty. And yet—I can't tell. I can understand Dad. I can talk with him and feel no irritation. When I talk with Dick I seem to lose my sense of humour... Sometimes I feel I am too old for the world I have come back to. Other times I feel I am too young... But I hold that somehow, somewhere, there is a Power in the world that works for good and that in the end the sacrifice will not have been made in vain. We are in a fog just now, a great fog that covers the western world and hides the sun from our eyes. But the light will break through—somewhere—somehow—and the new life will have begun. There are some who are already talking of getting back to normalcy, but those who have seen the light shining against the darkness that hung for four years over the fields of Flanders know that we cannot return to normalcy. We cannot return to the days when the people and even the parliaments knew nothing of what was going on behind their backs until they were asked to give their lives to vindicate the bad bargains of the diplomats. All that is past... I am sure of it. If it were not for that faith..."

The telephone ringing from the hall startled him. He got up from his table and went to answer the call.

"Yes?" he said in a voice that was heavily resonant, almost raucous.

It was Mrs. Nason, mother of young Dickie Nason. Her daughter, Marion, had told her that to-morrow was a day of more than ordinary significance in his life—she wanted to have an opportunity to offer her congratulations and good wishes—they had come in from their summer cottage at Minaki to meet Mr. Nason whom they expected back from England where he had gone on a business trip—he would be back to-night—she was having a few friends in to dinner with a little music afterwards and a little chat or a game of bridge—anyhow, would he join them at dinner to-morrow evening about seven—no dinner party was complete nowadays without its war hero—she would promise that he would not be asked one question during the evening, about his experiences at the front—and Marion would be there to tease him—and, well, would he come?

The Magpie listened until the flood of Mrs. Nason's chatter had ceased, then drew a deep breath and coughed slightly to clear his voice.

"Nothing could keep me away," he said. "I don't think I have had a real dinner since I sat at your table the last time, to say nothing of the other things you promised. I'll be there, Mrs. Nason."

"Quite informal, you understand."

"That makes it better still."

"Then we'll look for you at seven."

"Righto, and thank you for remembering me. Give my regards to Miss Nason."

A moment later he hung up the receiver thoughtfully and went back to his table. Mrs. Nason's garrulity always swept him off his feet. Her verbal assaults left him breathless.

Presently he drew himself forward and lifted his pen as he leaned above the book in which he had been writing.

"If it were not for that faith..." he read and then slowly put his pen to the paper. "...I could not live," he finished the sentence.

He closed the book quietly and laid it away in the upper right-hand drawer of his table.

CHAPTER II.

One

APART FROM A RATHER RAUCOUS QUALITY in his voice, there was little about Craig Forrester to justify the nickname his younger business associates in the Winnipeg Grain Exchange had given him within a month after he had sought his seat and opened his office on the seventh floor of the building on Lombard Street. In fact, the first man who had called him "The Magpie" had done so from a sense of humour that Craig considered somewhat perverted. He had been listening to an argument that had lasted for nearly an hour without his having taken any part in it. It was a habit of Craig's to let others do the talking.

"Have you nothing to say, Forrester?" one of the men asked.

"Forrester is the original magpie when it comes to talking," another remarked. And the name stuck.

Craig had often longed to be able to chatter about trifles as other men did. He found it difficult even to exchange ideas on matters of moment. Almost invariably, when an idea struck him relevant to the question under discussion, someone else had blurted out the very thing that was in his mind before he had more than half framed his thoughts in words.

"Craigie has a nimble wit but a heavy tongue," his father had said of him in the old days.

Both sides of his father's observation were true. Slow of speech as he was, he had a gift of quick analysis that was almost uncanny. While he listened to others talking, he fitted their opinions into a kind of geometric plan that rose instinctively in his mind every time he heard an argument. Logic for him was a kind of symmetry. Truth was a balance of form. He sensed an error in judgment as a carpenter might sense an error in length or breadth or height. His religion was a faith in the order of the world in which he lived. Friendship was an experiment in the harmony of human nature.

If his silence in the company of others was a source of amusement—and sometimes of annoyance—to his friends, Craig Forrester found in it little cause for uneasiness. Talkers, as such, were a terrible test of a man's patience.

"Besides," he protested, "I may learn to speak a few words—some day. Magpies do."

Two

If traditions were followed to the letter, Craig Forrester should be painted as a man in shirt sleeves, guiding a plow across a field at the other end of which a blood-red sun sinks in a sky of pale amber. The British emigrant would then recognize him immediately as a Canadian. His sleeves would be rolled above his brown elbows, the legs of his trousers tucked snugly into the tops of boots that reach to the knees. In the distance a group of grain elevators would lift their square forms against an aureole of light borrowed from a westering sun, while a railway train of prodigious length would creep over a gilded prairie carrying with it the highly romantic suggestion that ocean is linked to ocean across the measureless reaches of a vast continent. Or he might take the form of a sturdy figure hewing his way through giant forests, guiding a frail canoe on its perilous course down a treacherous river with walls of granite on either side, battling his way through blinding blizzards with a half dozen pelts slung over his shoulder, or dancing a jig on a log that leaps down the rapids and threatens him with instant destruction at every whirl of the current.

Craig Forrester, as a matter of fact, might have sat for any of the above posters-portraits and done credit to the subject. It was old man Forrester, Craig's father, who had ordained that his son should don a suit of business grey instead of the toggery of romance. Old Forrester had been a railroad contractor in the days when the West was still young and had invested some of his money in a section of land as an earnest of faith in the country's future. At twenty, Craig had been sent to college. At twenty-four, the year before the Great War broke out, he had been presented with a seat in the Winnipeg Grain Exchange as a gift from his father on the occasion of his graduation from the university.

There had been nothing accidental in the choice of a place in the business world for Craig Forrester. He and his father were alone in the world and were more like brothers in their treatment of each other.

"I'll stay on at the farm, Craig," old John Forrester had said, "and go on with the work on the soil. Go down to the city and learn the business of bringing the wheat to the people of other lands that can't grow it the way we can."

"Yes, John," Craig had said in reply; "I think I'd like that."

A little more than twelve months later the world was shaken by the news that war had broken upon Europe. Craig Forrester had closed his office one day and had driven out to have a talk with his father. When he returned the next day a new pride thrilled in his heart. The preachers who raised their voices on behalf of a violated Belgium and called a nation's Youth to the defence of an outraged Humanity gave Craig Forrester little or nothing to think about. He was twenty-five, clear-eyed and direct, sound in wind and limb—and his father had spoken!

But something had happened after that...

Three

One day, in the path of the retreating Germans, he had come upon trees denuded of their bark and left to die. He had touched their bleeding trunks with his fingers and had stood while the sadness in his heart turned to bitterness and then to hatred. As he turned away pride in the Great Adventure vanished from his heart.

Three days later word reached him that his father had died. He could not help thinking of the trees and their bleeding trunks. Had John Forrester's heart bled to death because it had been stripped of his son's companionship? The comparison was not apt, but Craig could not get it out of his mind.

That night he had written in his book: "The world can never be the same after this madness has passed. If we come out of it alive only to find that the world is standing where we left it, someone will have to pay. If I ever get back—"

He had added something more, drawn his pencil through it, thought for a long time, and finally set his diary aside without completing the sentence.

Henceforth there had been pride neither in youth, nor in birth, nor in nation, nor in empire. For days and nights he had talked as he had never talked before, not of England or of France or of Germany or of Russia—these things were interests of a day, of a month, of a year—but of things that old men talk of and that young men weave into the fabric of their dreaming. The world could never be the same—and please God the world would know it when the men got home and buckled to the task that awaited them.

Craig Forrester, it seemed, had grown suddenly old.

Four

For weeks, then, Craig had struggled to put out of mind the memory of the easeful days he had spent on the farm with his father. They had been good days, days full of the quiet purposefulness of the season's routine, rich days for all that they were filled with tasks that moved in a circle and brought one back again to seed-time and harvest and winter marketing if one had but the patience to wait. It was these days he remembered rather than the days at college and the later days of hurry and confusion on the exchange. More than once under French skies he had dreamed of taking to the fields in the morning, suiting his long stride to the gait of his team, lifting his face to the stirring breeze with the fragrance of the soil and the dewy grass. But those were the symbols of the old life. He struggled to put them all behind him.

The world had changed—it could never be the same.

Something of the spirit of blind patriotism had swept through him when, with the touch of the soft spring air on his cheek and the cries of his own people in his ears, he had again set foot firmly on Canadian soil. For a moment the old thrill had come back to him. Again he thanked God for his birthright and was unashamed. That, too, had passed.

The world had changed—it could never be the same...

Then had followed days and nights when he had luxuriated in the clean delights and warm comforts that had been denied him for more than three years. Unutterably weary in mind and body, he had rested till, at the end of a month, the old discontent had set in again. He had returned to his work. When the New Day broke it would find him in the market as it would find other men in the street and the shop. For try as he might, Craig could not put away the feeling that the change, when it came, would be a matter of days—weeks at most. It was to be a miracle brought about by the wise men who sat in the councils of the old lands and knew what the world expected of them.

For days Craig went about his work as a man might into whose ear God had whispered the Secret.

The world had changed—it could never be the same...

Five

And while Craig waited, the whole world waited, too, its great men silent, its leaders dumb, shocked by the war's close as it had been stunned by its coming, standing drunkenly at the cross roads not knowing which way to turn.

CHAPTER III.

One

WITH A COUPLE OF HOURS TO SPARE before he was due at the Nason's for dinner, Craig left his office and made his way across the street to where his car stood among a score of others in a vacant space beside a garage.

Half way across the street, he heard his name called and turned to see Claude Charnley, one of the younger brokers on the Winnipeg Grain Exchange, hailing him from the sidewalk.

"How about a game of golf, Magpie?" Charnley suggested.

Craig shook his head. "I'm due at the Nasons' for dinner," he replied. He knew that Claude Charnley counted himself a friend of the Nasons.

"The Nasons? Lucky Magpie! Give my best to Marion. Tell her I'm still waiting for that little game of golf she promised before she goes back to Minaki next week."

"I've got a poor memory, Charnley," Craig replied, but Charnley was already gone and Craig turned and crossed the street to his car.

There was something very characteristic in that last little speech of Charnley's. There was something, too, that made Craig feel a fool for having mentioned the fact that he was going to have dinner with the Nasons. Remind Marion of the game she had promised Charnley some day next week? Certainly, if the occasion presented itself. The thing that nettled Craig was the fact that behind the apparently innocent request was a thinly veiled suggestion that Charnley stood in very well indeed with the Nasons, especially with Marion, and that he wished to have the fact taken for granted. Craig was only too ready to take it for granted and yet—the fellow's manner annoyed him unreasonably.

He shook the thought of Charnley from his mind and climbed into his seat behind the wheel. Speeding south along Main Street, Craig found himself wishing, as he had wished many times since his return from overseas, that he could drive on out and find John Forrester waiting for him at the old place. Instead he sent the car round the corner of Portage Avenue and headed west through the city.

Two

Five minutes later his eyes fell upon a figure that seemed vaguely familiar. The man was walking westward along the avenue, his shoulders slouched forward and his head hanging. Craig drew closer to the curb and leaned out to get a better look at the man.

"Lord, that looks like Dyer," he said to himself.

As he spoke, the man turned his face slightly toward him.

"Ho, Dyer!" Craig called.

The man halted abruptly and turned. Suddenly his shoulders lifted and squared and a smile spread over his face.

"God, if it isn't the Cap!"

"Hello, Sarg! Jump in and take a ride. Where are you going?"

Dyer stepped toward the car as Craig opened the door. "I'm just thinking of striking for home, Cap. Take me as far as you're going—straight ahead. You can kick me out when you want to turn back. But how's tricks?"

"Fair. How goes it with you, Jimmy?"

"Not so good, Cap, not so good. We got back about a week after your lot and—"

"I remember seeing it in the papers. I kept track of the

units returning from day to day until I got tired of it finally and gave it up. But I remember—"

"So you're getting back to normal, too, eh? Kept track of them for two weeks and then gave it up, eh?"

Craig was sensitive under the cynical smile Dyer turned upon him. "I'm not getting back to normal, Jim, but—"

"But you find it too much to go on fighting the war here after you've done it over there, eh? Don't think I'm panning you for it, Cap. I began to forget about who was coming home in about a week. The fact is we can't go on thinking about it. What's more, if we do we'll be doing our thinking alone. They're all doing their damnedest to forget about it. They're sticking a few hundred of the broken ones in hospitals here and there and they're putting in a cenotaph and a bronze tablet here and there for the fellows who won't be back. For the rest of us they're putting green seats in the parks where we can sit down and go over our troubles if we want to without being asked to move on. In a year's time they'll send us a medal with a couple of inches of coloured ribbon and a form letter and the thing will be all over. Instead of shouting 'On to Berlin' they'll change it to 'Back to Normalcy.' We've spent four years of the best part of our lives fighting for the big fellows, and we'll spend the rest of our days working for them just the same as we did before the war. The only real difference is that we had a band or two and a banner or two and a chaplain or two to remind us that we were fighting for the glory of God and the brotherhood of mankind, and now we have the squalls of hungry kids and the insults of a few God damned slackers to cheer us on our way. That sums it up for me, just about."

They were whirling along towards the outskirts of the city and Craig's eyes were on the open sky before them while he listened to Dyer's talking.

"We've got to be a little patient, Jimmy," he observed quietly. "The war wasn't won in a day and the thing we fought for won't happen till the air is cleared of the smoke."

"It's all right, Cap, to talk of having patience, but the other fellows aren't losing any time, believe me. What about those strike leaders waiting their trials in the jail? What about the raids on the homes of the—"

"Perhaps we don't know everything about that, either, Jimmy. If we'd been on the ground a couple of months earlier—"

"Earlier—hell! Those fellows made mistakes—of course they did. They're only men, after all. But their hearts were right, Cap, whatever their heads did for them. Don't make any mistake about it, the reason these fellows were branded as Reds and Bolsheviki was because of what they had in here"—he struck his breast as he spoke—"not because of their wrong thinking. The guys on the other side of the business, the big fellows who called out the Mounties and had the streets cleared with bullets, don't worry any about how we think. It's how we feel that's got them worrying. They can think rings around us and they know it. They think in terms of policemen and reserves and penitentiaries and deportations. That's the machinery that does their thinking for them and it's dead easy, Cap, dead easy."

For some time, then, they were both silent, Craig's eyes following the road ahead of the car, Dyer's eyes lifted toward the open country that began to show itself already between the houses set apart from each other in the sparsely settled suburbs.

"The trouble is," Craig ventured at last, "if the Labour element took over the reins from the present governing bodies, it's a question whether we'd be any better off for it. Revolution of the sort they tried in Russia won't appeal to the people of this country. In the first place, Dyer, the Radicals have nothing to offer the workers. There is no peasantry here and the land isn't in the hands of the aristocracy. If they seized the industries and put themselves in the positions of management, it would only reverse the present order, it would only turn it upside down. There would still be a bottom and a top and the real problem would be as far as ever from being solved."

"Well, damn it—who has a better right to a turn at the top than the poor beggars who waded through filth to keep the top on the damned system?"

"Admitting that, Jimmy," Craig replied, "it doesn't seem to me to get at the rights of things. After what we've been through it seems to me there ought to be a new sense of justice, a new intelligence, a different ordering of things, somehow. This business of throwing one class against another ought to be left where it belongs. It ought to be left to the history of the days before the war. The world is looking for something else now. It's looking for men who will forget class distinctions at home just as they did in the trenches. There were no sects there—there should be at least less of that kind of thing now that the lesson has been learned. There was no Labour and Capital there—they should get together here. There was no high and low in the mud in Flanders—why should we begin to make the distinction as soon as we get back again to our own country?"

"I don't know why it is, Cap, but I know it isn't going to be any other way as long as two human beings are left together on the earth. The stronger one is going to beat the other and take what he wants. When he's got it he's going to make it wrong for the under-dog to take it back. You seem to forget that there isn't much difference between Might and Right in this world, Cap. The Boche didn't argue the point. Our preachers prayed that Right would win, but they were pretty damned sure it would win only if it had enough men and enough ammunition and enough money to back it. It doesn't help a man much to be right if he isn't strong enough to lick hell out of the man who is wrong. The kind of a world you'd like is the kind of a world a whole lot of us would like, but it's the kind of a world the dirty blighters in control won't let us have. You can stake your last dollar on that, Cap. It's a nice thing to dream of a perfect world, but we have to look things in the face and fight through."

They had come to the street down which Jimmy lived. They were in the heart of a little straggling suburban village and Craig drew his car to a stand at the curb near the corner. From where they sat they could look clear away over the wide prairies to the westward with only a house here and there in the distance to break the even line of the horizon.

The sun was still far from setting and a bank of dark cloud was lifting straight before them. A breeze had sprung up with a welcome promise of rain in it and the two men sat with their faces lifted to catch the fresh fragrance it bore them from the fields. A saucy jay shot down from a tree near the road and perched on a fence-post only a few feet away. Craig sat back in his seat and filled his lungs with the pure air.

"Jimmy," he said, "I'd rather work a nice farm out there on those plains than take the place of the Prince of Wales."

"Well, Cap," Dyer observed, "being a prince isn't as popular as it used to be—and it looks to me like it's going to be less popular than it is."

Craig laughed and let his hand fall heavily on Dyer's knee. "Let's leave princes and kings to themselves, Jimmy, and talk of cabbages for a while. Have you got a garden?"

"You bet I have. Get out and come up to the house for a

minute and meet the wife. It isn't often she has a chance to meet a self-respecting man these days. A man's got to hob-nob with his kind—that's a part of getting back to normal."

"Cut it out, Jimmy," Craig protested. "Don't let 'em get you to thinking less of yourself now that you're through with the big job."

They got down from the car and took the plank walk that led north from the pavement.

"Our mansion, Cap," Dyer announced as he halted before a gate and waved his hand for Craig to enter. "Built it myself and paid for it out of a little over four years' savings. Not bad, eh?"

"I'll say it isn't," Craig agreed.

The "mansion" was a little green and white "shack" standing well back from the street in the shadow of two small elms whose branches swept the roof. The low afternoon sun, striking the wild cucumber vines that cloaked the tiny porch, and pinning a bright disc of light on the stove-pipe that rose from the brick chimney, lighted a picture that touched Craig to the heart. A low straggling hedge was being encouraged with bits of string to grow along the wooden fence that enclosed the little patch of lawn. Stiff blue asters stood in a prim row on either side of the pebble walk that led to the door. Flanking the lawn on the left, boldly in sight, green tomatoes hung on their propped-up stems, separated by a narrow path from the potato-patch, dusty green in the sun.

As Craig and Jimmy approached the door, a lusty yell rang out from somewhere within, followed by a slamming door in the rear. Immediately Jimmy's wife appeared on the front doorstep, flustered but smiling.

"Kids raising Cain, Millie?" Jimmy greeted her, and threw an arm about her waist. "This is Captain Craig Forrester—

you've heard me talk enough about him to know him at first sight. Met him just when I was thinking of hopping on a car and coming home. What do you think of my wife, Cap?"

Millie Dyer blushed shyly and extended her hand to Craig. He noticed that under her retiring manner she was searching him with eyes that were full of understanding and shrewd insight. After an exchange of greetings she turned and led the way into the house. She had a quick, almost bird-like way of moving, and a pleasant, slow voice, as if she had all the time in the world to talk to one. But Craig saw in her face an old sadness the same expression he had seen in the faces of the English and the French women of the lower classes even during the height of the rejoicing that followed the close of the war. It had a certain ineradicable beauty—like shadow caught in a tree that is full of sunlight, thought Craig.

The pieces of furniture in the living-room to which Craig was ushered might have been counted in one sweep of the eye. There was linoleum on the pine board floor and the chairs were of cheap wicker covered with gay cretonne. On the walls were prints of "The Angelus" and "The Age of Innocence." A tall vase full of fragrant sweet peas stood beside a book on the table in the middle of the room. Somehow, in spite of the bareness of the place, there had crept into it the tender, unmistakable feeling of home, a feeling Craig had not experienced in many another house where he had been welcomed among luxurious surroundings.

"How about having a little supper with us, Cap?" Jimmy Dyer suggested with a glance toward his wife.

"I'd like that fine, Jimmy," Craig replied, "but I've a dinner engagement in town. Make it another time and I'll be out."

"We'll do that—sure! We'll drink a glass of something cold, then, and I'll take you out to see the garden. It isn't much of a place, this, but it keeps out the rain. Have to sit up most of the night in the winter time to keep the stove from going out and leaving us to freeze to death, but it's a good spot in the summer. Where are the kids, Millie?"

"They got so noisy that I shooed them out into the back yard," Millie answered from the kitchen. Presently she brought in a tray with a bowl of fruit punch and glasses, carrying it a little self-consciously.

"How long have you lived out here, Jimmy?" Craig asked.

"You mean, how long has Millie lived out here," returned Jimmie. "I say it's more like her house than mine. We moved into the place just six months before I enlisted and she lived here alone with the kids while I was away. Great life, eh, Millie, keeping the home fires burning and all that rot?"

Millie laughed and tucked back a little strand of hair that was faintly grey. "It was. I believed I was doing something that would count later. But I guess the women don't know much about what will come of it all. It doesn't look any too good for us yet."

"It will—it will," Craig said quietly.

"If it doesn't," she observed, "perhaps—next time—we won't be so careful about the home fires—we won't be so willing to look after them."

A little spark of light shone in her eyes—a spark, Craig knew, that might very easily kindle into a flame of anger.

"Let's take a look at the garden, then," Jimmy suggested.

In the backyard Craig came upon three sturdy youngsters engaged in the task of erecting a see-saw. The youngest, a tow-headed little girl of about five, stood admiring her brothers who were lugging a heavy plank from one end of the lot. The children, quite subdued, were introduced in turn to Craig and then went off with a matter-of-fact air to attend to their own affairs.

Millie accompanied the men to the chicken-coop, the exterior of which Jimmy had covered with tar paper and criss-crossed with pieces of lath. On the roof of the coop he had placed sod from which long silky grass and yellow sow-thistles had sprung.

"My chicks deserve a good home," said Millie. "They do their little bit very well."

Jimmie was inordinately proud of his garden. He went into great detail about his painstaking cultivation of the plot, from the preparing of the soil to the combatting of the insects that attacked the grown plants. The luxuriance of the growth was something good to look upon and Craig felt himself yielding to the old desire to be back again to the soil and the rich, free, growing power of it. He loved it all—the plumy, red-green beet-tops, the feathery tops of the carrots—the healthy pea-vines, heavily podded—the beans yellowing in the warm light—the lettuce plants, pale and transparent, still crisp and upright at the end of the season.

"You ought to be very happy here," Craig said to Millie Dyer. "There's nothing in the world that's quite so good as making things grow."

"Yes. You can be happy anywhere if you have the thing you want most," she replied, smiling up at him. "We don't ask for very much, either. We want a home—a little place is just as good as a big place if it's really a home. It wasn't a home with Jimmy away."

Craig smiled. "No—it wouldn't be," he agreed.

They took their way around the side of the little house and Craig paused before a small but well-kept bed of red poppies.

"That's our remembrance bed, Cap," Jimmy explained. "My old girl is a bit sentimental and—"

"You planted half of them yourself," Millie protested.

Jimmy laughed and winked at Craig. "I'll own up to it. We planted that bed the spring before the war broke out, just five of 'em. One for me and one for her and one for each of the kids. We were sitting on the porch there the night we decided that I had to go if the war wasn't over in a few weeks at most. Millie looked out here from where she was sitting and—we won't tell any secrets, eh?" he broke off suddenly, looking at his wife. "Anyhow, she's kept the seed and planted it every summer—and that's what she had to show when I got back a few weeks ago. What do you think of it?"

Craig was touched deeply by the little expression of simple sentiment the poppy bed symbolized and found it hard to say anything in reply to Jimmy Dyer's question. He looked from Jimmy to his wife and then back again to the poppy bed.

"Somehow or other," he said, "you've got the right idea."

Then he took his leave hurriedly, promising to call again without leaving it off too long. But the memory of the poppy bed was to remain with him for many a long day.

CHAPTER IV.

One

IT WAS CHARACTERISTIC OF CRAIG'S FRAME OF MIND in those days that when he made his way briskly up the walk that led to the Nason house, the place seemed stranger to him than on the first day he had seen it. Though he had spent only brief periods in England during his stay overseas, his heart had warmed gradually toward the English manner of living and especially toward the English home. He had often smiled to himself at the Englishman's inordinate capacity for arriving at results—in the laying out of his home—that would have driven the average Canadian to exasperation. In fact, the English home had never really been planned at all. It seemed to have simply grown. Its great hall, its countless rooms, its endless succession of doors leading mysteriously one never knew where, its "quarters" and its old fireplaces that were really designed to give warmth to the place—everything gave it an air of leisure and reminded one that life might be lived quietly and slowly and at the same time yield its fair share of genuine pleasure. There was always the softness of old memories about the places he had visited in the old country, always the mellowness of age. Generation after generation had left its bit of quiet romance that clung like a kind of fragrance to the shadowy walls and the old staircases. After a few visits to English houses Craig had forgiven the old men their patronizing ways and the youngsters their questions about wild Indians and cowboys.

There was nothing like that about the house that stood at the end of the walk down which Craig swung in pleasant anticipation of the evening he was to spend with the Nasons. As westerners reckon time, the house of Gilbert Nason was an old house. It had been one of the first houses built in that section of Winnipeg that lies to the south of the Assiniboine River and west of the point where the river describes a crescent before it joins the historic Red a scant half mile away. Gilbert Nason had been one of the men whose belief in the future of the city was as firm as their belief in God, and ten times more profitable. In fact, while his faith in the Almighty had wavered more than once when he had had trouble with Labour Unions, he could not recall one investment in real estate that had failed to vindicate his faith in the good sense and the vision that had prompted him to make it.

Gilbert Nason's house was a monument to those two qualities that were supreme in his personality. It was daily pointed to as the kind of thing that comes to a man who had the good sense and the vision that Gilbert Nason boasted. There was no fence, no wall, not even a hedge along the front of the plot of ground on which the house stood. A wide drive made a half circle which was cut in two by small clumps of shrubbery placed rather too precisely on either side of the walk. The house itself was almost majestic with its three full storeys topped by a roof of red tile and flanked on one side by a small wing composed mostly of windows, and on the other by a stone porch which served as a shelter for visitors entering the house from automobiles. At the back of the house stood a garage for the accommodation of three cars, and beyond, a sloping tree-covered bank that fell away to the river. The windows in the house were all large and Craig had never seen the shades drawn, even at night. It was as if Gilbert Nason wished it to be clearly understood that he had no secrets to keep from the world and disliked any man who had.

Craig's senses had always played him a trick on approaching the house from the street. They did so now as he crossed the drive at the end of the walk and mounted the short flight of stone steps to the door. He imagined he caught the pungent smell of lime in fresh mortar...

Two

Marion Nason opened the door in answer to Craig's ring.

"Hello, hello!" she cried and put out both her hands to him. "Congratulations and many happy returns!"

Craig stepped toward her and took her hands in his. "It's awfully nice of you to remember me in this way," Craig replied. "I hope you don't think I let the secret out the other day just to give you time to invite me to dinner to celebrate."

"I believe you did," Marion replied.

"I'm quite capable of it," Craig observed. "I'll do the same thing every year till I'm a doddering old fool if it produces the same results."

Marion laughed and shook her head. "Come on—we have some friends for dinner—one especially who wants to meet you."

She came close to him and dropped her voice almost to a whisper. "She's a war widow, but she's young and—come on, you'll see for yourself."

She took him by the hand and pulled him after her across the hall and through an open doorway into a small reception-room. Mrs. Nason got up from where she had been sitting and came forward to meet him. "So here you are!" she greeted him, extending her hand. "My, but you're looking well! Here's our hero, Jeannette." She turned toward a handsome young woman in her early thirties who lifted her head slightly and smiled as Mrs. Nason spoke. "Craig, you've heard me speak of Mrs. Bawden. This is Craig, Jeannette."

Craig acknowledged the informal introduction with a bow and a smile and seated himself in the chair Mrs. Nason indicated with a gesture of her hand.

"Mr. Nason is gone for a stroll down to the river with Mr. Bentley," Mrs. Nason explained. "They'll be back in a minute or two, Craig, if you think you can put up with the society of three women till they return."

"Lock the doors so they can't get in," Craig suggested in reply.

"But you can't have anything to eat till they get in," Mrs. Nason countered.

"In that case, I'll withdraw the suggestion," Craig laughed.

The conversation drifted along over meaningless trifles, Craig contributing very little to the chatter except when a remark was addressed directly to him. He settled comfortably in his chair and observed the three women from under his heavy brows, wondering how they would appeal to the man with whom he had been riding only an hour or so earlier. They were all dressed becomingly in gowns that were so simple that a mere man might have been startled to learn their cost. Mrs. Nason was a large woman of matronly bearing to whom a dignified manner was becoming. Yet there was a sparkle of roguishness in her eyes that made it almost impossible to be serious in her presence. Craig thought he had never heard a more musical laugh than hers when she was gay. He had often told himself that her sense of humour alone had made it possible for her to live her life contentedly with Gilbert Nason.

Marion had much of her mother's sprightly manner, though there was a touch of her father's coldness in her eyes when she was not smiling. Craig had given Marion a considerable amount of thought since their first meeting immediately after his return from overseas.

"She can drive a car better than nine out of ten men I know," Charnley had once said by way of praise, "and if she meets you on the street she's very likely to match you for a box of chocolates or offer a wager on the next prize fight."

Altogether, Craig had long since decided, Marion was not at all a bad sort. Perhaps she was unusually fine. He began to think so for the first time, consciously, as he watched her closely in conversation with her mother and Mrs. Bawden. She was about twenty-five and rather taller than the average, with a figure that was slight but well formed. Her brown hair, "bobbed" in the latest mode, was slightly waved, her cheeks showed a little the effects of a couple of weeks at the lake, but there was a softness to her skin that betrayed the fact that she had probably spent most of her spare time at the lake fortifying her rather delicate complexion against the attacks of wind and sun. Both she and Mrs. Bawden smoked cigarettes while they waited for the men to come in to dinner. Marion, however, secure in the presence of an indulgent mother, seemed ready at any moment to toss her cigarette aside at the first sound of approaching footsteps to announce the coming of her father.

Jeannette Bawden, however, gave Craig more to think about for the moment than either Marion or her mother. She was a new type to Craig. She smoked with an air of one who knew how to take the last bit of pleasure out of everything she did. She was a tall, full-breasted woman, with softly rounded arms and a voice that was almost a caress. Yet, in her eyes, there was a shrewdness, a keenness that pierced to the quick when she looked at one. Craig found it impossible to feel at ease in her presence, but for the life of him he could not tell whether his discomfiture was the result of her piercing glance or of her velvet voice. She was a passionate animal endowed with an intellect that was as coldly analytical as that of a judge. Secretly Craig hoped he might never become the object of her disfavour—though he prayed even more fervently that she might never single him out as the object of her affection. His first impression was that she was the sort of woman he was determined to have nothing whatever to do with, though every time she spoke he unconsciously retreated a little from the ground he had taken. It annoyed Craig terribly not to be able to put people in the places to which he felt they belonged. He could find no place for Jeannette Bawden. Even had he found the place and put her there, he felt sure she would manage to slip out of it somehow or other when he was not attending.

Craig awoke from his contemplation to discover that the woman had finally come round to a mention of British politics.

"I shall be interested to hear what Mr. Nason has to say of Lloyd George. I'd like to know just how long he'll succeed in his game of blind man's buff with the people of England and the other nations of Europe."

"I don't think you'll have any difficulty in getting him to talk about it," Mrs. Nason replied. "He's full of the situation in England. He's been home less than twenty-four hours and he's been invited to speak at six different club luncheons."

"Take a trip to London and get yourself invited out to luncheon every day in the week for a whole year after you get back," Marion commented. "I was rather hoping we wouldn't have any politics with our dinner tonight."

"Here they come, anyhow," Mrs. Nason said, getting up,

"so we'll just have to take what we get and be thankful. Perhaps we'll be able to inveigle them into a game of bridge after dinner."

Marion hurriedly pressed her cigarette into the tray on the table near her as Gilbert Nason crossed the hall and presented himself in the doorway of the room, the figure of a man in clerical garb following at his heels.

"Well, are we ready to sit down? Hello, Forrester—glad to see you! You know Bentley, don't you? No? This is one of our real heroes, Bentley. Shake hands with Captain Forrester—what is it—D.S.O.—I never can remember the tags you fellows have stuck on the ends of your names. Anyhow, he's one of 'em, Bentley, and they don't make 'em any better. Where's Dick?"

"He's gone over to the Frawley's for supper with Tom. He'll be back later. We can go in."

"Good—I'm hungry as a lion. Come on, Forrester—come on, Jeannette. We'll see what the old woman has laid out for us."

Three

The Reverend George Bentley was a Methodist and among those who had made themselves heard at the recent conference that had considered the cases of certain recalcitrant brethren who had shown themselves somewhat too kindly disposed toward the cause of the labouring man. As a leader of one of the largest congregations in the city George Bentley enjoyed a position of distinction that gave weight to his words when he expressed an opinion on questions of the day. He was a "successful" minister of the gospel, having risen mainly by his own efforts from a position of obscurity on a little country circuit to a place in the white light of public interest. Particularly brilliant had been his conference attack on the methods of teaching in the colleges that had graduated such radicals as had made themselves prominent on behalf of labour in the recent strike disturbances. He blamed Germany's downfall on the insidious teaching of the higher critics and had once in public prayer beseeched the Almighty to deliver the Kaiser into the hands of the hangman.

In fact, the Reverend George Bentley was everything his chief patron, Gilbert Nason, expected him to be. He differed from Nason only in the power of his voice and the extent of his worldly goods, but since Gilbert Nason applauded his denunciations and abetted his views, Bentley was content with the worldly portion which God and Gilbert Nason had seen fit to mete out to him.

It was Bentley's peculiar pleasure to continue his account, interrupted by his return to the house with Nason, of the strike disturbances during the month of June. Nason had been away since the first week of May and was particularly interested in hearing the details of the strike that had threatened to spread over the whole of Canada and had ended shortly after the leaders had been taken from their homes and thrust into prison to await their trials.

While Bentley talked, Craig detected signs of impatience on the part of Jeannette Bawden and wondered what was passing in her mind. Once he caught a glance which passed between Marion and Jeannette that plainly betrayed Marion's frame of mind. There was some understanding between the two women that intrigued Craig from the moment Bentley began his long story.

"Unless we restore our institutions to their status of the days before the war," Bentley declared, "there is no hope for civilization."

Jeannette Bawden broke through at last with a word of protest. "Why take the trouble to save it, Mr. Bentley?" she asked in her softest voice.

Marion chuckled in spite of herself—or because she had been awaiting just such an opportunity—and was reprimanded by a look from her father.

"Why take the trouble to save our Christian heritage?" the good gentleman asked, surprised.

"I wasn't aware that it was Christian," Jeannette retorted.

Craig caught a glance from Marion and the two exchanged furtive winks. He was beginning to like Jeannette Bawden and was pleased, for some reason or other, to find that Marion shared her views.

"Jeannette, you heretic," Mrs. Nason interrupted, "I'm not going to permit you to badger Mr. Bentley. Craig, can't you talk her off the subject."

"On the contrary," objected Bentley, recovering himself, "I think I rather enjoy being badgered by a woman when she is as charming as—"

"Gad, I like it myself, Bentley," Nason broke in. "There was nothing I missed so much on my visit to London as the old arguments I used to have with Jeannette. But I wouldn't advise you to be in a hurry to invite them, Bentley. You don't know Jeannette as I do."

"Don't you think it would be a good time for Mr. Bentley to get acquainted, Daddy?" Marion piped out.

But the Reverend George Bentley sought retreat without dishonour. "You haven't told us anything about how you found conditions in England, Mr. Nason," he observed, turning to his host.

"England is scared stiff," Nason replied. "I got to Liverpool the Sunday after the riots. The mob broke into the stores and handed the stuff out and divided it on the streets. The docks were under the protection of a couple of gunboats and over fifty boats were tied up. The people have been expecting to get back through indemnities the money they spent on the war. Now they realize how impossible it is. The government is carrying a debt of about eight billion pounds and is spending about eight times as much as it spent the year before the war. Japan and the United States are underselling Great Britain and her export trade is in a terrible condition. The people have gone on a spending spree and the cost of living is mounting every day. Europe is looking forward to five years that will be as hard to live through as the last four years of war. It may be harder. There's talk of revolution everywhere. Unemployment. No end of subsidies. War in Ireland. Disagreement among the allied powers. The fact is, we have no conception over here of the problem they are facing in England. I don't think they know how big it is themselves. There was never a day during my visit in London that I didn't thank God from the bottom of my heart that I lived in Canada. I wouldn't want to have to face what they're going to have to face there in the next few years."

"If it teaches them that war is a very foolish business," observed Jeannette Bawden, "it may be worth while after all."

"Bless my soul, Jeannette," Nason replied, "they're already beginning to talk of the next war."

"Who are beginning to talk?"

"Everyone."

"Did you hear many of the unemployed returned men talking about it?"

"Jeannette—Jeannette!" protested Mrs. Nason.

Gilbert Nason let his eyes rest for a moment on Mrs. Bawden, then shifted them to Craig. "Captain," he said, "you are sitting beside as hot a little Bolshevist as ever hailed

Bolshevist:
"supporter of majority faction of
the Russian Democratic Party"
= violent overthrow of capitalism
~ Marxism, Leninism, Sovietism, Stalinism
- radical revolutionaries

the name of Lenin. If she weren't so becoming in a well furnished drawing-room, I'd be afraid of Jeannette Bawden."

"May the Lord deliver us from the parlour Bolshevist!"
groaned the Reverend George Bentley, taking advantage
of his host's jocular mood to relieve the high pressure he
had suffered ever since his first brief passage with the soft-
voiced widow.

"Permit me to breathe a reverent 'Amen!' to your sentiment, Mr. Bentley," replied Jeannette Bawden.

And for the time being the discussion on questions of
public moment was dropped in favour of Mrs. Nason's account of a battle with a nest of wasps that had succeeded in
making their home in one corner of their summer cottage
at Minaki.

Four

"Don't you think Jeannette is just about the most wonderful
thing you ever met?" Marion asked Craig in a whisper as
they passed down the hall after dinner.

Ahead of them Mrs. Nason walked beside Bentley while
Nason himself, with Jeannette on his arm, led the way to
the drawing-room.

"She seems like an unusual woman," Craig admitted,
"though I confess I'm not quite clear whether she means
all she says." *Jeannette only allowed*
be one visually
"But isn't she positively beautiful?" *pts in*

Craig looked down at the slender figure of the girl
beside him and allowed his eyes to rest a moment on her
face. "I don't think she is the most beautiful woman in—
in the company," he said slowly, and with a feeling that
he had spoken awkwardly though he meant every word
of what he said.

"Did you learn to say those things while you were overseas?" she asked with a toss of her pretty head.

"No," he replied, "I had to come back here to learn it. I learn such things slowly—and not very well."

She responded with a smile as they entered the doorway that lead to the drawing-room. Craig heard his name called and looked up to see Nason beckoning to him from the farther side of the room.

"Come over here, Craig," Nason called. "I want to give you something to think about while you digest your dinner."

Craig left Marion's side and took a chair between Nason and Bentley. The ladies moved to the other end of the room where stood a large piano, its white keys gleaming under a soft light that fell from a shaded lamp. Marion seated herself on the bench and ran her fingers lightly over the keys, while Jeannette Bawden sat on the bench beside her and turned to face Mrs. Nason who had taken a deep chair close by. Jeannette and Mrs. Nason talked quietly, their voices mingling softly with the wandering notes that Marion set free as she listened, pausing now and then to add her word to the conversation of the other two women.

Craig, watching them from the other end of the room, thought he had never seen anything so peaceful, so reassuring, so soothing to the senses. It was with difficulty that he forced himself to listen to what Gilbert Nason was saying.

"Bentley and I were having a little talk to ourselves, Craig," the old man began, "before we came in to dinner to-night. I've just had a glimpse of a very serious set of affairs in London. Things have gone wrong there and no mistake about it. Before another year there may be civil war in England—bloody revolution in the streets, that's what. We've had a taste of it here, but we're going to have

renewal of socialism / enforcement of capitalism

more of it unless we get busy and look the thing in the face. If this Bolsheviki business is going to be beaten, it'll have to be beaten in every country in the world and the quicker we get at it the better. We're not going to do anything by waiting till we see how they're going to handle it in England and France before we start to handle it here. We haven't much machinery to fight it but we have enough if we go after it right from the start. The strongest organization in this country during the next few years will be the returned soldiers, the veterans of the great war. It will just about mean that the man who hasn't a clean war record to show will have to keep his mouth shut or take a beating. The men who have come back from the front will just about control the political life of this country for the next generation. There's no reason why they shouldn't if they go about it the right way and give this country the kind of government it needs. What we need more than anything else just now is the right kind of publicity for sane government to get us out of the hole we're in. These fellows have been lambasting the crowds in Victoria Park with sermons on treason and anarchy and revolution. They know how to work up sentiment, I'll say that for them. But we'll have to work up sentiment on the other side. We've got to talk more and we've got to talk louder."

enforcement of dominance / oppression

Craig lighted a cigarette and permitted his attention to shift momentarily to the strains of soft music rippling from the piano. For some reason he was beginning to feel uncomfortable listening to the argument Gilbert Nason was laying before him. Why was it that everybody was so keen to take sides and prepare the ground for a new struggle now that the great struggle had ceased? He didn't want it. He felt the men and women he met in the street day after day were as tired of struggle as he.

"Don't you think, Mr. Nason," he ventured, "that the world wants to be quiet for a little while now? Don't you think we've had just about enough loud talking for a while?"

"I'd admit that readily enough, Forrester, if there was any hope of the other fellow keeping quiet and giving the world a chance to catch up with itself."

Bentley shuffled his feet impatiently. "Captain Forrester has not been back long enough, Nason, to get his bearings. When he has been on the ground for a while he'll see the seriousness of the situation just as clearly as we do. If you will permit me to speak a word, I might give it as my opinion that if we don't get started on a programme of sane reconstruction at once, control will pass into the hands of a few unscrupulous agitators and we'll have another Russia here inside of six months."

"Don't you think the people of the world, including the people of this country, expect some sort of change to come out of the war?" Craig ventured. "Or do you think the world must go back to its position of the days before the war?"

"We don't know, Captain," Bentley replied. "God's ways are not known to man. If it is His good will to bring about a change we shall welcome it when it comes. In the meantime, nothing is clearer to my mind than the fact that we must do all we can to restore the world to the peace and harmony that prevailed before this terrible tragedy befell us. With the world in its present state of hysteria, there's no telling what may become of us. Any man who can make himself heard can get on a street corner and expound his doctrine for the salvation of the world—and get an audience. History never offered a better opportunity for a man with a wrong idea to lead the world to perdition."

"You put into words the very thing I've been thinking myself, Bentley," Gilbert Nason observed.

"If we could only know what the right idea is," Craig said quietly.

"Tell Craig what we had in mind, Bentley," Nason suggested abruptly.

Bentley coughed a little and moved his chair closer to Craig. "There are a few ideas that we know are right, Captain," he said, "and they're enough to work on for a start. Mr. Nason and I have been talking over a little plan I have had in mind for the past month or more. If the church of Christ has any mission in the world it is surely to bring peace to a war wearied humanity. We are going to start a campaign among the churches of the city by which we hope to do our part in helping our people forget the horrors of the past four years and turn their faces toward a better day."

"Don't you think it will be a little difficult to accomplish both objects at once?" Craig observed.

But the Reverend George Bentley permitted the observation to pass unnoticed. "We want to enlist a score or so of men of your type, Captain," he continued, "to work through the churches of the city." Craig noticed that the music had ceased and that the ladies were evidently listening to what Bentley was saying. "We want to cultivate a healthy spirit through the medium of our different church clubs by having our returned men lead weekly discussions on the problems arising out of reconstruction."

"A sort of forum?" Craig asked.

Bentley passed his hand slowly over his chin. "Something after the manner of the forum, only—well, the forum idea, as it has been carried out in the past, hasn't been a marked success. There has been too much disagreement—too much dissension, perhaps—and I don't look upon that kind of thing as particularly becoming in the House of God. I had in mind something more constructive."

["Something in which only half the truth can be told," Jeannette Bawden] suggested from the other end of the room.

"On the contrary," Bentley protested, "we want the truth—and we wish to have the utmost freedom in the discussion of the problems that arise. At the meeting of the ministerial association the other day, that point was emphatically stressed. There must be no barriers to the sincere expression of opinion."

"Was that the meeting of the association at which it was decided that the Unitarian minister was not qualified to ask the blessing before they began their luncheon?" asked Jeannette.

Craig could not repress a chuckle. Bentley appeared not to have heard Jeannette's comment. "What we want," he went on, "is the building up and the consolidating of a body of public opinion that will not tolerate the sort of disgraceful disturbances we have witnessed in our city during the past two months. We believe the church can do its part to create the sentiment we must have to offset the destructive agencies and to help preserve our Christian civilization for the future. We want you to come in with us, Captain, and help perfect the organization."

"Yes—what do you think about it, Craig?" Nason prompted.

Craig had been staring before him for some time at three objects that had supplied him with an amusing problem in geometry. He had discovered that a triangle formed by the two feet of Bentley's chair and the heel of Bentley's left foot would be almost exactly equilateral if the worthy gentleman would just shift his foot about one inch to the right. He could see the exact spot on the rug where Bentley's foot should rest to carry out the plan that had taken form in his imagination, and for fully ten minutes he had waited in vain for the foot to move.

46

At the sound of Nason's voice, Craig came to himself and gathered together quickly the fragments of Bentley's lengthy speech that remained somehow in his memory.

"I haven't been inside a church for a long time," he observed.

"That wouldn't make the slightest difference," Bentley assured him.

"A good chance to start in again," Nason commented.

"I couldn't say a half dozen words if I got on my feet before an audience," Craig protested.

"We can find the speakers," Bentley replied. "What we want just now is a man who will take the movement in hand and organize it and push it forward. Mr. Nason thinks you are the man we want and he rarely makes a mistake in his choice of men."

Craig, with his eyes on the foot he had been waiting to see move, smiled as he saw it shift a little more than an inch—in the wrong direction.

"I don't really know what to say," he said slowly. "I've never wished for anything in my life as I've wished for some way to help solve the tangle we've got ourselves in. But the fact is, I don't know how it is to be done. It's too hard a problem even to decide who's right and who's wrong in the business. I'm afraid you'll have to count me out, much as I'd like to help."

"If you change your mind about it, Captain," Bentley suggested, "I'd like you to call on me and give me a chance to go into the details with you as I have them worked out in my mind."

Mrs. Nason laughed as she got to her feet and came toward the men. "You've talked enough politics or whatever it is you call it to do us for the next month. If this is what it means to have peace I'm going out to start another war. If you don't come and join us in a game of bridge, I'll let Jeannette loose on you again."

Gilbert Nason got up at once and put his arm about his wife's shoulders. "That last threat does it, eh, Bentley?" he said turning to the man who had been the centre of Jeannette's attacks during the evening.

Bentley got to his feet quickly. "If you don't mind," he said, "I'll leave you to your game and get back to some work I have to do sometime between now and tomorrow morning. I'll call you or drop you a card, Captain Forrester, and I'm very pleased to have met you and have had this little chat."

He made the rounds, with a handshake for Marion and one equally as warm for Jeannette, and then went into the hall with his host and hostess.

"Exit a representative of the class who are doing their best to bring on another war," said Jeannette Bawden in an undertone.

And right there Craig resolved to reject the invitation the Reverend George Bentley had extended him.

Five

It was late that evening when old Gilbert Nason suggested that Marion should sing for them. They had tried cards without much success. Jeannette Bawden was again the chief barrier to the pleasure Mrs. Nason had hoped to infuse into an evening that had thus far proved a disappointment to her. Jeannette was not in the mood for cards and Gilbert Nason drifted so frequently into fragmentary accounts of his visit to London and the conditions he had found there that the game died a natural death when it had only begun.

"Sing for us, Marion," Nason said at last. "I'm tired of talking and tired of thinking. I want to listen."

Without waiting to be urged, Marion went to the piano and sang a number of quiet songs in a clear, rich voice full of simple beauty and stirring feeling.

When she was through, Jeannette spoke up. "Sing that new song, Marion, that one about the sunrise."

Marion struck a chord and began to sing again. Presently her voice lifted into a melody that touched Craig strangely. He listened to the words.

"Dear one, the world is waiting for the sunrise,
Every rose is heavy with dew;
The lark on high his sleepy mate is calling—
And my heart is calling you!"

A hush fell upon them as the song ceased and the last notes from the piano died away. And in the silence Craig lifted his eyes to find Jeannete Bawden looking at him with a searching gaze. As he looked at her, he saw her lips move—though she did not speak—shaping the words:

"The—world—is—waiting—for—the—sunrise!"

And those were the words he wrote in his book that night when he returned to his apartment.

CHAPTER V.

One

IT WAS VERY LATE that night when Craig Forrester finally got to sleep. His talk with Jimmie Dyer and his visit with the Nasons had left him in a state of mind that made sleep impossible. It was not so much what they had said that caused him to lie awake wondering. Even Jimmy's outbursts were probably the result of a bad case of "nerves." But there was something about the cool deliberateness of Gilbert Nason and the supreme confidence of the Reverend George Bentley that perplexed him. It made him feel afraid. If they had blustered more, if they had reacted less politely to the sharp thrusts that Jeannette Bawden had aimed at them, if they had been somewhat less deliberate in their manner, Craig could have smiled at the whole business and gone to sleep.

As he lay awake, he reflected that both Bentley and Nason were probably enjoying the most peaceful slumber while he struggled with his perplexity. It made him almost angry. They had been so sure of themselves and of the future, they had been so damned reasonable about everything. They could see nothing dramatic in the world as it existed before their eyes. Nason had seen rioting in the streets of Liverpool, he had seen gunboats lying in the harbour, but such things were mere incidents in his trip. He had seen unrest and uprising but only as passing phases of the return to peace. There might be more of it, certainly, but in the end the authorities would restore order and the world would go on as smoothly as ever. Gilbert Nason feared nothing. What few fears the Reverend George Bentley entertained were

[handwritten margin note: Craig is accustomed to unstable condition of the world and not believing in their false hope beliefs of the world]

completely taken care of by his faith in the world's ability to recover itself before anything serious could happen.

What would these men do, Craig wondered, when they found the ground shaking under their very feet!

He could not help thinking a great deal about Jeannette Bawden. He wondered if his first impression of the woman had not been a little unfair, after all. He had wanted to know more of her and had been tempted to ask Marion Nason something of her history. He realized now that his first reaction had been prompted wholly by fear of her as a woman. Her soft voice, her almost languishing manner, her strange way of looking at one as if she were on the point of asking some intimate question, had put him on the defensive at once. Now as he thought of her, however, he did not remember these things except in so far as they threw into greater relief the shrewd glance that always preceded her quick question and the sudden lift of her eyes before she spoke. The more he thought of her the more convinced he was that Jeannette Bawden was sincere, that she was intensely in earnest, that she was the kind of woman who would halt at nothing once she set her face toward a goal. He resolved to know more of her.

[handwritten margin note: his opinion about Jeannette]

It was to Marion, however, that his thoughts turned. He had said very little to her during the evening and she had entered the conversation so seldom that Craig knew little of what she thought. Strangely enough, he gave no thought to what her ideas might be. She had declared her liking for Jeannette Bawden and had applauded her gibes, but Craig realized that she was attracted more by the older woman's daring before Bentley and her austere father than by any philosophy Jeannette had enunciated.

As a woman, Marion Nason stirred him strangely—and somewhat differently from Jeannette. While the latter prompted him to fall back on the defensive at once, Marion made him conscious of his manhood and of a desire to possess. Her fresh young beauty had quickened his pulse every time he had looked at her during the evening. The sound of her laughter and her voice singing was still with him. It had seemed that her singing was for him, that she had set herself to reassure him and to restore his faith in a world gone suddenly topsy-turvy. After all, the heavy burdens in life were for the stout hearts. Perhaps such creatures as Marion Nason, beautiful creatures whose lives were compounded of laughter and light, had been sent to the world to fill a finer purpose. Men had their sterner moods, moods that possessed them in their hours of struggle, but they had their hours, too, when they wished to forget the struggle and when they longed for rest. Perhaps these creatures of light and laughter were sent into the world that romance might live and that men might be coaxed to forget their sordid memories and yield to tender allurement.

As Craig closed his eyes and drifted into forgetfulness, it was the memory of Marion's voice that soothed him, it was the image of her vivid face that stilled his perplexity and made him less afraid.

Two

When he awoke in the morning it was with a sense of relief that he had his day's work ahead of him. The doubts of the previous day had left him groping and confused. The more thought he gave to the world in its present condition the more difficult it became for his mind to function. There was something even in the orderliness of his rooms and in the broad outlook along the avenue beneath his windows that strengthened his faith in the universe and in the God of Things As They Ought To Be.

When he drove down the avenue in the fresh morning air and sped up Main Street toward the business section of the city, his heart was lighter than it had been for days. While he sat at breakfast he opened the morning paper and glanced hurriedly through it. At once ne found himself gazing upon the picture of a civilization in the agonies of a death-struggle. At the top of the front page, its headline stretched across two columns, stood a despatch from London in which Arthur Henderson was quoted for the benefit, Craig thought, of just such men as the Reverend George Bentley and Gilbert Nason. The British leader predicted a "terrible spasm of rage and despair among the peoples of Europe in which the final remains of civilization might be totally annihilated." Craig glanced at other headings—"Tanks to Quell Police Strike In Liverpool"—"International Plan To Check Profiteering"—"Have Lost All Faith In Political Parties"—everywhere turmoil and unrest and upheaval—and western civilization hovering on the brink of destruction!

On an editorial page he lingered over three sentences that caught his eye: "Old ideas have been scrapped; new ones have taken their places. The great masses of society are demanding a day of better things." Was this but a voice crying in the wilderness? Maybe so. And yet, it was a voice that spoke from the heart of the human race. Here and there, all over the world, small voices were making themselves heard above the tumult. In the end they would speak together, millions of them—and the old order would pass.

Three

Half an hour later, Craig entered the building on Lombard Street that housed the Winnipeg Grain Exchange. It was not yet nine o'clock, more than half an hour still remained before the opening of the market, but the place presented the busy activity of mid-day. Craig had never wholly recovered from his first wonder at the shifting contrasts the Exchange brought before his eyes. While half a dozen messenger boys were scurrying in all directions, three were furtively matching pennies while they waited for an elevator to take them back to their offices. Well groomed men whose manners proclaimed their standing as men of wealth and influence in the city chatted with seedy, unshaven individuals who might have spent the night in the cells, if appearances counted for anything. Trimly dressed stenographers stepped into elevators alongside farmers' wives who, with their rustic husbands, had dropped in to make sure of a place in the visitors' gallery when the market opened. There were busy men who brushed past without offering a good morning to their best friends, and there were idlers in groups where discussion centred about the chances of the New York Giants in their battle for the pennant of the National League. From open office doors came the ceaseless chatter of telegraph instruments that echoed everywhere in the corridors above the cat-calls of office boys and the loud shouting of men.

The confusion, however, was only on the surface. Here was the great funnel through which a billion bushels of grain passed annually from the broad acres of the Canadian prairies on its way to the nations of the world. Here was the nerve centre of a great industry to which hungry men and women of practically every nation in Europe looked to be fed. Here could be felt the nip of early frost in northern Alberta or the shock of a bomb tossed into the streets of Budapest. Once inside the walls of the building, a man became a citizen of the world, he saw from afar the hands of millions uplifted and heard from beyond the seas the ceaseless cry for bread.

It was this aspect of his work that had appealed to Craig Forrester from the first. The "scalper" who was content to gamble on the fluctuations of the market from day to day and the broker who depended for a livelihood on the commissions he drew from "customers" who nursed dreams of "beating the market" and becoming millionaires in a season, were types to whom Craig could never quite reconcile himself. He had gambled somewhat in futures on his own behalf with such marked success that he had made a reputation for being able to "smell" a change in the market and predict its status an hour or a week in advance. But when he gambled it was to satisfy the sporting instinct within him rather than to realize any dreams of sudden wealth. He had seen gamblers come in from the streets with their savings, some of them with money enough to last them for the rest of their lives, and had seen them go out again penniless and disillusioned. Some of them lasted a week, some a year or even more, but it was always the same old story. The game was too much for them and in the end they were beaten and shoved aside. Some day, perhaps, his business would expand until he could number among his clients men of sufficient wealth to make the game not only worth while but sufficiently interesting to justify his taking a part in it. In the meantime, his interest was bound up with the export end of the business and here his imagination found enough play to satisfy him.

For half an hour before the opening of the market, Craig went from one office to another of the firms with whom he had been dealing during the past month and arrived at the entrance to the trading-room within a few moments of half-past nine. The room was a huge enclosure with great windows along one side flooding the place with light. Beneath the windows a row of telegraph operators sat behind a long desk that ran the full length of the room. On the opposite side stood the telephone booths above which ran a long narrow platform where stood the recorders ready to mark up the fluctuating prices of grain sold on the markets of Chicago, Minneapolis and Duluth. Before the blackboards that covered the walls, the recorders stood, brushes and chalk ready, awaiting the sound of the gong and the first announcement of prices at the opening of the American markets. Above the blackboards was the "clock," an octagonal dial on which was recorded the price of each trade as it occurred on the local market.

Craig went at once to the "pit," an octagonal enclosure in the centre of the floor where the trading was carried on. Fully fifty men were already standing in the pit waiting for the gong to ring as a signal that the day's trading had begun. Others were coming from every direction, trading cards in their hands, telegrams and orders folded and sticking from their pockets. The telegraph keys kept up their incessant chatter, telephone bells rang almost continually, boys blared names through megaphones or darted in and out among the gathering traders with despatches clutched in their hands.

Craig glanced at the clock that hung on the wall beside the dial and mounted the steps of the pit. He took a moment to look over the orders he had been given to execute, then thrust the papers back into his pocket and looked about him at the faces of the men in the pit. On the farther side he saw Charnley crowding toward the centre, his right hand raised, his body poised like a runner set for the start of the race, his eyes darting from one to another of the men beneath him. Not till that moment did Craig remember that he had neglected to give Marion Nason the message with which Charnley had entrusted him.

Suddenly the gong clanged and a deafening chorus broke loose from the throng in the pit. Arms were up, fingers spread, hands clutched and tore madly, men hurled themselves half a dozen at a time upon a trader whose voice barked but once from the very centre of the pit, the red figures flashed upon the dial—the first trade was made! For fifteen minutes, then, the tumult was deafening. The market that had been only recently opened for trades in wheat after a period of government control throughout the war, was running contrary to the expectations of everyone. Losses from drought in the United States and Canada had been serious and the price was jumping at every trade. Already it had passed the two-dollar mark and three-dollar wheat was predicted before the October deliveries were due.

Craig watched the trading at first in silence, a little puzzled at the steady upward trend of the market. Then, suddenly, he became alert, he leaned toward the centre of the pit and listened. Charnley threw both arms into the air.

"Sell October at seven-eighths!" On a strong market he had offered to sell at an eighth of a cent under the price.

Craig threw himself at him. "Sold! Sold!"

He seized Charnley and drew him toward him. "A hundred?"

"Twenty-five," Charnley replied and Craig made a note on his trading card.

Charnley turned and went back to the centre of the pit. Craig watched him quietly. Why was Charnley selling short on a rising market? Almost immediately the young trader raised his arm again.

"Sell October at three-quarters!"

A half dozen traders were upon him at once. Craig crowded through till he was within earshot of the men who had surrounded Charnley. A young broker had succeeded in getting Charnley's eye and was setting his pencil to his card.

"Twenty?"

"Ten!" Charnley replied.

On the wall the dial recorded the trade.

"Does Charnley think he can pound this market?"

Craig turned and looked into the eyes of one of the oldest traders on the floor. As he did so, Charnley's voice rose once more, shrill above the hoarse cries of the other traders. "Sell October at five-eighths!"

"Sold!" said the trader who had just spoken to Craig.

But Charnley had caught the eye of a youth standing in the centre of a group of men of about his own age. The youth seized him with both hands and pushed him to the edge of the pit. In a momentary lull, Charnley's voice reached Craig's ears. "Make it five hundred!"

"Nothing doing—make it five!" the young trader replied.

Craig became suddenly angry. He threw himself half way across the pit and brought both hands down upon Charnley's shoulders. "Are you acting according to instructions, or are you just a plain damned fool, Charnley?" he asked.

Charnley was well aware that his conduct was uncommercial and contrary to the rules of the association, but he smiled at Craig and tore himself free as the tumult increased about them. With a dozen orders to execute, Craig turned his attention to the bids that were being called and for the next half hour pushed and mauled the men about him until he had filled his card.

Then, in a moment, the tumult ceased. A few traders still barked at each other across the pit, but even these grew silent as no response came to their bids, and one after another they stepped down and strolled about the floor. Craig stood a moment at the top of the pit, his hands thrust into his pockets, and looked around from one to another of the men on the floor.

He made an unusual picture as he stood there, with his great height and his broad shoulders and a neck and head that were considerably heavier than the average. His dark brown hair, with a faint suggestion of a curl in it, was ruffled from his strenuous hour of scrambling in the pit. There was already a mere suspicion of greyness above the temples that had crept in there during his last year in France. His dark eyes looked out from beneath heavy brows that gave him the appearance of almost constantly frowning.

A paper pellet flicked his ear and caused him to turn and glance toward the telegraph desks where Charnley stood talking with another broker, the two regarding him with smiles. Charnley was a very different type from Craig. There was something in his bearing when he was not struggling in the pit that gave one the impression of good breeding. His head was small and well-shaped, the lines of his face finely drawn, his black hair smoothed back with a patent-leather finish to it that betrayed the fact that he had used the brush since the activity of the market had fallen away. There was nothing Charnley disliked more than to be caught with hair dishevelled and clothes awry. He was older than Craig and had managed to see more of the world and boasted a knowledge of "life" that always made Craig a little conscious of his own unsophistication and limited experience. That was Claude Charnley, of Cade and Charnley.

As Craig stepped down and approached him, Charnley made a pretense of running to cover from an expected attack. But Craig came forward quietly. "Trying an old joke on the crowd this morning?" he asked Charnley.

Charnley approached him cautiously. "Honest, Magpie," he said, "I'm getting out of the market. I was long about five hundred and—"

"You don't have to lie to me," Craig observed quietly. "One of these days—"

"You get me wrong," Charnley said. "This market is riding too fast. Some of you fellows think you're going to have three-dollar wheat. Well, I'll tell you what I think. You're going to ride this market to two and a half and then the government is going to close it without warning. That's what I think. You can do what you like about it, but I'm not going to be left with a pocket full of contracts I can't cash in on."

Craig did not reply. He leaned on the desk behind him and allowed his eyes to run over the stragglers in the pit.

"The fact is," Charnley went on, "your darned old world is going topsy-turvy—and it's getting there pretty damned fast."

"Give it a chance to right itself," Craig suggested. "If some of you fellows had a little more faith in—"

Charnley laughed. "Faith!" My God, Magpie, why aren't you working for Billy Sunday? I'm getting suspicious of you lately—you're getting so damned religious or something. Next thing we hear you'll be taking up the ouija board and raiding the market on tips from the Almighty."

For the first time since Craig stepped down from the pit to join Charnley, the man to whom Charnley had been talking took a part in the conversation. "If the government closes the market now they're just going to cheat this country out of its one best chance to get back some of the money it has spent in Europe."

Craig turned sharply on the speaker. "You'd like to get rich on Europe's bad luck, eh?"

"Forget it—forget it," Charnley protested. "I'm fed up on the war and Europe and the whole damned business. We've got enough to worry about here without fighting the war over again on the floor."

Craig frowned. "What you fellows seem to be blind to," he observed, "is the fact that you can't forget it—that you may be more fed up than you are—and that you won't make things any better here or anywhere else by robbing one part of the world to make the other part rich. Sooner or later you'll find that out for yourselves if you don't know it already."

Charnley laughed. "Go ahead, old man, and be a Good Samaritan to the blasted world. It won't hurt the world and it may do you some good."

Craig saw the two men turn away slowly, laughing at him as they went off. He put out his hand to arrest them while he struggled for words to express what he felt.

"I—you—"

He followed them for a couple of steps, then halted. His brows came down over his dark eyes as he watched Charnley and his companion move away out of reach and finally out of hearing.

"But—I—I say—you can't—"

His voice ceased abruptly as he realized that he was talking to himself and that three or four others, without knowing the cause of Charnley's laughter, had nevertheless taken their own cue from him and had playfully cut off Craig's pursuit.

"Forget it! Forget it, Magpie! No matter what it is—forget it!"

They tossed paper balls at him and one man threw a handful of torn fragments of paper over him.

Craig's good humour got the better of him presently and he moved back and made his way slowly toward the entrance.

And although there was nothing vindictive or surly in his disposition, Craig looked back once when he reached the door and felt his blood warm as he caught sight of Charnley standing with a half dozen others in a far corner of the room, their faces turned toward him wreathed in smiles.

He turned away abruptly and went to his office.

Four

Late that afternoon, Craig swung slowly about in his chair, leaned back with his hands locked behind his head, and let his eyes wander out over the tops of the grey buildings that lay in jagged, irregular pattern under his office window. On returning to his work a few weeks before, he had opened an office on the ninth floor, from the windows of which he could look out to where a wide avenue led to the westward, past the farthest limits of the city and lost itself in the wide reaches of the prairie beyond.

From the corridors came the din of men's voices and the sharp calls of messenger boys. From the street below came the sound of a band leading the way up Main Street before a long line of men in weathered khaki who had arrived from overseas during the afternoon. Craig stood at the window watching the files go up the street, then turned and seated himself again as the door opened and let in the din from the corridors. It was old "Dad" Robinson, the halls janitor, come to take away the waste paper. He raised his bent figure and his eyes lighted up as he met Craig's smile.

"Hello, Dad," Craig greeted him cheerfully. "How's the garden coming along these days?"

The old man made himself busy at once with the waste paper in the basket that stood beside Craig's desk. "Aye— you must be comin' roun' soon, sir. It be a treat to see 'ow the stuff is comin' on. The celery as I tried out in that ground, sir, you remember—it'd fair make you laugh to see the jumps they've took, sir. It's the right weather we're 'avin' an' the ground 'as the growin' smell to it, if you knows what I mean, sir."

"I'm coming round to see it some night next week, Dad," Craig replied. "Let me know what night suits you best and I'll run you out in the car."

The old fellow turned to the door, holding in his hands the bag stuffed with paper he had collected in his rounds. "I'll put you in mind of it, sir, that I will," he said with a broad smile. "You'll like to see some petunias that's got a bit o' rare colour in them for all—"

"I'll be glad to see them, Dad."

With a bow of deference and dignity, too, the old man retreated through his door and dragged his sack after him. Craig turned again and gazed from the window.

Out there where the sky was a pale blue canopy above the open fields, the summer was warm with life. "The growin' smell," old Dad had said. The growing smell of the soil! The feel of the soft mould underfoot, the steaming fallow and the dust from the fields, the rush of the blackbirds alighting, and the dart of the sparrow in the freshly turned furrow!

And, in line with his thoughts of other fragrant things, Craig's mind came back again to Marion Nason. In obedience to an impulse that awakened in him early that day, he lifted the telephone and in a moment was asking her to take a drive into the country with him before dinner.

She was in a mood for chasing the wind, she said, and would be ready for him as soon as he would call.

For some reason, the sound of her voice and her quick, odd little laugh left him as excited as a schoolboy.

He lost no time in getting the car around to Nason's. Marion was already on the steps waiting for him. Craig thought he had never seen anyone so dainty, so—what was it?—so *chic*. He didn't like the word but it sprang into his mind as he saw her come down the walk toward him, arrayed in a frock of some shimmering yellow knitted stuff. Over her arm hung an enormous motor coat. She stood poised and delicate as a flower while she waited for him to turn the car.

"Do you know, I was just *hoping* you would call and ask me for a spin," Marion confessed while she made herself comfortable beside him. She touched his little finger where it rested on the wheel. "What large hands you have, Craig!" The playful contact gave him a quick thrill.

They left the pavement a few minutes later and took a winding, shaded road that led southward from town. The road was a soft cushion under the speeding car and ran through wooded country where the branches of the poplars that lined the trail swept the top and sides of the car as they passed.

Marion exclaimed at the beauty of the country through which they were passing.

"Has it ever occurred to you, Craig, what a lot of sheer *gladness* you have to make up for to yourself now that the war is over?" She looked at his strong profile against the light as she spoke. "You could go on playing now forever and be perfectly justified. You have earned a good time for the rest of your life."

Craig looked at her. How alive she was! Her eyes, as clear as a child's, fairly danced with eagerness for living. What a spur she would be for a man's ambition! He thought of her question.

"Just what do you mean by a good time?" he asked her.

"I mean—just that. A good time. You're so very serious—aren't you? After all, there's a place in life for—well, for a little frivolity."

Craig's thick, dark brows knotted together for a moment. He smiled at her and she put her hand on his arm.

"I think a returned man has a right to be—perhaps a little selfish," she asserted. She was looking at him as she spoke. What a gentle, firm mouth he had...

Craig was silent for a moment. He did not know how to reply to what she had said. She could not have meant precisely what her words conveyed. She was just being generous, that was all. Or perhaps she didn't realize—everything.

"In the end," he observed, "I'm not so sure that being selfish would lead to any good."

She tossed her head and laughed. "Let someone else worry about that."

Craig smiled—a slow smile. Marion's words had brought to mind an old saying of his father's. "Worry is bad medicine," he used to say, "so don't give me anything to worry over."

He thought of John Forrester's words now. Off to the left there, some twenty miles to the south, lay the old farm he and his father had worked together.

"Out there," he said pointing ahead to the left of the trail, "I learned not to let anyone else worry about anything that was my business."

"Out there?"

"That was where I lived with my old dad on a farm. We didn't worry about much of anything in those days. We had a good neighbour—old Farmer Lane—and we had a pretty good world—or thought we had—we had enough to live on comfortably and enough work to do to make us happy. Some day I'd like to take you for a spin out there. Farmer Lane had a daughter—by gosh, you'd like her, Marion."

"I've often wondered if there wasn't a woman somewhere," Marion teased. "These very quiet men—"

Craig laughed. "Don't be foolish. She wasn't of our world. She went away to the old country—had some ideas she wanted to work out in art or something—she used to draw and make things out of clay. I haven't heard of her since the year before war broke out. We grew up and forgot about each other—whatever there was to forget. One of these days—"

As they rounded a quick turn in the trail, Craig stepped suddenly on his brakes. Ahead of them, in the road, something had happened. Three or four towsy children were bending over a mongrel dog that lay yelping at the roadside.

Craig brought the car to a stand beside them and looked out at them.

"What's the matter?" he asked the eldest of the group, the only one of them all who was not crying.

"They run over his leg," he informed Craig, pointing down the trail where a car had evidently vanished a few minutes before.

Marion shrugged impatiently. "Oh—Craig, I can't stand that noise—do go on!" she begged, covering her ears with her hands.

"Wait a minute, please," he said, throwing open the door and jumping down.

He picked the mongrel up in his hands and examined it. One of the hind legs had evidently been broken, but the dog was otherwise unhurt.

"I think we can fix that," Craig commented. "Where do you live?"

The boy pointed toward an unpainted shack set back from the road and half concealed under the trees.

"Just wait a minute, Marion," he said. "I'm going to give the kids a hand. Here—come on, kids, and let me show you how to be a doctor."

The children had stopped crying and looked in dumb awe at Craig. He gathered the dog in his arms and started away in the direction of the house.

"Whatever are you going to do, Craig?" Marion asked him, frowning slightly.

"Just going to be a little frivolous for a minute or two," he said, smiling back at her. "You don't really mind, do you?"

"Do anything you like," she replied. "Only stop that awful yelping!"

It was several minutes before Craig returned to Marion in the car. She greeted him with an odd smile.

"You're funny Craig," she said in a low voice, as if she were making the observation to herself.

"Maybe," Craig admitted.

He started the car and they drove away, a strange silence having fallen between them that challenged all Craig's efforts before he brought Marion back to the gay mood in which she had started out.

Five

During the week that Marion remained in town before she and her mother returned to their summer home, Craig saw

Marion as often as he could make an excuse for calling her over the telephone.

They motored out almost every trail that led into the country from the end of the paved streets.

And after she had gone, whenever he thought of her, it seemed the most reasonable thing in the world that Claude Charnley should be in love with the girl.

He couldn't think of any reason why anyone in the world should not be in love with her.

CHAPTER VI.

One

THE END OF AUGUST brought Craig an invitation to spend the week-end at the Nason cottage at Minaki. They were celebrating the close of the season with a house party and had asked some friends to come out from town on the late train, Friday.

Looking for a seat in the crowded day-coach of the camper's "special," Craig came across Charnley with two other men of about his own age.

"Gad, if here isn't the Magpie!" Charnley greeted him as their eyes met and Craig paused in the aisle. "You're not on the way to the Nasons' by any chance?"

Craig nodded. "It's a fact—you're a good guesser," Craig replied.

"Sit down here, we're all headed in the same direction."

Charnley introduced his two companions. One turned out to be a newspaperman by the name of Croker, a pale-faced, under-sized chap whose comments on the European situation had excited some interest during the last months of the war and the uncertain days that had followed the armistice. The other, a man of about thirty, dark, almost handsome in appearance and of athletic bearing, was Ayers, a recent addition to the staff of the University, a Rhodes Scholar whose career at Oxford had been abruptly terminated by the outbreak in Europe.

Craig thrust his bag under the seat and sat down beside Croker.

"Forrester, here," Charnley elaborated, after the introductions had been made, "is a hero with a record that reads like a fairy tale. On the exchange he's better known as The Magpie, not because he chatters a great deal, but because he never has a word to say on anything until he's forced to speak. His favourite word is 'Sold' and he has a reputation of knowing just when to speak it."

Craig smiled. "Rather when not to speak it," he corrected.

"His only real weakness," Charnley continued, "is a belief in—"

"It isn't quite fair to complete the dissection on the first meeting," Craig protested. "You haven't told me a thing about either of your two friends."

"Croker, here," Charnley said, brushing his hair back with a quick sweep of his hand, "is our free lance purveyor of punk opinions on almost any subject you want to ask him about. Trouble with Croker is he has to have a sheet of copy paper and a typewriter in front of him before he can say anything. You two would get along famously, Magpie. You ought to go fishing together. If Croker would only leave his typewriter at home, the two of you together wouldn't have enough to say to startle a trout out of his mid-day snooze."

"You come highly recommended," Craig remarked, smiling at Croker.

"Croker's pet philosophy is that the world would be a very decent place to live in if there weren't any people to bother one," Charnley added.

"Don't you think Ayers ought to share a little in the special mention?" Croker suggested mildly.

Charnley drew himself up and looked across at Ayers. "The professor thinks the university would be a pretty decent place to live in if there weren't any students to bother one— that's just about where he stands. He got that idea when he was at Oxford. He might have been a pretty fair Canadian if he hadn't been unfortunate enough to be selected for the Rhodes scholarship. Heaven for him would be a chair in a British university with a small class—no co-eds—tiffin about five—and a specially constructed printing press that could be counted on to turn out the results of his research without groaning."

The men laughed at Charnley's witty analysis of Ayers' character. In spite of a kind of instinctive dislike for Charnley, Craig could not help admitting to himself that the fellow could be entertaining when he chose. He liked Charnley at such times and inwardly upbraided himself for harbouring any dislike for him.

And yet, before they had been on the way an hour, Charnley perpetrated one of those little annoyances that always left Craig in a state almost of hostility to him. They had been discussing the order-in-council by which the government had suddenly and without warning closed the wheat market after only a week of open trading. What had prompted the action was still a mystery and was likely to remain one for some time to come.

The conversation had gradually turned to modern methods of doing business and Charnley had listened for some time to Ayers and Craig who had differed mildly with regard to the extent to which the spirit of fair play entered into business tactics. The argument had been informal and neither man had urged his point of view with much fervour.

"Business, to my mind," Ayers said, "proceeds on compromise. A man will probably do the thing that pays, whether it is fair or not, until—until it ceases to pay. Honesty is the best policy—provided it shows dividends at the end of the year."

But Craig resented the thought of the disorder that seemed to lie badly enough concealed in such a philosophy. "That sort of man," he protested, "the man who follows that rule goes to the wall sooner or later. You forget, Professor Ayers, that there must be a broad principle of good faith in the business world in general or you couldn't have any valid contracts anywhere."

Charnley dismissed the whole question with a sudden puff of breath from between his thin lips. "All bunk, Magpie—and the same to you, professor," he said. "It was a wise guy that said 'All's fair in love and war' and we've put business in the same class. The morning the Germans let poison gas loose on the Canadian front—that morning we learned that the wise man is the one who begins by forgetting nine-tenths of what he learned in Sunday school and then throws his conscience out-of-doors. If you're fighting—well, fight! If you're out to make money, forget the ten commandments and go ahead. When you turn Romeo, go in through the lady's window and lock the door to keep everyone else out. Whatever you want—take it."

"If you can pay for it," added Crocker.

"And if you can't, take it anyhow," Charnley concluded.

Two

They were met at the train by Gilbert Nason himself who blustered up to them excitedly and tried to seize all their hands at once. He was dressed in an old pair of khaki coloured overalls and a cast-off shirt, a slouch felt hat pulled rakishly over one ear. Gilbert Nason believed in affecting, at least, the strenuous and simple life of the care-free camper while he was away from the city.

"Hello, Charnley—and you Forrester—glad you got away. And this is Professor Ayers, isn't it—Marion told me to look for the handsomest man in the crowd, ha! ha! You, too, Croker—this is bully! Come on, the launch is down this

74

way. Here, give me your bags. We'll stow the baggage and I'll come back to find Marion. She's looking for a couple of girls to complete the party. Hey, Dick! Give a hand here!"

In response to his call a youth of twenty shuffled his way through the noisy crowd and joined them. He was rather too tall for his slender build. His clothes revealed something of the same studied carelessness as those of his father, but his face wore none of the older man's eager expression. The arrival of guests for the week-end very evidently bored Dickie. For that matter, life in general might have been pretty much of a bore to the boy, if there is anything in the old epigram to the effect that the face is a mirror of the soul. His cheeks were sallow and gave the appearance of actually sagging. His lips were heavy and loose, his eyes constantly moist and the edges of his eyelids inflamed.

Craig was the only one who paid the boy any attention when he joined them. "Hello, Dick," he greeted him and held out his hand.

Dickie thrust his hand forward and permitted Craig to shake it. Then his father pushed a couple of bags toward him and invited the three men to follow him. As they walked down the path that led to where the launch stood moored to a small dock, Dickie fell into line beside Craig.

"Well, Dick," Craig began at once, "what's the latest thing among the moderns? Or do you do any reading down here?"

"What else is there to do?" Dickie responded. "I don't swim, and fishing is my idea of nothing to do. I might get a thrill if I went sailing with Dad, but I consider that taking too great chances. And while I don't think much of life the way it's lived here, I'd rather not drown. It suggests cats and superfluous puppies."

"You refuse to be classed with—"

"I refuse to be classed at all," Dickie interrupted. "When a man allows himself to be put into a class he becomes vulgar."

"Perhaps it's just a sign that he's getting older, Dick," Craig suggested.

"There isn't much difference. The older a man gets the more hopeless he becomes. All the old men are doing to-day is trying to kill off the younger generation."

"You mean the old men brought on the war because there were too many youngsters in the world?" Craig never knew just what Dickie Nason was driving at.

"The war? Pooh! They did some of it there, but it's nothing to what they're doing now. If they had their way they'd kill off every modern poet and novelist that didn't use the same forms as Tennyson and Scott. There's James Branch Cabell's 'Jurgen' for example—"

But they had already reached the bottom of the path and Gilbert Nason was busy piling the bags into place under the diminutive forward deck and exhorting his guests to get in and sit down while he went back to meet Marion and her friends. In the end, however, after the bags had been stowed in their place, the four men went back with their host, leaving Dickie to look after the launch till they should return.

They met Marion and her friends at the top of the hill and together the crowd of them swept down the path to the launch, chattering and laughing and disposing of introductions as they went. In the few moments it took them to reach the launch they had all become acquainted and Marion's contagious gaiety had infected the whole group.

"This is going to be the duckiest party of the season," she declared as she took her seat in the launch and looked round at the others while her father busied himself with getting the engine started.

And as the boat moved away from the dock and was turned toward the open waters of the lake, Craig caught Marion's eye and held it for a moment while they exchanged smiles. She was sitting between Charnley and Ayers.

Three

The "cottage" came into view about half an hour later as the launch nosed its way through a narrow channel and came out into another smaller lake dotted with countless islands covered with evergreens. It stood high up above the water on a bluff that rose almost sheer from the edge of the lake for a distance of more than fifty feet. The bluff fell away on one side and sloped gradually to the level of the water where a small floating dock had been built in a miniature bay at the farther end of which stood the boathouse. Gilbert Nason steered his craft rather expertly to its berth beside the dock and held it with his hand while Dickie clambered out and secured it with a line.

"Now, then—all out!" Nason called and at once his passengers proceeded to carry out his instructions hastily, if a bit awkwardly, the men helping the women up and throwing the bags out upon the float.

Marion led the way through the evergreens and up a winding path that brought them to the house that topped the bluff. It was a huge, one-storey affair, built of logs carefully selected for their smooth roundness and their trim straight length, and dove-tailed into place at the corners with a precision that was nothing short of artistic. A wide porch ran along the western and southern sides, the whole structure having been roofed with split shingles that gave just the desired rough-and-ready effect to the exterior. The centre of the house was one large room with a great stone fire-place at one end large enough to accommodate a good-sized log when the weather turned chilly. The place had been used as a winter hunting lodge, as well, a fact that was suggested by the trophies that hung from the walls, a large moose head above the fire place and several smaller heads on the other walls. The floor was bare save for a couple of small bear skins before the couches which stood one against each wall on either side of the fire-place. Doors on the northern and eastern sides led to the bedrooms ranged side by side in a partitioned annex. The roof above the living-room had been only partly finished so as to reveal the stout rafters from one of which hung a large, heavily shaded gas-lamp. Someday Mr. Nason would install his own electric plant, but for the present he preferred the rustic touch and derived no small satisfaction from the feeling that his "cabin"—as he insisted on calling it—was thoroughly and typically Canadian.

Mrs. Nason greeted her guests in the large central room, kissing the cheeks of the girls and even permitting Charnley the liberty of kissing her own. Nason arrived in a few minutes and Marion took the girls to their rooms to prepare for supper.

"You fellows will have to herd into one room to dress," Nason informed them, "that is unless you want to eat the way I do—in whatever clothes you happen to have on."

He "herded" them into a bedroom which was quite large enough to serve as dressing room for all four.

"Don't get the idea that you're all going to sleep in one room," their host reassured them when he had closed the door and laid out a half dozen towels for them. "The old lady has covers for a dozen cots and we have a screened porch that's proof against mosquitoes. You'll be able to lie with your eyes on the lake and wake up to as nice a picture as you ever saw. It's got the real outdoor Canadian touch to it. However, fall to now—I'll go and get a little refreshment ready."

The men dressed hurriedly and emerged presently to find a row of cocktails awaiting them on a shelf beside the fire-place.

"My own blend," Gilbert Nason said as he handed the glasses about and picked up one for himself.

They drank the cocktails, Croker pronouncing his drink of finer flavour than anything he had sampled in the days before such things as cocktails were forbidden—Croker's favourite pastime was to damn prohibition and all its attending evils—and the men went out to view the sunset from the western porch.

Half an hour later they returned from a stroll along the edge of the bluff to find the table laid and ready for supper in the large living-room. The sun had set and the air had turned almost suddenly cool so that the men in the white flannels and the ladies in their "sport" clothes fell in readily enough with Mrs. Nason's suggestion that her husband should start a small fire to take the chill out of the air.

The company that sat down to supper was noisily gay and in keen spirits. Having left the city for a few days of relaxation, they set about the business of enjoying themselves with fully twice the amount of energy they would have given to their occupations in town. Craig found himself seated at the table between Marion and one of her friends from the city, a Miss Howard, to whom, it was plain from the outset, he was expected to show a great deal of attention. Miss Howard had spent the past three years in a bank—she was the daughter of a well-to-do citizen and had taken up banking as an inoffensive means of "doing her bit" during the war—and had never quite recovered from the thrill which she experienced on receiving her first salary check. She was in her early twenties, of medium height, could have been called plump with perfect safety, and rolled her soft eyes up to Craig whenever he spoke as if she were pleading with him not to strike her. "Soft," Craig labelled her at once and began to think of ways of escape that would not outrage his innate sense of courtesy to the poor girl. Across the table from him sat a very beautiful girl who, Miss Howard informed him in a confidential whisper that brought her lips perilously close to his ear, was a nurse and the daughter of Mr. Frawley who owned "ever so many" ranches in the west and had a packing concern in the city. "She's rather—rather interesting—but I'll tell you about her later," Miss Howard said in a murmur that entailed no risk in the noisy chatter that prevailed about the table. Concerning the third of Marion's girl friends Craig knew nothing but that her name was Smith and that she seemed as matter-of-fact as her name. Miss Howard informed him that she had joined the staff of a newspaper in town and had written some short stories and a one-act play that had been produced by the leading amateur company of the city. Craig could see nothing in her outward manner that held promise of a brilliant career in the literary world, but he was wise enough to know that such qualities do not always appear on the surface. At any rate, the girl and Croker seemed to be having an interesting time of it between them, their position at one corner of the table affording an opportunity to carry on their own conversation without being forced to join in the general chatter.

The company presented a perplexing mixture to Craig as he looked about him and listened to Miss Howard's low-murmured account of each one. He was aware that the war had broken through many old lines of distinction and had brought together people who would never have known one another under ordinary conditions. But he was quite convinced that in Marion Nason herself could be found the real reason for the existence of such an assembly under one roof and about one table. These were Marion's friends, men and women, and the more or less motley aspect of the group was but an expression of Marion's tastes in the matter of human contacts. The more thought he gave to this newly discovered quality in Marion's mind, the more Craig found in it to admire—and the more resolutely did he hope for a moment when Miss Howard's cooing voice might subside simultaneously with a pause in the rapid fire talk of Claude Charnley who sat next to Marion and seemed bent on permitting no one else to get a word with her. It was annoying. Miss Howard paused only when Charnley was busiest. Charnley's voice halted only when it would have been rankest discourtesy for Craig to turn abruptly away from something Miss Howard was telling him, always in a tone of confidence.

At last the moment arrived, and Marion, as if she had been waiting for the opening with fully as much impatience as Craig, startled him by seizing the advantage before he was able to frame a sentence with which to address her.

"Have you seen anything of Jeannette during the past month?" she asked him.

"I haven't seen her since the night I met her at your home," he replied. "She spoke that night of calling me up and having me attend some meeting or other in which she was interested, but I guess she's put me out of her life."

He smiled as she shook her head. "No—I won't believe that of Jeannette," Marion responded. "Jeannette does put people out of her life, as you say, but only after she has found them to be helplessly mummified. I have good reason to believe—"

"Don't you think you can persuade Captain Forrester to tell us some of the heroic things he did when he was in France, Marion?" Miss Howard cooed, with her cheek touching Craig's left shoulder.

"I should think you could get him to do that, Vicky," Marion suggested. "I've never known how to get a returned man to tell of his experiences."

"I've heard some—some perfectly wonderful stories from men who have come back—one boy in the bank—"

Damn the woman! She was in control of the conversation again and Craig would have to listen and, a moment later hear Charnley's voice begin again on the other side of Marion.

"I know it must be very unpleasant to awaken some of the horrible memories," Miss Howard ventured when she had told the story of the hero who worked on the ledgers with her at the bank, "but don't you think you could tell me some of your experiences—later, perhaps, when the conversation isn't quite so general. I'd love to hear about it."

Craig had to study his reply to avoid being rude. "I'm afraid, Miss Howard," he said, "I'm a poor talker and besides, I seem to have forgotten everything that happened over there, so far as the fighting is concerned."

Miss Howard lifted her great eyes to him and smiled. "Of course, I think it's rather wonderful of you not to want to," she breathed, and Craig felt very much an ass.

His attention was diverted, however, by the voices of Gilbert Nason and Professor Ayers who had evidently disagreed over Canada's right to have equal voting power with other nations in the League.

"While, from the point of view of the British Empire," Ayers was saying, "it would be a very desirable thing to have six or seven votes, it seems to me rather a difficult thing to establish that right before we have satisfactorily established Canada's place as a nation among the other nations of the world. Perhaps I—"

The words had been addressed to Nason, but Croker lifted his head suddenly and spoke up. "I'd like to know what a country has to do, Professor, before it establishes itself as a nation. And when you've told us that I'd like to know if Canada hasn't done it."

"I was hoping Daddy would stay off politics till after supper," Marion said in an aside to Craig.

But Marion's wishes, it appeared, played a very small part in determining the course of the evening's conversation. With Charnley's assistance, and with Miss Howard's soft voice constantly cooing an undertone, Craig and Marion contrived, with more or less success, to keep up a four-sided discussion of their own. Marion seemed bent upon talking over the plans of the dramatic club for the coming season.

"I think it's just about time we were thinking of getting a stage of our own. There are a number of smaller movie houses—I should think we might find one somewhere in the north end—"

From the other end of the table came Ayers' voice. "If the United States can't be persuaded to join the league we might just as well give up the project. If Wilson is defeated at the next election, the league—"

"I think the question of finding a stage of our own might be left over for another year," Charnley suggested, "until we know whether the club is going to hang together or not. These things have a way of falling to pieces before they are old enough to stand alone."

"Perhaps you're right, Claude," Marion admitted, "but it would look more as if we were really trying to create something if we had some sort of permanent workshop in which to try out any new ideas we may have."

"—the American people have been taught to believe that they won the war and they'll not come in unless we give them a vote for every state—"

"Don't you love the theatre, Captain Forrester?" Miss Howard asked.

"I confess I don't know very much about it," Craig replied. "I once saw a good comedy and I liked it, but I'm afraid I've forgotten it. I saw a couple of burlesque shows in London, but—"

"Oh, you shouldn't admit any such weakness in Marion's hearing!"

But Marion was much too intent upon what Charnley was telling her at the moment to hear either Craig or Miss Howard. Craig overheard a half dozen words from Charnley in the brief interval that Miss Howard granted him.

"—a play by Andreyev, called 'Anathema,' I think—"

Croker's voice rose again above the sound of Charnley's.

"—never can be such a thing as permanent peace so long as there are two people left in—"

"Of course, we look upon the theatre as a means of expression rather than as a place to go for entertainment," put in Miss Howard. "We think Ibsen has brought the stage back to its rightful place as a mirror of contemporary society." Was she quoting from some book she had recently read? "We are experiencing new emotions that aren't getting themselves properly expressed and we think it our duty to experiment with new forms that will be adequate to express them."

"You think they should be expressed?" Craig ventured from sheer stubborn resistance to the girl's attempt to draw him into any form of conversation. "Why not leave them alone where they are without dragging them out on the stage for the audience to see them?"

"Well—well—"

She paused and rolled her eyes up to him in helpless appeal.

Croker again: "We don't need to have a real issue to bring on another war. All we need is a new slogan."

But Miss Howard smiled at Craig. "I think you're the most original person. I wish someone would write you into a play."

"O God!" Craig groaned.

Four

A few minutes later the company got up from the table and Gilbert Nason led the men out of the house to the porch where they smoked their cigars in the twilight and continued the political discussion they had begun during supper. Presently the strains of a lively fox-trot being played on a phonograph issued from the doorway leading to the living-room and Marion came to order them into the house for a dance.

Craig was reluctant enough to leave the discussion to which he had been listening with a satisfaction that was greater because he found it quite unnecessary to take any active part in it himself. He lingered a moment until the other men had gone in, then went in with Gilbert Nason.

"Come on, Craig," Nason encouraged him, "and get your joints loosened up. These arguments on the European crisis are likely to make a man stiff in the knees."

They were already dancing, each man having chosen for the first dance the same partner that had sat with him at supper. Craig looked across the room to where Miss Howard was standing expectantly beside Mrs. Nason. There was nothing for it, apparently. It must be Miss Howard! In his heart he was almost thankful that he was a clumsy dancer without the slightest knowledge of the new steps that gave zest to the fox-trot and kept the dance interesting for one's partner. He didn't want to prove interesting to Miss Howard. He let his eyes follow Marion moving lightly about the floor with Charnley's arm about her and wished he could induce Miss Howard to throw herself over the edge of the bluff.

Nevertheless, he strode resolutely across the floor and did his best to muster a smile.

"Come on, here, Craig," Mrs. Nason cried to him when he had covered scarcely more than half the distance that separated him from his hostess and Miss Howard. "Vicky has been waiting for you to come in out of the cold until I thought we'd have to go out and capture you."

Craig bowed and offered his arm to Miss Howard. "I'm a rotten dancer, Miss Howard, but—"

"Make him call you 'Vicky'," Mrs. Nason admonished Miss Howard. "It's our chief business in life to keep some of the best looking men for ourselves and to keep them from getting old. Make him call you 'Vicky' and shake him up a little so he'll know he's alive."

"Come along, old girl," Gilbert Nason greeted his wife, and Craig was left to the mercies of the soft, plump person who moved toward him and put her hand on his shoulder.

They danced their way half the length of the room before either of them spoke. Craig was experiencing the temporary embarrassments consequent upon adjusting himself to his partner's movements and with an ear turned to catch the music, striving as best he could to put a little of his own sense of rhythm into the motion of his feet. His task was causing him no little concern and for the present he was conscious most of his ill-concealed awkwardness, fearing momentarily the sudden miss-step that he felt sure would bring disaster of some kind to his partner.

The sound of Miss Howard's voice, for all its softness, smote across his fear-taut consciousness with a suddenness that startled him.

"I wish you *would* call me 'Vicky'—I'd like it," she said.

"What is your first name?" Craig asked evasively.

"Victoria."

"I see—of course. I might have guessed it—I beg your pardon!"

Something had happened—they were out of step—they halted a moment in the middle of the floor and started afresh.

Thereafter, the question of how he should address her was left in abeyance while she directed him through the intricate movements of the dance and introduced him to a couple of new "steps" which he took up with a facility that surprised him and won expressions of delighted approval from his partner. After that they returned to the simpler movements with which they had begun the dance and Craig found himself drifting into the swing and rhythm of the thing in a way that brought a thrill of great satisfaction to him.

He ventured presently to turn his attention to the other dancers and finally found Marion and Charnley. They danced well—as if their understanding of each other went much further than the mere requirements of dancing. He admitted, rather grudgingly, that they seemed to be nicely mated in height—she was just tall enough to rest her head on Charnley's shoulder—and in some other indefinable way that he could not easily explain. Nothing could be more natural in the world than that Marion and Charnley should—no, he wouldn't admit that Marion was meant for Charnley.

She looked over Charnley's shoulder and caught his eye. Smiling a little, she lifted her hand a moment from Charnley's shoulder and waved her fingers toward him.

And then the music stopped. Miss Howard disengaged herself more slowly than Craig felt the occasion demanded and stood with one hand on his arm.

"Why, I think you dance wonderfully!" she exclaimed.

But Craig's eyes were upon Marion where she came skipping gaily across the floor toward them, her bobbed hair shaking as she tossed her head.

"I want the next, Craig," she called when she was yet several paces away.

And then, in a moment, the music had begun again and they left Miss Howard to the mercies of Ayers who came up at the proper moment and asked if he might dance the next one with her.

Inwardly Craig was not sorry he had danced the first with Miss Howard. It had broken him in, so to speak, and he was less conscious of his awkwardness as he moved down the floor with Marion. They did not speak at first. Craig was experiencing a new sensation, a consciousness that the girl whose slender body he held in the circle of his arm was moving about with the ease and smoothness of a skater. No wonder Charnley could dance well with her. Who couldn't? He believed he was doing very creditably himself.

"Has Vicky been trying to vamp you yet?" Marion asked with a roguish smile.

"I haven't observed it," he replied.

She laughed and tossed her head as she looked up at him. "She will, sooner or later. It's a little way she has with good looking men."

"That leaves me safe," he replied.

"How modest we are. But I mustn't be catty. Vicky is really

a very good sort when you get to know her. She has really
worked very hard for the dramatic club and we all like her...
I didn't know you were such a good dancer. You always told
me you never danced."

"I don't believe I do. With you it seems different, though.
I couldn't imagine anyone not dancing if he had you for a
partner."

Somehow he wished he had not said that. It seemed
so palpably the thing that was expected of him. He felt
that the expected thing was precisely not the thing to offer
Marion Nason. He wished he could think of something
original, something witty—no, he didn't want to be witty.
Charnley could be that on occasion. He wanted most of
all to be serious. And yet, knowing how serious he was by
nature, he curiously enough sought some way to avoid
being so.

Everything he could think of saying seemed so futile, so
uninteresting, so provokingly inappropriate...

"I thought you danced very well with Vicky," Marion
stated. "I watched you from the corner of one eye."

"On the contrary, I got along very awkwardly—especially
at first."

"You'll do better when you dance with her again."

"Are you going to insist on my dancing with her again?"

She tossed her head again and looked at him in mock
surprise. "You're not trying to shirk, are you?"

"Lord, no—only—"

"There's the moonlight dance."

"The moonlight?"

"Yes. We always have one moonlight. Daddy turns the
light down and we dance in the light from the moon. It's
almost full now and you'd be surprised how the place is
lighted."

"If you don't mind, I shall try to find another partner for the moonlight, then."

"Why—Craig!"

"I beg your pardon. That was rude. But I'm inclined to be a little rude when I'm off my guard."

"Besides—we make it a rule here that you dance the last with the same partner you chose for the first."

Craig wanted to tell her that he had had nothing to do with choosing a partner for the first. But a better impulse seized him.

"I'll do so—cheerfully, if you'll dance the moonlight with me."

"We don't arrange our dances ahead. You'll have to dance the last with Vicky—and no conditions attached."

"I guess I've shown myself in a bad light," Craig apologized. "Well—just forget it and in the meantime I'll do my best by Miss Howard."

"I think you're ungrateful. Vicky likes you. I saw that the first moment she set eyes on you. And she's really a very nice girl."

"Lord, yes, I admit it. Now, will you dance the moonlight with me?"

She laughed up at him. "Didn't I tell you the rules were—"

"I'm in a mood for breaking any old rule that happens to be in the way of what I want. In fact, I'm in a very destructive mood right now."

"It wouldn't be fair."

"I don't want to be fair. I want to dance—"

"Sh-h-h!"

The music had stopped suddenly and Craig's voice sounded above the chatter that had begun immediately.

Charnley was upon them at once, bringing Miss Frawley with him, and together the four went to a couch and sat down.

Craig danced the next with Miss Frawley and afterwards went the round of the ladies in the company, including Mrs. Nason, who danced very prettily indeed.

The "moonlight" was sprung upon them so suddenly that Craig was taken entirely off his guard. He looked quickly for Marion, found her in the farthest corner of the room, and gained her side just as Ayers stepped in and proffered his request. Craig watched them go away together and felt himself very much of a soldier as he stepped before the little woman of the newspaper and bowed as he offered her his arm. The effect of the dance was highly romantic; Mr. Nason had softened the music and lowered the lights till there was scarcely a glimmer left to compete with the moonlight that streamed in from the porch, and the dancers moved about like eerie figures making scarcely a sound save for the soft brushing of their feet upon the floor.

When the music stopped a clamour arose to have the dance repeated.

"Change partners, then," the host announced and as the music began once more Craig turned quickly in the hope of picking out a slender figure in white and a tossing head with bobbed hair shaking in the half-light. He discovered her at the other side of the room, standing between Croker and Charnley, both of whom apparently begged for the honour of dancing with her.

Craig stepped quickly toward her, saw her hesitate a moment before yielding to Croker, then turned and found himself looking into the soft eyes of Miss Howard.

"I really believe you are trying to avoid me," she murmured as she moved a little closer and put out her hands to him.

"On the contrary, you have been so much in demand—"

"I didn't think you would stoop to flattery."

And then they danced.

"Let me put my arm under yours...there, I like that better."

Craig did not. The position she took brought her very close to him and made graceful dancing almost impossible. More than once Craig attempted to change the position in such a way as to leave his legs free to execute the easy striding movement which he preferred to the short shuffling step necessitated by the position they had taken. But the girl re-adjusted herself to every change and Craig silently accepted the inevitable. She was not tall enough to rest her head on his shoulder, but she laid her cheek close against him so that her dark hair, faintly perfumed, brushed his chin. There was something too frankly intimate in the way she pressed her soft body to him and closed her fingers warmly about his hand. His senses were stirred strangely, and in spite of himself he found his breath coming unevenly.

Almost as if she sensed what was happening within him, the girl laughed lightly and Craig felt her arm press against his shoulder. For a moment a brutal and primitive instinct flamed up within him and he was tempted to crush her mercilessly in his arms and leave her.

The music stopped suddenly and Miss Howard drew back and stepped through the door opening onto the porch. Craig followed her, urged on by he knew not what impulse, and stood beside her with his eyes turned toward the lake lying glassy-smooth under the moonlight.

Then he looked at the girl beside him.

"Do you dance with everyone like that?" he asked bluntly.

She moved till her shoulder pressed his arm and turned her large eyes up to him softly. "Not with—everybody."

"Don't do so again—with me," Craig requested in a voice that had not yet regained its usual firmness.

"I really believe you are afraid of me," she said shyly.

"I really believe I am," he admitted. He struggled to keep a note of anger out of his voice.

"How very—" She strove to find the exact word she wanted. "How very—how very pre-war-ish you are!"

Which was only another way of telling him that he was hopelessly old-fashioned and out of step with the times. He was glad that others came out of the house to view the lake in the moonlight just then.

Presently Marion left Croker's side and rushed upon Craig and Miss Howard. "You old mooners," she said as she threw her arm about the girl and looked at Craig with a smile. "Craig Forrester, you're not growing romantic suddenly, are you, standing out here in the moonlight? I didn't think it was in you."

"As a matter of fact you know I am the most romantic person you ever met," Craig countered. "Otherwise I should not have insisted on having that last dance with you. Probably if I had not been quite so romantic—if I had been more like Ayers or Croker—"

"Oh, you couldn't believe how incurably romantic both of them are!"

Craig looked at her as if he had never seen her before. What witchery, what full-blown beauty was hers!

"Will you let me take you for a canoe ride as soon as we are through dancing?" he asked abruptly. "Or are you booked up for that, too?"

She glanced toward Croker and Miss Howard standing apart talking quietly with their faces toward the lake.

"I'd like that," Marion replied. "And no one has thought of suggesting it—yet."

"Sold!" Craig cried, borrowing from the jargon of the pit.

"Don't you think you'd better—what do you call it?—

don't you think you'd better *hedge* a little—just to be safe? You might get an option on Vicky."

Five

Craig and Marion were not alone as they hurried down the little pathway through the evergreens and came to the boathouse where the canoes were kept. Charnley was there and Ayers and with them the Frawley girl and the inevitable Miss Howard. Croker and his quiet young friend had remained behind to talk with Gilbert Nason.

There was some discussion as to how they should pair off for the trip on the lake—the matter had not, it seemed been settled definitely before leaving the house—but Craig put a hand firmly on Marion's arm and let Charnley and Ayers settle a question that was quite clearly their own.

They were soon on the water, the three canoes striking straight out in the golden path the moon threw upon the lake. The burden of taking care of Miss Howard had fallen upon Charnley and Craig could not help feeling that somewhere in the universe, after all, was a divine power that kept the balance of human affairs even.

Two small islands lying directly before them prompted Charnley to suggest that the three canoes should separate to take different courses around the islands and meet on the farther side.

"I wonder if there are such nights as this anywhere else in all the world?" Marion exclaimed.

The shore line with its black silhouette of pointed spruce, the islands lying like dark, sleeping creatures on the water with here and there a glint of light on the topmost branches and stems of the trees, the dark water with a narrow strip of rippling gold running from the bow of the canoe, and in the distance a slow creeping of mist-cloud out along the water from a low level of grassland where the tall reeds stood white and shivering in the moonlight...

They came to the other side of the island to find that Charnley and Ayers had taken still another direction. The low murmur of their voices came clear to them over the water.

They had gone along for some distance without speaking, yielding their spirits to the magic of the night. There was no sound but the soft dip of Craig's paddle in the water and the intermittent murmur of the voices from the other canoes—and over all the constant trill of the frogs.

It occurred to Craig that he would never find another setting so perfectly fitted to speaking the thing that was in his heart to say.

"I hope you did not think me too rude to-night in what I said about Miss Howard," he said. "I did my very best to make it up to her later. The fact is, Marion, I can't find anything interesting in any other girl when you are around. I may as well confess to you at once that I have been in love with you ever since the night you sang for us—the night Jeannette Bawden was at the house for dinner. I have no way of making phrases—like Charnley for instance—and I can't tell you what I want to tell you in the way—I'm just awkward at such things and I can't help it. But I'm in earnest—terribly so—and I want you to know how much I—love you."

Marion was dipping slender fingers in the water just where the moonlight fell alongside the bow of the canoe. Little flecks of silver and gold leaped up and fell away as the canoe glided slowly past. Marion's head was bowed with the moonlight doing strange things in her hair. She did not speak when Craig paused after his rather blunt confession.

"I want you to know that it isn't the effect of the night

or—or anything that has just happened on the spur of the moment," he went on. "I have thought it all out—quietly—seriously. There was one other woman once—I'll tell you about her when you wish—but she isn't of our world and I have forgotten all the love I thought I had for her before I went away."

"Did you promise to marry her?"

"No, no! I never told her a word of what I felt. She was the girl who used to live on a farm next to ours—we used to see a great deal of each other—it seemed the natural thing to look forward to marrying her some day, that was all. But she wasn't of our world, Marion. She wasn't of the new world where things are changing. We are, and I need you. I need you to help me, and I know you can do it as no other can. I want you to be my wife, Marion. Tell me—can I hope—will you let me plan a future for us two?"

"I had a feeling you were going to tell me about—about this to-night," she said quietly. "I believe it's sort of in the air. Yours is not the first proposal I have had to-night."

"You mean Charnley has spoken before me?"

Marion laughed lightly. "Oh, Claude proposes every week or so. Sometimes I think I ought to marry Claude. We've been such good friends and we understand each other as well as if we'd been married for years. But it wasn't Claude. Perhaps I'm a poor sport to tell, but it has struck me since as being rather funny."

"You don't mean Ayers?" He couldn't think of Croker doing anything so sentimental.

"I was offered the honour of becoming a professor's wife. I don't mean to treat it lightly and I am trusting you not to say anything about it. But I couldn't stand the thought of being the centre of college-hall gossip among the sophomore girls and I couldn't face faculty teas after listening to mother's accounts of the affairs for what she calls the 'faculty wives' and I—well, I just couldn't think of it, though I like Mr. Ayers very much. I think he's handsome and cultured and I find him very interesting to talk to. I believe we could become very fast friends."

Craig had a feeling that she was getting away from the subject. He brought her back to it promptly.

"Then, at least you haven't given your affection to anyone else?"

She was silent for a long time before she spoke.

"No—I haven't—I'm not sure that I want to. I don't know that I want to be married at all. After the first year married life seems to get terribly dull, if one is to judge from the husbands and wives one sees about one."

"But you expect to be married some day?"

"Yes—probably. It seems the thing to do for women. But I love to be free more than I love anything else."

wants to be free
doesn't want marriage dynamic

"I would not bind you—you would be as free as you chose—as long as I could have you to come home to at the end of the day. Marion, perhaps you do not care for me as I hoped you might, but let me ask for myself. I never needed anything in my life quite so much as I need you. Let me hope—a little."

"Oh, dear—how does one decide such things? There are so many things to—"

"Tell me anything—ask me anything," Craig pleaded.

And for fully an hour they talked until Marion sounded a warning that it was time they should be getting in.

"What is your last word, then?" he persisted when they had covered more than half the distance back to the boathouse.

"Don't ask me for my last word yet," she begged, "I want time to think it over. Would you mind—very much—if I mentioned it to Claude?"

Craig did not know how to reply.

"I must leave that to your own judgment," he said finally.

As they rounded a corner of an island they came suddenly upon Ayers and the Frawley girl making for home. Ayers hailed them and the two canoes drew together and a few minutes later came alongside the float.

Craig and Marion led the way up the hill to the house. Half way along the path they found themselves considerably in advance of the other two.

"When shall I know?" Craig whispered.

"Soon—perhaps to-morrow night," Marion replied. "Don't be impatient."

From the porch they hallooed to let Charnley and Miss Howard know that they had come in. From far out on the lake Charnley's voice came back to them.

The cots were in place on the porch and Gilbert Nason and his wife were already preparing to retire. In a few moments Craig found himself alone on the porch with Ayers and Croker. The two latter were getting ready to turn in, but Craig was too restless to follow their example immediately.

Hearing the sound of a paddle striking the edge of a canoe, he decided to stroll down to the boathouse and meet Charnely. At the foot of the path he halted abruptly. They had landed and were standing in the shadow of the boathouse talking in subdued tones. All at once Charnley took the girl in his arms and held her close to him while he kissed her lingeringly. Then they stood for some time in close embrace, and presently started up toward the path.

Craig retreated noiselessly and hurried back to the house ahead of them, wishing with all his heart that he had gone to bed at once when Ayers and Croker had done so.

He hurried out of his clothes and was thankful to be

in bed when Charnley finally arrived after showing Miss Howard into the house through the door at the back.

Six

Late that night, when the moon had set, Craig opened his eyes on a world that was still as death. From where he lay at one end of the porch he could see the night sky studded with stars and up from the northernmost point of the horizon a single shaft of the aurora borealis rose to the zenith, its gold and crimson folds swaying slowly back and forth among the stars.

As he gazed, two meteors shot together athwart the shaft, a thread of white light in the wake of each.

"Perhaps it is an omen," he thought to himself.

But he did not observe that the light in the wake of one died suddenly, while the light that followed the other made a path half way to the horizon before it died also.

On the following night, while they were alone in a canoe watching the sunset from the lake, Marion promised to marry Craig before the end of the year.

PART TWO | MARTHA

CHAPTER I.

One

IN NOVEMBER Craig and Marion were married.

For four months they occupied a suite of rooms in the Fort Garry while the work was being finished on the interior of a snug little house they had chosen in Crescentwood, only a few blocks from the Nason home. They were four months of unalloyed happiness for Craig, months during which he all but forgot the problems that had perplexed him during the restless days following immediately upon the close of the war. Marion was the beautiful, the impulsive, the radiant fulfilment of his dreams, the creature of light and laughter that he had loved that night when he had heard her voice singing to him and stirring his heart with high hope for the world in the days to come.

There had been great moments during those first four months when Craig felt that the sun must have already risen on the new day the world awaited. In the light of his own happiness it seemed impossible that there could be very much wrong with the world in which he lived. They had entertained at little dinner parties in the hotel and Craig had met again the members of Marion's "set," the Frawley girl and Ayers, Croker and Miss Howard, and a host of young people whom Craig had never met before. He had withdrawn engagements of his own to accompany them on snowshoe tramps, taken early leave of congenial company to join them in moccasin dances, striven to anticipate every wish of the indefatigable young person who had become mistress of his heart, and was happy if only a smile

lots of Craig's experience — not Nenor

or a perfunctory kiss rewarded his services. It was as if they were all on a great lark that would come to an end only too soon when the affairs of life began to press. And Craig gave himself to the enjoyment of it all with scarcely a thought of what lay before him.

At Christmas Craig took a couple of weeks from his business and planned a holiday among the cities in the south. He had felt for some time that he must visit the exporters in Chicago and New York and establish new connections for the coming season. It was during their stay in Chicago that the first cloud appeared in Craig's bright skies. He had been asked to join a small group of men who had met to talk over the prospects of the European market for the coming year. Marion had been left to herself for the evening and Craig had come back to the hotel to find her already asleep. As he prepared quietly for bed, his eyes fell upon a letter lying on a small table near the door. The envelope was addressed in Marion's handwriting and bore the name of Claude Charnley.

Ordinarily the incident would not have disturbed him. Charnley had been a frequent visitor during the past few weeks and Craig had discovered much that was really likeable in the fellow. He had been at great pains to assure Charnley that he was welcome whenever he wished to call. He had striven to overcome his instinctive dislike for him and had succeeded marvellously. At the sight of the letter, however, a twinge of the old feeling shot through him and left him bewildered. All evening he had been with men who had mulled over questions of foreign markets and international exchange until he had grown weary for the want of someone to talk to for whom such things as markets and exchange held no interest whatever and very little meaning. He had come back in the hope that Marion might listen while he told her something of the old dream that had returned to him during the evening while his friends talked of Germany and France and Russia. While they had talked of practical problems of finance and politics he had dreamed again the dream of those first days of his return home. It had come to him during the evening that he had not spoken much of late of his great hope of a new world and he felt as one feels who has betrayed the trust of a friend. It had been the thing he had held closest to his heart when his love for Marion had blossomed there. He determined to tell her about it at once, to let the hope that was in him mount into full flame once more—perhaps to lie awake in the warm comfort of their love and talk far into the night.

Now, to find Marion asleep, the letter she had written during his absence lying on the table—strange how great impulses are often turned aside by the merest trifles! For a moment after finding the letter he stood and looked at it, wondering not so much what might be written there as why the sight of it should disturb him so unreasonably.

At the sound of Marion stirring in her sleep he turned abruptly and looked at her. Her head upon the pillow held the mysterious lights—like the mingling of moonlight and shadow—that he had loved from the first. One hand was under her cheek and her bare throat white and moving with the slow rise and fall of her breathing. He tip-toed to the side of the bed and leaned above her for a moment. The coverlet was turned back revealing the soft lines of her breast and the round curve of her shoulder. A sudden hunger leaped up within him and he put out a hand to touch her hair. She moved slightly and a great tenderness filled him as he withdrew his hand quickly for fear of waking her.

A few moments later, as he slipped quietly into bed, she awoke, and turning, drew his arm about her and sleepily murmured her goodnight.

He drew her gently toward him and felt the soft warmth of her slender body against him.

A great content filled him and a happiness swelled in his heart so that he had to grip his hands to control himself.

And yet, it was scarcely more than five minutes since he had doubted her... no, he hadn't doubted her... it was not doubt... such a thing could never enter his heart.

Two

And then spring came.

Nowhere in all the world does spring come in as it does in Canada. After the long weeks of frozen rivers and white lakes and forests lying deep with snow there comes a week of sunshine and soft clouds and warm breezes from the south. The bear comes out, so the hunters say, sniffs the air, and turns back again into his hole for his beauty sleep. He has probably not closed his eyes before the skies turn grey, the sun-dogs stand on either side of the rising sun, the wind ceases for an hour and there comes a feeling of rain in the air. Presently there rises a sound as of a wind stirring far away. Then from the north it comes, the white driving blizzard that gathers all the last chilling breath of Winter in his death agonies and sends it down laden with fine snow that comes in swirls and eddies and fitful gusts that seem to meet from all directions at once. Three days, perhaps, it takes the old fellow to draw his last breath, and then he is gone. Almost overnight the change comes. Before a week has gone the water is lying in pools in the lowlands, the fields are steaming under the sun, the plains are brown with patches of new green showing here and there in the higher spots, the birds come north in great flocks that fill the night with carolling, the purple crocus pushes up its head, and the farmer sings as he puts his team into the fields in the early morning.

It was difficult, walking down the street under the warm sun, to realize that all was not well with the world, that old hatreds were rankling, and that new hatreds were being born. Bolshevism had risen like a black cloud in the east and was threatening to overcome Polish resistance and sweep down upon Europe to shatter the remains of civilization. France and Britain had already begun to distrust each other. The prospect of a great republic, saved from the crushing heel of a militarist Empire, itself becoming a menace to the peace of the world, was being spoken of in the streets. Guarded criticism found its way into the columns of the daily papers. The Turks had returned to their slaughter of the Armenians, only now the Powers looked on afraid to move lest they should upset a sensitive diplomatic balance and precipitate a crisis as great as that of 1918.

And yet, deep in Craig Forrester's heart lived still the hope that had sustained him ever since that night in France when he had caught a vision of the new world that must rise from the ruins of the old. The conditions in Europe were but passing phases, the necessary after-effects of four years of drunken delirium.

It was thus he argued with himself as he walked westward along the avenue thronging with late afternoon shoppers. Hearing his name called, he turned to see Jeannette Bawden waving her hand to him from the doorway of one of the stores.

He had not seen her for some weeks, not since before Christmas when she had called on them at the hotel and spent a quiet evening with Marion. He remembered that night now. He had been forced to spend the earlier part of the evening at a local club where he had been called to help entertain a number of Montreal exporters who were leaving that night for the east. He had broken away in order to get back in time for a chat with Jeannette, only to find upon his arrival that she had already left.

She gave him her hand as he came up to her and searched his face with her shrewd gaze.

"You're looking awfully well," she said. "I don't know whether to congratulate you or scold you for it."

Craig could not frame a reply that fitted the occasion. Jeannette's remark seemed to call for something facetious, but for the life of him he could think of nothing to say except to ask blunderingly what she meant.

"I mean," she replied, then paused. "I mean—you look as if you were going to vindicate my fears."

"Your fears? And what are they?"

She smiled in the strange way he had often seen her smile before, half cynically, half pityingly.

"You were made of the right stuff, Craig," she said finally. "But you look too comfortable. I liked you better when you had the pucker between your brows. You used to be worried about things, but you're getting over it like all the rest of them. You're too comfortable. If you don't take care, you'll get fat and easy-going and before another ten years you'll buy yourself a bull-dog and a fan and spend the afternoon on the front porch with a glass of lemonade and a love story, and your wife will have to wake you to get you to dress for dinner. That's the way with the world, Craig. It gets married, then it gets fat, then it grows old and falls asleep in its chair—and then a war comes along and wakes it up and gives it a chance to become young and start all over again."

She laughed as she spoke, but Craig's face was serious. Somehow, this woman who had suffered so much in ways and never spoke of, this woman who carried herself with such confidence and spoke to him in a voice that never seemed to lose the charm it had held the first time he had heard it—somehow, she had probed a wound in his conscience. For weeks he had been struggling to throw off a feeling almost of lethargy that he had felt coming upon him for some time. Was it possible that Jeannette Bawden could actually see that he had changed since that night, almost a year ago. when he had chatted with her in the Nason home?

The man in him refused to be cornered—even by a woman as brilliant as Jeannette Bawden. He affected her facetious manner.

"You don't seem to think much of married life, Jeannette," he ventured.

The smile died suddenly from her lips. "That's where you are terribly mistaken," she said quietly. "I do—but I don't think there are many men who can stand it, or women either for that matter. When one is married the only thing worth while seems to establish one's position securely in society and then spend all your energies fortifying it."

"Is that the reason you haven't been around to see us lately? We have moved into our house. Marion was speaking of you just the other night."

She gave him a quick, darting glance. "Was she?"

"Yes—certainly! Why, Jeannette, what's the matter?"

She stepped out of the doorway and started down the street. "Go along with me, Craig," she suggested. "I have another purchase or two to make and we can talk just as well along the way."

He fell into step beside her.

"There's nothing the matter, Craig, not a thing in the world. But I can't—somehow—go visiting people as easily as I once could. Marion least of all. It may seem foolish to you—I may be unkind in saying what I am about to say, but I know what the truth is and there's no reason why we should deceive each other. Marion is doing what she thinks is right. I did the same thing when I was her age. I don't know whether they ever told you much about me."

"Marion has told me a little."

"I married a man—a brilliant man—because I loved him with all the passion of my young life. I thought it was my part in life to love, and love—and in my own way do all I could to make a home where the man I loved could come for rest and comfort when the day's work was done. To keep him so that he would be glad to come back to me from the office and find quiet with me in the long evenings when we were alone. I was jealous of everything that kept him from me and I was sentimental to the point of silliness over such trifles as learning how to choose his favourite brand of cigars and how to place his slippers and his house jacket and—you know very well what I mean, Craig. You've had a few months now of the very same thing with Marion. I learned to talk with him about the cases he argued before the judges and how he brought men out of tangles where it was thought escape was impossible. I can't describe all I did—and we were very happy, as happy as two lovers from the first day of our married life till the day he left with his battalion. I moved in his circles, played bridge with the wives of his chief clients, sought for ways to help him make his position secure. We might have been just as happy now—would have been just as happy if the storm in Europe had not broken. I lost him."

She paused a moment as her voice grew unsteady.

"The night after I got the message telling me that he had been killed was a night of heavy fog. I sat alone in the house where we had spent so many of our evenings together and he came to me there, Craig, just as surely as he had ever done in the years that had gone. He came and sat with me and I talked with him. Craig, he told me what I have never forgotten, that the price he had paid, the price I paid, the price millions of women in the world had paid—he told me the price, great as it was, was none too great if only the women of the world would keep their men from forgetting the vision they had all seen in the terrible days and nights in the trenches. It was the soul of the world that had been lost, Craig—that's the way he put it—the soul of the world had been lost, and it had been found again in the fields of France, in the mud and the rain and the stench and the— oh, Craig, you know what I mean."

"I know—I know," he told her.

For a moment she walked in silence, then she paused before a shop doorway and gave him her hand.

"I must go in here," she said with a smile. "Don't think ill of me, Craig, if I can't forget easily and if I'm a little impatient with my old friends who are making it their chief business to forget as quickly as possible—everything except production and reparations and this thing they call reconstruction and all such. I just can't go it—not yet, at any rate."

Craig pressed her hand and held it a moment. "Then perhaps you will let me come to see you?" he suggested.

"Would you—would you?" she asked eagerly.

"I think I—I ought to," he said.

"Whenever you like," she replied. "Call me any day before noon. I'm never out before one o'clock. If you can, I'd like you to come and have tea with me some afternoon.

Give me a ring."

"I'll come," he replied.

And then she was gone. Craig watched her until she had disappeared into the shop, then turned and took his way along the street.

Three

Craig was rather pleased that night when he returned home and found Marion in one of her quiet moods. He didn't want to talk. He wanted time to think. He wanted to go back over the ground he had covered during the weeks since his marriage and discover, if he could, just where he had begun to let himself drift with those around him back into the swirl of the current that was sweeping the world into the old channels.

When he was ready for dinner he sat down in his library and looked from his window toward the west where the sun was already nearing the horizon. Presently he got to his feet and went to a cabinet that formed the lower section of one of his bookcases. Opening it, he rummaged about until he found a book—*his* Book. It had not been opened for months.

He closed the cabinet and picking up the book from the floor, went and sat once more in his chair before the window. He opened it slowly, as if he feared to find his fate written somewhere in the pages he turned.

The last entry he had made in it was dated a few days before he had been married. The discovery was like a pronouncement of judgment. He closed the book and laid it on the table beside him. Then through half-shut eyes he watched the changing hues in the clouds that lay just below the sun.

When he had sat for some time, he turned and opened the book once more, found the last page upon which he had written, turned it down and passed to the next page clean and white under his hand.

He took up his pen, dipped it in the ink, and wrote slowly: "The soul of the world was lost." Those were the words that Jeannette Bawden had used.

He read the entry over and over, then dipped his pen once more and added the words: "Judas Iscariot."

That was it, he thought to himself. He had forgotten. He had been a betrayer. He had been untrue to the light that was in him. His heart had been the heart of a Judas.

He read the entry once more, set his pen aside, and blotted the ink.

From the dining-room came the sound of Marion's voice calling him to dinner.

Four

Dinner was almost half over before Craig noticed that he had scarcely spoken a word since he sat down.

"I saw Jeannette Bawden on the street this afternoon," he said when he realized that his silence might have become offensive.

Marion smiled to herself. "Is she still trying to find some antidote for the world's ills?"

Craig sensed a little annoyance in his wife's manner as she spoke.

"I thought you two used to be very good friends," he ventured.

"I don't know that we were ever what you could call good friends, exactly. Mother used to have her up to the house quite often before Bawden went overseas. I used to find her

113

interesting sometimes, but I think she has grown tiresome of late. After all, one likes to talk about other things than the 'system' as she calls it."

she's right though [marginalia]

Craig was silent for a moment. "There are other subjects, of course," he observed quietly at last, "but there are also less interesting subjects."

"I shouldn't mind so much letting her choose her subject, either, but Jeannette wants to quarrel about it, as if the world wouldn't go along at its own gait anyhow, whatever she thinks of it. She's too serious about it to make her company pleasant."

"Without quarrelling about it, Marion," Craig remarked, "how much time have you given to thinking about such things during the past two years?"

She looked up at him suddenly as if she wondered whether or not he was serious. "I think I have enough to think about without giving my time to worrying about things I know nothing about. I don't think it's a woman's concern, anyhow, and I'm not so sure but that the men would be as far ahead if they would leave it all to those who make it their special business to look after the world's welfare."

"In other words, leave it all to the men who made it their business to plunge the world into four years of war while the rest of us were dreaming of what a wonderful world we were living in."

"I think we were living in a very comfortable world, at least, before the Germans set out to bring the world under their control. Now that the thing has been settled to our liking, I don't see why Jeannette and her kind want to keep us in hot water with their disturbing questions and their ceaseless arguing. If they got out and really did something that would strike one's imagination, one could forgive them for being dull in company. But they're just tiresome. Let's not talk about it."

Craig accepted the suggestion and said no more on the subject. He debated with himself whether he would ever bring it into their conversation again. It was clear that Marion didn't like it.

He took another track. "Charnley kicked his oats out to-day and took off a profit of pretty close to ten thousand dollars."

"He called me on the telephone this afternoon about four and told me about it," Marion replied. "He seemed to be pleased to get out of the market before the price started back. He wants to celebrate with a little party somewhere this week and has asked us to go along."

"I wonder why he didn't mention it to me when he was in the office. It must have been about that time when he called on me and told me he had got out of the market."

Marion expressed no interest in the fact that Charnley had not spoken of the matter to Craig. She placed her two hands on the table before her and looked up at him with question in her eyes.

"I have often wondered why you don't do a little speculating in the market," she observed. "It seems to me that you should be able to do it if Claude can do it."

Craig had rarely discussed his business affairs with his wife. Once or twice he had made some mention of the uncertainty and confusion that had been introduced into the grain trade by the government's action in closing the wheat market. But the subject had never roused her interest and Craig had kept their conversation clear of any reference to business matters.

"Just why would you like me to speculate?" he asked.

"I haven't said anything about wanting you to do it," she protested mildly. "But after all there's something rather romantic about it—the idea of taking risks and staking fortunes to win on a chance turn of the market."

He looked at her steadily for a moment. "I'm beginning to think there are very different ideas of romance in the world," he said. "I seem to see a little romance in keeping close to the export end of the business. To buy a bushel of wheat from a farmer in some little valley in northern Alberta and to carry it across a continent and across an ocean and sell it to some hungry man or woman waiting to receive it in a village in southeastern Europe—isn't there romance in that?"

"You get your thrills by long distance, don't you, Craig?" she replied with a laugh. "Personally, I like to look a little closer for mine. I got more real excitement the day the Mounted Police drew their guns on the mob on Main Street in front of the city hall than I got out of the whole war. It was our Main Street and our mob. After all, the war was so far away. We never saw a Zeppelin raid and never heard the sound of a gun. And that's the way I feel about your work. I don't understand the kind of romance you profess to get out of it. I really believe I'd sooner stand in the visitors' gallery in the trading-room and see you lose your last dollar than sit at home and watch you make a fortune by what you choose to call legitimate methods. Life is a gamble no matter how you treat it. The dramatic moments make it worth living."

Craig smiled across the table at his wife. He wondered how long she would continue to enjoy the dramatic in life after her sense of security in the world was lost. He resolved to tease her into making the admission that would betray her real nature.

"If you had been in the front ranks of the mob when the mounties drew their guns?"

"But I wasn't."

"If the losses in the pit came slowly at first—and then crashed before we had a chance to cover?"

"There would be another chance."

"Did you ever hear of what happened to old man Prout and—"

"I've heard it all, but—"

"I bought him a ham sandwich and a glass of near-beer in the Grange at noon to-day. He came up like a beggar asking for a hand-out."

"You're not Prout. I don't hear of Claude asking anyone to help him to a sandwich and he's been speculating in the market ever since he bought his seat on the exchange."

"Claude's been lucky."

"You're so safe, dear!" she remarked.

a system must for him allow his luck

Five

When Craig was still a boy, his father had taught him a lesson he himself had learned in the years when he was a railway contractor on the railways in Western Canada.

"Save the odds and ends, my boy. You never can tell when they may come in handy."

On the farm in the old days they had kept a box in the back kitchen where the "odds and ends" were gathered against the time when they should be of use about the place. Odd bits of old iron, discarded bolts and nuts, fragments of wire and broken leather straps, all manner of "useless" things found their way, sooner or later, to the odds-and-ends box.

The box had justified its existence in more ways than one. Not only did they dig out, time and time again, something that exactly suited the purpose to which it was ultimately put, but the box gradually took a permanent place in Craig's simple philosophy. He had never been able to give any place in his mind for the idea of waste in a well-ordered world. As a boy he had picked up a jagged piece of broken mirror and laid it away in the odds-and-ends box where it had lain for some time. He had finally taken it out, broken it into small irregular pieces, and used them to decorate the harness for his sleigh dogs.

Though only a few weeks had elapsed since they had left their hotel apartment to move into their new house, Craig had gathered together bits of waste material the builders had left lying about the place and had laid them away in a small box in the basement.

Marion came into the library where Craig had gone immediately after dinner to smoke his cigar and glance over the evening papers. She paused by the table and looked down at the book in which he had made his entry before dinner.

She read the words in silence, then spoke without raising her head.

"What is this? 'The soul of the world was lost'... 'Judas Iscariot'... What is it?"

Craig took his cigar from his mouth and smiled at her.

"That," he said, with a pretense of great importance, "that is a great secret, my dear. You must never ask me what—"

She closed the book with a gesture of impatience. "It sounds more like something Jeannette Bawden might say," she remarked abruptly, then paused. "By the way," she continued, "I do wish you would move that boxful of truck out of the basement. I would have had the woman take it out to-day when she was cleaning, but you can't expect too much of these people nowadays."

"As a matter of fact," Craig answered, "I was going to leave it there till I got the garage into shape."

"Till you got the garage into shape? You mean you are going to keep all that stuff?

He smiled, a little self-consciously. "That's the beginning

of my odds-and-ends box, Marion. I'm going to get a bigger chest put into the garage where it will be easy to get at and out of the way."

She straightened herself and looked at him with a characteristic toss of her head. "Well, it begins to dawn on me—you never know a man till you have lived with him. What any man could possibly want with scraps of tin and old nails and—"

"They'll come in handy sometime," Craig interrupted mildly.

"But you never work with anything like that," she insisted. "And I don't see any sense in cluttering up the place with—"

"Marion!" Craig got to his feet and tossed his paper aside as he stepped toward her and laid his hands on her shoulders. "Are you going to start in making me over before we're a year married? I've had a box like that, only bigger, as long as I can remember."

She stood motionless with his hands still resting on her shoulders. "They gave you a good name when they called you the Magpie. From now on I shall express no surprise at anything I find you carrying home to your nest—only please don't expect me to grow enthusiastic over every new bit of bright ribbon or broken china you discover in your foraging during the day."

"I always sort of liked that name," Craig replied, smiling down at her.

"I don't."

"It's a mark of affection to be given a nickname of any kind."

"You may mistake it for something it was never meant to be."

He let his hands slip down from her shoulders to her elbows and drew her close to him.

"My old kid has been doing too much to-day, that's what's wrong with her. She's dog tired—that's what. Come, let's forget the house and snuggle down in our big chair while I tell you what it's like to be married to the sweetest girl I ever knew. Come on."

He drew her gently toward the chair in which he had been sitting, but she resisted him and shook herself free from his arms.

"It would please me far more if you'd just carry that box of truck up and put it out on the ash-heap. Besides, I'm not in a sentimental mood to-night. I've had a headache all afternoon. I think I'll go to bed."

Craig went to her and put his arms gently about her.

"You haven't been well for several days, Marion," he said. "Is it possible that—do you think—"

"No—I hope not."

He stooped and touched his lips to her hair, then moved back before the pressure of her hands against his shoulders. She turned and left the room and Craig made his way slowly toward the basement.

A few minutes later he carried the box out of the house and set it inside the half-completed garage.

Six

Craig sat in his library late that night and tried to account for a feeling that had crept unconsciously into his heart. When affairs in a man's business life are not running smoothly, he goes back over his records and tries to find the cause. He does so anyhow as a matter of routine to make sure that nothing is escaping his attention. Craig spent a full hour or more going back over his relations with Marion since the day of their marriage, searching for anything that might be amiss, wondering if he was disturbed without cause.

Was it possible that marriage was nothing more than what the cynics described it, after all? He had once heard Croker say something characteristic about married life. He tried to recall it now... He had cited an old philosopher... Marriage doubles a man's responsibilities and cuts his joys in two... That was it. But of course even Croker scarcely meant what he had said. Marion had been an unfailing source of joy—he had even regarded his responsibilities toward her with affection.

His talk with Jeannette had disturbed him. He didn't want to drift from the ideal he had set himself to seek in the world. He had begun to feel that too many were already drifting with the current. He might not be able to do much, but he would do his part. Perhaps, somewhere—maybe in millions of hearts—there was just now the wavering between the ideal and the thing men called "practical." He would speak, if no one else would. He would remind them of what they had so soon begun to forget.

But why could he not do that and keep fresh the young love that brought him and Marion together? He could. He would not permit himself to think he couldn't. Wrong thinking prepared the way for actual evils. He would not give a place to the thoughts that had arisen in his mind since dinner. He would sweep them out of his mind. He got to his feet and realized that it had grown quite late. He shrugged his shoulders as if he wished to relieve them of a burden.

Then he locked the doors and went upstairs. He was in an exalted mood as a result of the thinking he had done. He had not felt so sure of himself for days. From this time forward he would master his fears and his doubts, he would be once more the man who had raised his eyes and seen the vision in the dark skies above the shell-pocked fields of Flanders. The world would be a different place... a better place... it could never be the same.

As he turned on the light, Marion awoke and looked at him.

"Craig—are you—"

She paused sleepily.

"Yes, dear?" he prompted.

She turned her eyes from the light and laid her head on the pillow. "Did you put the box out?" she asked.

He smiled in spite of himself.

"Yes, dear."

CHAPTER II.

One

DURING THE NEXT WEEK Craig was at pains to set himself right again in the world outside his own home.

It was a world in which things were happening behind closed doors, as they had happened in those strange faraway years before the war. He had thought that those days would be no more. He had thought that hereafter the people of the great nations, in particular, would demand to know what was going on. And yet, would they understand even if they were told? They would have to learn to understand, or fall back again into the old ways.

Perhaps they were falling back... Perhaps his hopes were foolish... Perhaps—but no! There were men in the world whose voices were still ringing with the prophecies of a new day. He thought of President Wilson. There was a man whose utterances were still radiant with hope. He had probably made some practical blunders, but he had a great people behind him and his spirit was right. Craig wished the president of the American Republic had spoken louder, had made his voice heard above the din and confusion in Europe. Wilson's spirit and Roosevelt's thunderous eloquence—that would have done the thing! And yet, Wilson's illness had proven the man's courage and stoutness of heart. His letters written from his bedside declaring his unwavering adherence to the league he had fathered and calling his subordinates to task for acting without his consent, as if they regarded him as good as dead... that was the spirit of the new day. Fight for the ideal! Never say die!

Craig was not so sure of the British premier. The words of Lloyd George carried farther, he spoke in a louder voice and he was too clever for his opponents. But—well, he was too clever. Craig believed Wilson meant every word he said. He *hoped* Lloyd George did.

The Prince of Wales had started on his journey around the world. There was a real prince. He might have stepped from the pages of an old book of fairy tales. Everywhere he went he was acclaimed—and loved. What an opportunity to bring a message of goodwill to a broken world and so make ready for the incoming of a better day!

It was not long before Craig fell back again upon his old habit of looking at things as if they were parts of a scheme. As he saw it there were three sides to his life—he could see it as a sort of triangle. One side was his personal life since his marriage to Marion. He thought he had drawn that line straight. He refused to believe he had not. Days would come—like the day when they had had the little difference about the odds-and-ends box—when the line might seem not quite true. But those days came to everyone. Overwork—a little nervousness—almost anything might do it. But where people were as healthy as he and Marion, where they had little or nothing to cause them any immediate uneasiness, where living was as secure and as comfortable as it was with them, such days would pass. The line would become true again.

John Forrester had helped him to draw the second line years before. "A man can't go far without faith in some kind of a god, if it's no more than a block of wood," he had once said. Craig had never been very sure about his faith in God., Since the turbulent days of his early youth when he had given too much thought to the subject he had worried very little about it. And yet, deep within him was an unreasoning faith in Something—call it what you might—that helped to save life from futility and utter waste. No... he couldn't reason much about it... but the line once had been drawn true and he had left it there.

It was the third line that had caused him perplexity. Somewhere the world that was neither God's world nor his own, the world in which the war had been fought and in which race prejudices were even yet threatening civilization with destruction, the world that had sent its prayers up to an unheeding God, the world where the days had been filled with the thunder of guns and the nights with the cries of dying men—somewhere that line had broken or taken a wrong direction. The world should bring God and Man together...

And so for a week following his meeting with Jeannette he had thought the matter over to himself. It had been a week of glorious spring weather. Marion, as if to make up for her one day of impatience and irritability, had been the soul of good humour and high spirits. They had laughed together over trifles like children at play. Craig wondered how a man could be happier. The line was true, after all.

Waking one morning when the first glow of dawn was in the sky, he heard a carolling of birds and crept out of bed to go to the window. Thrusting his head out into the fresh morning air, he listened. The world seemed filled with birds, thousands of them, winging their way northward in flocks that made the air alive with their fluttering wings and their ceaseless singing. It was as if the gates of the far south had suddenly been thrown open and the birds, impatient to be free, had come north in one great rushing wave of song.

For several minutes he remained at the window listening to their singing, then turned and crept back quietly to bed. He had had a glimpse of God's world. Well... that line was true...

Two

At the breakfast table that morning, Craig found an article on the front page of the paper that startled him.

As a man of affairs, Gilbert Nason was too enterprising to place all his eggs in one basket. He was a director in at least a half dozen of the leading industries of the city. He had invested his money in a pulp and paper mill in Northern Ontario, drew a yearly dividend from a successful venture in copper mining in Northern Manitoba, was known to have a voice in the direction of a substantial shipping enterprise with boats plying between Fort William and eastern points on the great lakes, and had been one of the first figures in a company formed to insure western farmers against losses from hail. But his pet enterprise was the Adanac Metal Works, a venture that Gilbert Nason spoke of with pride and that others invariably referred to as a "going concern."

For the past year the Adanac Metal Works had been Nason's chief anxiety in life. A disturbed labour market, a falling off in the demand for metal products, and the necessity of relying almost wholly upon foreign labour in the shops had made him uneasy. The workers had recently made demands that Gilbert Nason could not see his way clear to meeting without incurring heavy losses at the end of the year.

Above all, Nason prided himself on his "human" attitude to the men who were on his pay-roll. He had spent many days in the shops, moving about among his men, talking to them and "getting their point of view," as he so often expressed it. Among his more conservative business associates, in fact, he was looked upon as somewhat too liberal in his treatment of his men. He went to unnecessary extremes to make them feel that he was "one of them" and had come up from the lower levels of the social complex by just such honest effort and patient industry as he now expected of them. In short, the Adanac Metal Works stood as a monument to Gilbert Nason's determination to prove to his friends that a man could treat his workers as if they were human beings and yet make a handsome profit out of the business. It was his City of Refuge to which he flew every time Jeannette Bawden set upon him in defense of the "system." When she had driven him from a self-respecting defence of his mining schemes, when she had called him a robber and a thief in his defence of freight rates on the great lakes, when she had harried him without mercy on what she called his "insurance swindle," he had still a comfortable retreat behind the Adanac Metal Works. And Jeannette would laugh and call the enterprise his little "soul saver." And truth to tell, Gilbert Nason himself, in his quiet moments, felt that if he were fortunate enough to be in his modestly furnished office within easy hearing of the clangour of his factory when the angel Gabriel should blow his trumpet, the Lord would have little fault to find.

And yet, everything was not well with the Adanac Metal Works.

Craig read the brief article and looked across the table at Marion.

"Looks like more trouble down at the factory," he said.

She did not reply at once. Marion had always had her own opinion of her father's experiment.

"There's a little note in the paper here," Craig went on. "The men met last night and drew up another list of demands to present before the end of the week."

"Perhaps when Daddy reads the list he'll know more about the kind of people he's trying to humanize," she commented.

"I suppose Gilbert Nason has the same right as anyone else to try experiments in modern methods of doing business," Craig responded quietly.

"I suppose so," she admitted. "I suppose we all have a right to our pet delusions."

It was very evident that Marion's anxiety in the troubles that were beginning to cast a shadow over her father was very slight, if indeed she did not actually view them with a certain inward satisfaction.

She turned the conversation quickly to other subjects.

"You won't forget that I am having some women in for tea this afternoon," she reminded him.

"That's as much as serving notice that I am to stay discreetly out of the way till about seven o'clock, I suppose," Craig remarked.

"If the strain is not too great," she smiled. "You aren't forgetting that we are to go over to mother's for dinner, are you? They are having Mr. and Mrs. Blount over. Daddy wants you to meet him. You'd better be home by about half-past six and we'll go over together. They'll all be gone by that time."

Craig had not forgotten. Particularly he had remembered the fact that Blount was to be a guest of the Nasons. Blount had only recently come to town. His coming had been much spoken of in the press. He was taking over the management of a local trust company though the fact scarcely justified the inordinate amount of publicity he had already received. Craig felt strangely uneasy at the thought of meeting the man in the house that had been Marion's home. He had never seen Blount, but he had already formed an instinctive dislike for him. Perhaps it had been the man's name... He remembered Blount's picture as it had appeared in the daily papers. A heavy head, almost square, with a great jaw and no neck.

He wished he had been asked to meet Blount some-where else.

It was this thought that lingered still in his mind as he left the house and went to his garage to get out his car.

It was a rare spring morning... just the kind of morning to get into the country and watch the farmers at work on the brown fields...

Blount...

He had not been out to see old Farmer Lane since the week after he had returned from France...

But he would have to be at the Nason's for dinner to meet Blount...

Perhaps Martha Lane might be back again on the farm. He would like to see Martha...

Blount...

Three

On a quiet market, Craig executed the orders he had been given to fill, then strolled about the floor of the trading-room where the members chatted in groups or stood leaning against the telegraph desks with their eyes on the blackboards, studying the "spreads" between prices in Winnipeg and Chicago, or watching the record of the trading on desultory markets in Minneapolis or Duluth.

In the pit only an occasional trader barked a bid and turned away when he drew no response from the by-standers.

Craig left the floor and went out into the corridor.

As he swung around the corner on his way to the office, he all but bumped into old "Dad" Robinson, the janitor.

"Hello, Dad," Craig greeted him, "how do you like this weather for the garden?"

Dad grinned. "Can't be beat, sir. You never did get out to see that little place o' mine last year, sir, did you? We kept lookin' for you all summer and—"

Craig put a hand on the old man's shoulder. "Dad I'll run you home in the car this afternoon if you say the word. How about it?"

"There ain't very much to see there yet, sir."

"I don't want to see much. I'd go out into the country to-day for a spin and take a look at the old farm, but I've got to be back before six and I can't make it. I'm in a mood for getting my hands into the ground, Dad. I'm going to put in some flowers of my own as soon as the ground is fit. But what do you say to letting me run you home?"

"There'd be no harm in that, sir. The missus has been wantin' to meet you for the last twelve-month. I wish you could take a cup o' tea with us while you're out."

"I'll take a cup of tea—sure I will—as long as I can get back again before six. What time are you through?"

"This is a short day for me, sir. I'll be ready to go home any time after two."

"Better leave it till about three. I have to clear my trades after the close. Come around to the office and wait for me if you get through before three."

"Right, sir," the old fellow replied, beaming, "that I will."

A few minutes later Craig returned to the floor to find that trading had been resumed after the lull. He moved toward the pit where more than a score of traders were crowding in, their arms raised above their heads, their fingers thrust out to indicate the number of "eighths" included in their bids or offers above the last flat price recorded.

Someone had evidently entered the market for barley. Craig glanced at the blackboard where the trading prices in coarse grains were recorded. Barley for July delivery had opened that morning at a dollar and sixty cents a bushel. The price had crept down till it had stood at a dollar fifty-nine and three-eighths. Now it stood at a dollar sixty-four, flat. Even as he stood looking at the blackboard, the recorder set down a trade at an eighth advance. Immediately there was a clamour of voices in which none but an experienced trader could have distinguished one word from another. A dozen men threw themselves forward toward the centre of the pit, their fists closed and turned downward from the wrists. They were offering to sell barley at a dollar sixty-four, flat.

It began to look as if a battle was on between the "longs" and the "shorts." Craig stood undisturbed at the edge of the pit and looked on. The offerings had all been snapped up and buyers were bidding furiously again, their hands raised with one finger pointing upward, then with two.

Just now the activity was almost wholly the result of a sudden desire on the part of a dozen scalpers who sensed a formidable raid on the part of the "bulls." They were buying in small lots of one to five thousand bushels in the hope of selling out before the close at an advance of a few eighths of a cent.

Craig paid no attention to the small fry whose significance in the day's trading was in indirect proportion to the amount of noise they were making. He looked about him from one to another of the men standing in the circle till his eyes fell upon Sharples of the Continental Grain standing with his eyes upon the excited men in the pit. Craig watched him. The market fell off an eighth and Sharples stirred a little. It now stood at a dollar sixty-four and three-eighths. A young fellow standing near Sharples threw his hand up with two fingers pointing downwards.

"Sell July barley at a quarter!"

"Sold!" Sharples had jerked him half way round before the words were well spoken.

Craig knew that Sharples was not in the market on a mere speculation. Someone was buying barley in large quantities.

Three other traders offered lots at the same figure and Sharples was upon them like a wildcat.

Craig felt someone touch his arm and looked behind him to see Claude Charnley moving away slowly. He caught a glance that Charnley threw at him over his shoulder and knew that he was being asked to follow. He stepped down with a casual air and came up with Charnley a half dozen paces away.

"Get me fifty July barley—at the market," Charnley muttered in a low voice.

"Right," Craig replied and turned away.

Charnley, however, laid a hand on Craig's arm. "Don't let it go below sixty-three—buy everything in sight at an eighth above."

Craig returned to the pit and stood opposite Sharples.

A moment later an offer was made at a dollar and sixty-four and Craig's heavy voice broke from him—"Sold!"

Sharples had spoken almost at the same instant, but Craig took the trade and recorded it on his card.

The market became dull again and remained so until within a few minutes of the close when Craig bought three lots, though Sharples was his competitor on each occasion.

When the gong sounded, Craig found himself carrying, for Claude Charnley, of Charnley and Cade, forty thousand bushels of barley for delivery before the end of July.

Half an hour later he went out for lunch while he waited for his returns from the clearing house.

Four

As he drew his car to the curb before the doorway of his favourite restaurant, Craig's eyes fell upon a slender figure of a girl entering a shop a short distance down the street.

He was reminded of someone... one's imagination plays strange tricks at times... perhaps it was only because he had been thinking of Farmer Lane when he was on his way to the office that morning...

With his hands on the steering wheel, he sat until the figure vanished into the shop. Then he got down and walked slowly along the street till he stood before the doorway through which the girl had disappeared. In the window were artist's materials and a couple of small landscapes resting on easels for display.

Just the kind of place where he might expect to find Martha Lane... He stepped into the shop and looked about him.

The girl whom he had seen entering the place was standing with her back to him. Her hand was resting on the counter. Craig looked at it, a graceful, strongly-shaped hand, the fingers of which were spread fan-wise and looked peculiarly capable. An odd cuff of oriental colours fitted closely about the wrist.

The girl was tall, almost as tall as Marion, and her body had a finely-knit, willowy contour. A wave of hair beneath her hat was almost bronze.

Craig moved a step toward her and was about to speak a name when she turned her head suddenly and their eyes met. The girl's eyes were for a tiny moment wide and startled. They were the bewilderingly deep, olive grey eyes that had been for years but a memory for Craig.

"Martha!"

The girl laughed and a flush mounted to her cheeks, which had an almost transparent pallor.

"Why, Craig!"

Craig felt momentarily embarrassed. She had changed so. Her dress—he remembered that she had been away... it was five years since... or was it more?

He used to think her a rather plain girl. But now... she had grown beautiful... in a frailly vital way.

"I was just buying some special clay I ordered... yes, I've actually realized at least part of my ambition. I'm doing something at my old hobby," she said after they had had a few words of pleasant surprise at meeting each other again.

Her voice held a new note that Craig did not quite understand. It was if she were regarding him indulgently. Not patronizingly. She was too warm, too glowing for that. But somewhere she must have gained a wealth of knowledge, of understanding. It radiated from her.

"This clay of yours," Craig said, "will be here for you when you come back. Just now you're going to have a little lunch with me and we're going to talk over old times and what has happened since we both were kids. Come on."

He took her arm and led her, unresisting, through the doorway and into the street. A few moments later they chose a small table the white cloth of which was made warm by the rose-shaded light that stood against the wall.

Craig ordered for them both, then turned eagerly to his companion.

"Now, then," he prompted her.

She laughed at him. "Not till I've heard your confession first," she replied.

He told her something of his years in France—what he could of his father's death, of which she had heard quite as much from her own father—described his return to Canada—spoke a little of his marriage—his work.

She wanted to know more of his marriage, but he refused to tell her until he had heard something of her own life since he had last seen her.

"After you left and went to London," he said, "I wrote to you at the address your father gave me, but you never deigned to reply."

"I intended to, but the war came and everything was upset so suddenly. You could have no idea—"

"I think I have a pretty good idea of it. I was there not so long after it broke. I tried to find you one day. I found the house, but the old lady told me you had left. She didn't seem to know very much about you."

She laughed, her full, tender mouth curling up at one corner. "During my first year away from home I was scared stiff for fear of anyone finding out who I was and what my business was. I think I must have been a woman of mystery in that old house in London—but I did tell her that I was going into service until things settled down a little and made it possible to work again."

"I didn't know you had enlisted till I got back home," Craig said.

"I wrote for Dad's consent and then left for Egypt where I went to work nursing until his letter came giving me permission to go. I think he was afraid I had heard you were going to France and that I was using the war as an excuse for looking you up. Poor old Dad—I think we used to worry him a lot in the old days. However, I just went off to Egypt— it was wonderful." She looked at him with eyes full of warm laughter. "I don't believe I could live here—after all that— if it weren't for my work. But when are you coming out to see us? I have quite an exhibition to show you. I did some sketches in Egypt and—but you will come and let me show them to you. Perhaps your wife—"

"I have been planning to go for some time," Craig interrupted her. "I feel a little ashamed of myself for not having been out long before this. I went out as soon as I got back and settled up affairs out there and then I got into town and started to work at once. I just didn't feel like loafing after the first week or so of resting up. Then I got married and—well, the months slip past without your knowing about it."

She looked at him soberly. "Are you happily married, Craig?"

"Very. You must see her. I'll drive out just as soon as the roads dry out. Marion may not seem as much at home on the farm as she might, but I know she'll enjoy the visit. You know—I can't tell you why—but I'm glad you haven't left the farm, Martha."

"I look as if I belonged there, eh?" she laughed.

He disregarded her little taunt.

"I can't somehow, think of you anywhere else."

"I do belong there—right on the earth—close to it as possible," she said. "Nothing else seems real after—well, after everything over there. Perhaps you have had the same feeling. Don't you sometimes wish you were back?"

"Gosh—don't I!"

"Do you remember your old odds-and-ends box?" she looked at him very seriously and then burst into laughter.

"Don't tease me about that now," he pleaded.

"We have it standing in state on a shelf in the barn. I thought you might like to see it some day, so I salvaged it just a few days ago when Dad brought a man and his wife into your old house to work the farm for the summer. I used to make fun of you and your old box, but I think I've thought of it a hundred times since I went away. I believe I liked you for that. I don't know—there was always a sentiment about it. And there really were some useful things in it, too."

Craig wanted to tell her that he still had an odds-and-ends box, but he couldn't, somehow. It seemed out of place. They laughed together over her reference to the box and Craig felt mellow under her sympathy.

And then, all too quickly, the time came for Craig to return to the office and await his "error-slips" from the clearing house.

It was arranged that he should come out as soon as he could get away and bring Marion with him to meet Martha and her father. Craig asked Martha to let him know the next time she came to town and he would show her the market in operation. And then he left her.

But as he went back to work, there came to him again the memory of a girl he had kissed furtively under a silver poplar tree one day when he was still in his 'teens... little Martha who had "loved the whole world"... he remembered her words, too.

And now, it appeared, she had gone out into the world to prove her love for it... and had come home beautiful.

Would Marion like her?

He had told Marion that Martha was "not of our world." He wished he had not said that.

"Rather," he might say, seeing her now, "we are not of her world."

He went on wondering, and felt, for some reason, a twinge of apprehension at the thought of her meeting with Marion.

Martha had understood about the "odds-and-ends" box...

Five

Before he left the office that afternoon to drive out for a look at "Dad" Robinson's garden, Craig called Marion over the telephone and spoke a half dozen words to her.

He wished her good luck with her little afternoon affair.

He assured her that he would be home in time to take her to dinner.

He told her once again that he had the sweetest wife in the world.

But he did not tell her that he had had a visit with Martha Lane.

Six

Marion's late season reception of the women who claimed a place in her social world was the first affair of the kind she had given in the new house. But Marion exhibited none of the nervousness and very little of the excitement that might have been expected in a young bride entertaining for the first time in her own home. Her mother had offered the use of the Nason home earlier in the season, but Marion had stood out arbitrarily against any such make-shift. As a consequence, the novelty of her new station in life had somewhat worn off and she was wholly at ease among the observant matrons who descended upon her in response to her invitation. With a cool bearing that would have done credit to a middle-aged duchess, she received her guests, and with a fine sensitiveness that belongs to women who are born to the part, knew that she was already being taken for granted by the most critical.

And, indeed, there was no reason why she should have felt otherwise. Dressed in a flowing garment of soft "sunset" shade, her radiant personality had never expressed itself more becomingly. In her determination to remain young she had conceded nothing to her position as a young society matron. Although her mother had once hinted that longer hair might be more becoming in the wife of Craig Forrester, she had refused to forsake the "bobbed" hair mode that she had affected before her marriage. Narrow cuffs of black velvet at her slender wrists and a string of jet beads served to enhance the vivid effect of her frock and seemed to suggest a murky depth in the soft brown of her eyes.

Nor could the most observant of her guests find anything to offend the taste in the rooms on the ground floor of Marion's home. Craig had very wisely left the matter of decorating and furnishing the place in Marion's hands. He had had something to say about the effect he desired in the library, but even there Marion's wishes had been served. The walls had been treated so as to produce the appearance of mingled gold and dark green laid on a ground of deep brown. The floor coverings and the hangings were of a hue that afforded sufficient contrast to lighten the whole effect and make it the most cheerful room in the house.

With the other rooms it was the same—everywhere one looked there was more evidence of good taste and discriminating judgment.

"You have the nicest little home I have ever seen," one of Marion's guests told her, as if in confidence, though the remark was overheard by at least three others who pressed forward and added their praise to make it complete.

Marion was pleased, thanked them, and left them to discuss interior decoration while she moved away to join another group.

A healthy-looking middle-aged woman put out a hand and laid it on Marion's arm as she came up.

"We've seen your library and your dining-room and your drawing-room, Marion," she said, "but you haven't shown us the nursery."

A flutter of laughter greeted the remark and the women turned their eyes upon Marion, wondering, no doubt, if her blush would be well-timed.

sexually

But Marion did not blush. She had been prepared for something of the kind.

"There isn't any—and I'm not planning anything of the kind for some time at least," she replied.

The woman affected surprise. "Oh, my—where do you expect to spend your spare time?"

The flutter burst into a small storm, but Marion only smiled.

"I don't expect to have very much of that, either," she said.

She felt it would be safer to move along and leave the women to make their own pronouncements on the shocking neglect of duty that prevailed among "these modern wives."

Presently she came upon Miss Frawley and Victoria Howard with a group of the younger women, most of whom had been her friends for years before her marriage to Craig Forrester.

Victoria drew her affectionately into the group and held her for a moment in a warm embrace.

"I think it's all too perfectly lovely, Marion—and we all think the same."

They chattered together very much as in the old days.

"Don't you feel very much superior, now that you're married?" Victoria Howard asked after a little.

"I'm doing my best not to think of myself as married at all," Marion replied.

"I don't blame you," one of the "smarter" members of the group commented. "I don't see why marriage should change anyone—especially in these days when husbands are beginning to get a little sense."

"When they're too sensible they're not romantic," Victoria put in, "and I think I'd just about die if I woke up some morning and found that my husband had turned sensible during the night."

"I don't think I should worry, Vicky," the smart one remarked. "The man who marries you will never be in danger of that."

The girls laughed and Vicky pouted prettily. It was evidently the habit to make Victoria Howard the victim of jibes.

"I think the man who marries you," Marion comforted, putting her arm about Victoria, "will be very lucky."

"It hasn't taken you long to learn your part as a hostess, Marion," the smart one added. "You know in your heart that the man who marries Vicky Howard will live in hell if he doesn't come home from the office to kiss her at least once every hour of the day."

"A man should do exactly as his wife wants, no matter what it is," Marion smiled.

"And a woman—exactly what she wants, herself, no matter what the husband wants," she of modern thought concluded, and Marion left suddenly as her mother beckoned her from the other side of the room.

"I'll bet Marion Forrester will be like the rest of them before a year," one of the girls surmised as Marion left them. "I can see a change already. It won't be long—babies and feeding and a home spelled with a capital 'h' and—Lord, but it's a beautiful prospect!"

But Vicky Howard paid no heed to the comment on Marion's metamorphosis. There was a wistful look in her eye as she watched Marion glide across the floor toward her mother. "And to think that all this might have been mine," she thought to herself.

Marion reached her mother's side to find her talking to an elderly woman who had just come in.

"Marion, dear, this is Mrs. Blount," her mother announced as soon as she had joined them.

Marion gave the older woman her hand and the two greeted each other with smiles. Mrs. Blount was a large woman whose appearance bore every indication that she had lived a life of comfort and ease. She was, perhaps, a little over-dressed for the occasion, but Marion remembered that she was probably going home with her mother and had come out dressed for the evening. And yet, there was something almost vulgar in her appearance, as if she was quite willing that the world should know that her husband was blessed with a substantial income and that she was fully aware of the responsibility her station in life laid upon her. That she was quite capable of carrying it, no one who looked at her with half an eye could seriously doubt.

"What a charming little place you have here, my dear," she said to Marion. "I'm so pleased to think we are going to meet your husband."

"He's a handsome husband and a very clever one, too," Mrs. Nason informed her. "If only he would not worry so much about the world we're living in. I thought he had stopped worrying about it, but I think he has started again."

"I don't see what a man has to worry him with a home like this and a young wife as beautiful as your daughter," Mrs. Blount observed. "I should think that would be enough to make any man happy."

"Craig insists on carrying the weight of the world's problems on his shoulders, too," Marion said. "I really think that is what makes him happiest of all. I think he likes to worry about such things."

"Well, things aren't just as pleasant as they might be," Mrs. Blount remarked. "After all, it's perfectly proper that we should honour the men who fought for us. They did their duty and did it handsomely. But I can't understand their wanting to turn the whole thing upside down now that they've saved it from the Germans. My own opinion is, though it may not be worth much, that the war has spoiled a lot of men. There was some talk about our men fraternizing with the Germans in the field. I think it would have been better for all concerned if there hadn't been so much fraternizing between some of our own men. They seemed to forget themselves over there and made friends with each other no matter who they were before they entered the army. It's making trouble for us now. Democracy is all right in its place, but—after all—we're not all born equal, or if we are we don't all remain equal, do we?"

She had delivered her lengthy speech with her eyes on Mrs. Nason, and she had done it with an air of having thought it out to an unassailable conclusion.

But Mrs. Nason seemed disposed to evade the question, since if she had not done so, she would have had to disagree mildly with the woman she had invited to her home for dinner.

"I think the world has never been so much in need of divine love as it is at present," she said.

Marion's lips bore the faintest suspicion of a smile.

"Mother has gone off on this New Thought business during the past year," she explained to Mrs. Blount. "She used to be the life of every party she was on, but someone gave her a pamphlet and now she's turned evangelist."

"I believe some get a great deal of comfort out of it," Mrs.

Blount replied. "The only thing I have against it is that it doesn't seem to get things done. Who was that old king who tried the power of his mind on the tide or the waves or something? I never can remember things of that kind."

But Mrs. Nason spoke up before Marion had an opportunity to reply. "If men's minds were in tune with the infinite mind, there wouldn't be any such thing as war in the world. The problems that are vexing the great men of the world to-day would disappear if they paused long enough to put themselves in touch with the source of all Power."

"Will you try to get mother on another subject, Mrs. Blount?" Marion pleaded. "I see two of our guests preparing to leave."

Half an hour later Mrs. Nason found Marion where she had just turned away from chatting with two or three women who were going out. She drew Marion aside and walked across the room with her hand on her arm.

"I wonder why Jeannette hasn't come," she said in a voice that was loud enough for Marion alone to hear. "I called her yesterday and asked her to be sure to come. It is so long since we have seen anything of her. I hope she hasn't taken any offence at anything. Jeannette is so funny, though, one never knows—"

"Jeannette has ceased to worry me in the slightest, mother," Marion shrugged. "I wish you hadn't called her. She would have been here if she had wanted to come. She can be positively annoying when she wants to."

Mrs. Nason sighed. "I'm afraid she hasn't been just right since her husband was killed."

But Marion had already flitted away to attend to her duties as hostess.

Seven

Craig arrived promptly at half-past six and found Marion helping her two maids to get the house in order after the departure of her guests.

She had not changed her dress and Craig, entering cautiously as if he feared he might have come too early, looked through the doorway into the library and saw her standing beside the table.

He stood up to his full height and regarded her for a moment without speaking. Then he threw his hat into a nearby chair and went to her with his arms outspread.

"By gosh, girl, you're a picture!" he exclaimed.

She permitted him to put his arms about her and offered him her cheek, then pushed him back from her.

"Don't be so rough, Craig," she said.

He laughed. "But what's a man to do when he's as foolish about his wife as I am about you?"

"There are surely other ways of showing it besides putting her dress out of shape," she protested.

"There may be," he replied, "but they don't suit me half so well."

He drew her to him again and kissed her on the lips.

"Please go away and get ready for dinner," she urged. "I'm tired. Besides, we have only a few minutes to get ready."

He withdrew a little and caught her hands in his. She dropped her eyes till they fell upon the large hands in which her own white ones were imprisoned.

Suddenly she started back and withdrew her hands quickly.

"Why—Craig! Where *have* you been?"

He looked at his hands. The back of one of them had been smeared with mud that had dried and left a dark grey splotch on his skin.

He laughed to himself and looked up at her.

"Gosh, I forgot all about it. I intended to wash it off first thing, but the sight of you put it out of my mind."

He turned her about to see if he had left any of the clay on her dress.

"But where did you get it?" she asked again.

"There's none on you," he observed. "I've been out farming with old Dad Robinson."

He laughed again as he looked at his hands, and rubbed the dried mud off with his fingers.

"Don't—don't do that in here," she exclaimed. "And who in the world is Dad—you don't mean that old janitor friend of yours in the exchange, do you?"

"Sure I do! I got the old boy into the car and ran him out home to get a look at his garden. By the Lord Harry, I'm going to have a garden of my own in another year. And you should know old Dad's wife. Some old lady. She served me with the best cup of tea I ever tasted in my life."

He paused as he noticed a strange look coming over Marion's face.

"What's the matter?"

"Well, I must say you go a long way to choose your friends. I just hope you haven't asked them to dinner."

"No—I haven't done that, but I accepted an invitation for the two of us to run out and have tea with them some evening this summer after the garden has had a chance to come along a little."

"You did?"

"Certainly. Shouldn't I have—without—"

She hurried out of the room. "Will you please go and get ready. You know how mother dislikes having things late when she has guests for dinner. The Blounts will be there—"

146

"Oh—yes—the Blounts! Your commands will be obeyed without a moment's further delay."

He hurried away to dress for dinner, fell into marching step as he mounted the stairs, and teased a little as he kept time to his step with a—

"Blount—Blount—Blount, Blount, Blount!"

At the head of the stairs he waited and listened for Marion's laugh. She was coming up the stairs behind him.

"You have just ruined this dress," she remarked, and Craig slipped quietly into the bathroom and closed the door.

Eight

Lasker Blount was very much, in outward appearance, like the pictures Craig had seen of him in the local papers. Nor was it long before Craig began to feel that the sizing up he had given the pictures would stand for the time being as an estimate of the personality of the man himself.

Craig and Marion had found the Blounts already on hand when they arrived about seven. Mrs. Blount had accompanied Mrs. Nason when she had left Marion's late that afternoon and Blount himself arrived with Gilbert Nason who had called for him and brought him from the office of the trust company of which Blount had been appointed local manager.

When they had chatted a few moments in the drawing-room, Nason invited Craig and Blount to the library where he asked them to join him in the inevitable cocktail that prohibition measures had made doubly popular with those who could afford them.

"I think it's time to tell you, Craig," Nason said when they had emptied their glasses, "that Blount here has come to the city to do more than hold down the job he is supposed to be devoting his time to."

"I wasn't aware of it," Craig observed.

Nason glanced at Blount. "There can't be much harm in letting Craig in on the secret, Blount?" he asked.

"None whatever—none whatever," Blount responded promptly.

"It isn't generally known—and I may say we don't wish it to be generally known, either—but Blount is here by arrangement and largely in response to an invitation on the part of the leading business men of the city."

"That's interesting," Craig said, doubtfully.

"Blount, here," Nason went on, "was the man who saved the day for the mine operators in the maritime provinces— he was chief organizer of the forces on the side of law and order in steel-workers strike in the New England states a few years ago, and he's been coming right along ever since. Personally, I'm glad to have Blount on the ground in case this trouble over at the factory grows into something bad. You never can tell how far a bunch of men will go when they—"

"They'll go till they're stopped," Blount commented in a loud voice. "My idea is to stop them before they get started."

Craig was glad that Mrs. Nason appeared just at that moment to ask them in to dinner.

Nine

It was not long before the conversation at the table, which had begun casually and had wandered aimlessly over a wide field, assumed a more serious tone and narrowed finally to the one subject that was of interest to the chief guest of the evening.

In fact, Gilbert Nason was more than a little upset by the recent turn affairs had taken in his factory. He had spent the day going about among his men and had received a formidable delegation with whom he had arranged a formal meeting before the end of the week.

"The devil of it is," he said, much perplexed, "the men seem to be friendly enough when I get out among them. They don't seem to be discontented, and yet—well, before another month there may not be a wheel turning in the whole works."

"I don't see any reason why you should be puzzled over it," Blount said. "The trouble with you, Nason, according to what I hear from your best friends, is that you've been nursing the delusion for some time that these men you have working for you are men like yourself and deserve the same consideration as you do. There's no need to go into any long winded working out of the proposition, but the fact is, they are not like you. The fact is, society—modern society—is divided into two camps. In the modern world there is only one ideal and that ideal is Progress. Civilization and Progress are one and the same thing. The men of the Middle Ages never heard of Progress. We never hear of anything else. Progress means control and efficient direction under settled conditions. That simplifies the whole question. We know where the responsibility for good management lies and we know where the responsibility for disturbance lies. There is only one cure for the condition in which we find the world to-day. Deal with these professional agitators as you would deal with enemy spies in camp. Use wartime methods till the thing is settled and then use the same methods to keep them settled."

"That sounds almost Prussian," Mrs. Nason ventured with a smile.

"I admit it," Blount confessed. "And now that the war is over, there is no harm in saying that the Germans, how-

Marx was a German *sobbing*

ever foolish their ambition to bring the rest of the world under their flag, could teach us a good many things it would do us no harm to know. Don't you think so, Captain Forrester?"

Craig had not spoken a word during the whole discussion on the industrial situation in the world. To begin with, he was not quite so sure of himself as Lasker Blount appeared to be. Besides, he could not help the feeling that Blount, no matter what he thought on the subject, and no matter how convincing his arguments might be, must ultimately prove to be wrong.

By the time that Blount had finished his lengthy speech with an appeal for Craig's approval, something almost like anger had arisen in Craig's heart. He cleared his throat and gave himself time to get his impatience under control before he replied.

"I think it depends, Mr. Blount," he said finally, "on what we wish to learn from the Germans. If we could learn anything that would make the world a better place to live in, I'd say let us learn it."

"There you go worrying about the world again," Mrs. Nason accosted him.

But Lasker Blount was eager to have Craig express his ideas concerning the world that "worried" him so much.

capitalism

"The best world possible would be the most efficient world, to my way of thinking, Captain," he said. "What do you think of that?"

Craig was silent for some time. In fact they waited so long for his answer to Blount's question that Marion felt it was time to remind him that he had been spoken to and that some sort of response was expected of him.

"Craig, dear, don't keep us waiting so long," she said.

Craig sat up slowly and raised his eyes to Marion as if she

had forced him into a position he had no desire to take. But her eyes were almost hostile.

He looked at Blount who had been watching him ever since he had asked his question.

"If you would like to know what I really think," he said at last, "I'm afraid I don't think much of the idea of a world built on the idea of efficiency."

Blount became patronizing. "Your point of view is rather unusual in a man of business, don't you think?" he observed.

"Perhaps it is, Mr. Blount. I don't know enough about business men to know what their point of view is. And I confess I've come to whatever conclusions I have reached without much reference to business men at all."

He felt a little excited as he spoke, knowing that the eyes of everyone were on him and that they were waiting to see just how he would extricate himself from the predicament into which he had permitted himself to fall in his answer to Blount's questions.

"Perhaps you can tell us just what you think is wrong with the world and how we are going to overcome it," Blount went on.

His patronizing manner was growing more evident. Craig indulged in another trying pause. Strangely, too, he derived a certain perverse pleasure from being badgered by this blustering champion of the *status quo*.

"No—I don't think I can," he said deliberately. "I've heard so many answers to that question that I'm more confused than ever. A banker told me the other day that the unrest in the world was due to an unstable condition of international exchange. He thinks the world will re-adjust itself when the trade balance is restored."

"There's a measure of truth in that," Blount admitted. "But how are we going to restore the trade balance?"

Craig took the liberty to ignore the question.

"A friend of mine who happens to be a crank on economics says that what we need is more production, especially on the farms in the country."

"That's efficiency," Blount interposed.

"Croker says what we need is another war to kill off a little more than half of the population still alive on the earth," Craig resumed. "There's a travelling preacher in town at present who thinks the end of the world is near and that all we have to do is sit tight and prepare for the next life."

"And after all, the problem is so simple," Mrs. Nason put in.

"Mother!" Marion reproved her.

"With the exception of the preacher," Blount said, "I don't see much for any reasonable man to disagree with."

"I haven't disagreed very much, except quietly—and to myself," Craig said, almost apologetically, "but if you don't mind, I do disagree—with all of them, more or less."

Gilbert Nason suddenly put in a word. "I never heard you talk like this before, Craig. Go on and tell us some more about it. It's interesting, at least."

Craig looked at Nason and saw that the old man was really sincere in what he said. He was interested.

"I just mean," Craig explained, "that to my way of thinking there isn't very much wrong with the world and there won't be if you let things take their natural course and don't waste time trying to force them back into the old grooves."

"You'd have us stand just where we are, then?" Blount asked.

"No. I'd have the world go on to where it started when the war broke out."

"Make yourself clear, Craig," Nason encouraged him.

Craig paused again while he collected his thoughts. He had set out, without knowing it, on an adventure that promised already to provide more genuine thrills than he had ever got from a night raid on the German trenches.

"I don't know whether I can or not," he said slowly. "Mr. Blount, here, belongs to what we have come to know as the 'reconstructionists.'" Blount nodded his head. "It seems clear that what he wants is to restore the order of things that prevailed before the war. In other words, he wants to restore the order out of which the war grew. When we went to the front to fight, it was with the idea that we were fighting to bring in a new order. We regarded the German nation as the last word in the old order. She had progressed in one generation to a place among the leading nations of the world. She was the very symbol of Progress and Efficiency. We went out to defeat that—that machine. And we did defeat it—not by a machine of our own, but by something else—something that we knew only as the spirit that was in us. We muddled a good deal, but we were almost proud of our muddling, because we knew there was a soul there and not a mere machine. The men who faced the German armies on the west front died for something they were taught to call 'The Cause'... It was The Cause against The Machine. We were on crusade. The strange thing now is, that we hear nothing about The Cause for which we fought. The men who preached to us from the street corners and exhorted us from the pulpits and made heroes of us in the newspapers are the same men who to-day have nothing to say about The Cause. They tell us a lot of stuff we don't understand about lost trade and reparations and new treaties and indemnities and a lot of other things. I tell you, Mr. Blount, we didn't want to be made heroes of and we don't want to be blindfolded now that the thing is over. We want to know if these men were lying to us when they told us to join up. If they weren't, we want to know why we never hear any more about it. Has The Cause been won? If it has, what good did it do us to win a cause and come back to a world that is being pushed back again into the old ruts? If it hasn't been won, why did they stop us before we were through with the job? Either there must be a lot of poor fools in the world—or a lot of damn liars!"

"Craig! Craig!"

It was Marion's voice. Craig had wholly forgotten himself. Suddenly all his excitement vanished. He was abashed.

"I'm sorry—I forgot we were not alone," he said, looking from Nason to Blount.

Gilbert Nason laughed. "By golly, Craig, I didn't think you had it in you to make a speech like that."

But Blount apparently did not see anything to laugh at.

"Just—just what is this 'Cause' you speak about, Captain Forrester?" he asked. "It seems to me a little vague—or something."

For a moment only, Craig's anger threatened to return. He checked himself suddenly, however, and his voice dropped to its lowest pitch as he answered.

"It wasn't too vague for us to leave home and go out to fight for it, Mr. Blount," he said. "I don't see why it should be too vague for us to expect some change in the world we have come back to. Do you?"

"Yes, but what kind of change?"

"If the men who stand as leaders in the affairs of the world to-day would spend as much time considering that question, Mr. Blount, as they spend on secret treaties by which they hope to benefit in the next war, there wouldn't be any need for you to ask it. The young men who fought the war want to know what the old men who made it are going to do, now that it is all over. Are they going to give us another war—and another—and another—till the human race is wiped out or are they going to stop it now and forever and give the human race a chance to work and love and make the world beautiful? That's a fair question."

For a moment Blount lost his patronizing manner.

"It may be a fair question, Captain," he said, "but I'm not in a position to answer it—not knowing what's in the minds of our world leaders."

"Exactly, Mr. Blount," Craig replied. "In the meantime, you are doing your best to consolidate your forces, *like* the forces of wealth and property, in a fight to the finish against the forces of revolution and radicalism. The fight doesn't interest me very much. You have only to read history a little to learn whether you will win ultimately or lose. You may break up the One Big Union and you may split the enemy's camp in a hundred different ways, but in the end they will smash you, because they are going to muddle through. You may have the machine, but the men you fight have the spirit."

Mrs. Blount spoke finally in a voice that betrayed the effort it had cost her to remain silent for so long.

"I should think such views were very dangerous in these days—very dangerous, indeed," she commented in a cold voice.

"You haven't been calling on Jeannette lately, have you, Craig?" Gilbert Nason said with a good-natured smile.

Mrs. Nason laughed at her husband's jibe and began to tell Mrs. Blount about Jeannette Bawden.

Blount mentioned something to Nason about the Ruhr and made a reference to the latest massacre of the Armenians by the Turks.

But Craig, for the time being at least, was left out of the conversation and Marion ate her dinner in silence save for a word now and then to her mother or Mrs. Blount.

Once, looking across the table at his wife, Craig saw her lift her eyes to him with a look he had never seen in them before. It was a look from which all the softness had gone and there was left only the dark flame of resentment.

It seemed that he had committed a grave error, somehow or other, a fact that would not have disturbed him very much but for Marion's attitude. She seemed to take the whole incident as a personal affront.

Craig could not help smiling to himself as he remembered how she had adored Jeannette Bawden for her expression of similar views in that very room less than twelve months ago. Could it be possible, Craig wondered to himself, that Marion was losing her sense of humour? Or was it her courage that was failing, now that she had become the mistress of a home with all the attendant responsibilities?

Ten

Craig had never felt more alone than he did during the two or three hours the Blounts spent in the Nason drawing-room after dinner that evening.

He tried to think over what he had said to find where he had offended...

Was it really his views they objected to... and had he not won even the right to hold views that were contrary to the accepted views of the people about him?

Or was it his manner... his way of expressing himself? He knew he was "heavy"... he had been told about it often enough, God knows!

He was actually thankful when Dicky came in a little after nine o'clock and drew a chair up and sat beside him.

He ventured to say to him. "Gosh, Dick, I'm glad you came in." He smiled as he spoke. Dicky looked at him quickly, then squinted oddly as if he had discovered something.

"Has the gang cut you?" he asked in an undertone.

"What makes you ask that?"

Dicky looked about at the others in the room. "Well, they don't seem exactly clubby—and you've just said you're glad I came in."

Craig laughed quietly. "I feel like a whipped schoolboy, Dicky," he replied.

Dicky grinned, a little bitterly. "I never feel any other way around here," he said. "That's why I don't come home till I have to."

"Well, now you're here—say something, for the love of Mike!"

Dicky fell upon his favourite subject, his latest discovery among the "moderns" and Craig struggled to follow him until he gave it up finally and returned to wrestle with his own problem again.

He thought he ought to say something to Mrs. Nason... he wanted her to know that he had not meant to be offensive...

When the opportunity presented itself he left Dicky abruptly and followed Mrs. Nason into another part of the house. He found her in the kitchen giving her maid orders to prepare a cup of tea before the Blounts left.

He put his arm about her waist and leaned close to her white hair.

"I'm afraid I made a mess of everything to-night," he said.

She patted his hand affectionately and looked up at him.

"We all make our mistakes, Craig," she replied.

"I just wanted to tell them that living shouldn't be as hard as ever—in spite of everything that has happened in the last few years," he said.

"I know, Craig. And I think I understand. But God's ways are not our ways."

Craig withdrew quietly and wandered back again to join the company.

So there it was... God's ways... our ways... Blount's way.

CHAPTER III.

One

IT WAS CHARACTERISTIC OF MARION that she did not offer to discuss with Craig the unpleasant situation he had created by his outburst before the Blounts.

Returning home late that night Craig endured his wife's stern manner and her brusque responses to his questions without making any reference to what had occurred. He had already learned the unwisdom of trying to coax Marion out of a bad mood.

The longer he avoided any mention of the matter, however, the stronger became the desire to explode the bomb at once and have the worst over with.

When they had finally gone to bed, Craig felt that he could not go to sleep without at least begging her forgiveness for having spoiled her evening. He could not feel sorry for having spoken his mind to Blount. In fact, he felt as if something had been set free within him at last. Never before had he spoken at such length in any argument touching questions of the day. That idea, he thought, of the Machine and the—the Something-or other that was not the Machine—that was a good way of putting the case. He couldn't help feeling pleased with himself for having thought of the metaphor. He wished he could have found a word to express what was in his mind—the name of the Something-or-other that was opposed to the Machine. He thought of calling it by various names. The Soul. Humanity. The Spirit. Perhaps it was the Ideal. Perhaps there was no word for it in the language. And yet the thing itself was more real to him than the Machine could ever be to Blount. It was the only real thing in human life, the undying flame in the human heart, the fire from the altars of the gods.

No, he could not feel. aggrieved over having spoken out at last, especially when the man to whom he had spoken was Lasker Blount. His only regret was that his words had given Marion fresh reason for treating him as if he were a stranger. She had found many such reasons of late, it seemed. It did not occur to him that they might, after all, be strangers in fact. His only care was lest he should do something to estrange them.

He loved her... passionately... if only he might explain that he had not meant to offend... that it had been simply his own awkwardness...

He resolved to make the attempt.

"Marion, dear... if I did wrong in speaking to Blount as I did to-night..."

"You will—please—say nothing about that—just now, at any rate."

There was no mistaking her mood. If he insisted on speaking of the matter there would be an ugly "scene" and Craig thoroughly hated "scenes."

And yet, why should he not speak of it? Was he going to permit Marion to regulate his thinking and his utterances to the end of his days? As he thought of it, he became impatient with her petty mood. If she loved him half as much as he loved her... he became angry.

"My trouble seems to be that I am so often in the wrong," he said aloud. "The trouble with you is that you're always so—so damned right!"

Almost at once he regretted having spoken. It wasn't exactly the way to address the woman he loved. Somewhere he had heard that a passionate love can be converted in a moment into a passionate hatred. The very thing had happened—for a moment! Now he was the lover again, suddenly tender, awkwardly humble.

"No—I didn't mean that," he said softly.

When she did not reply he put out a hand and laid it very gently on her shoulder.

She did not speak. She did not stir under the touch. She lay as if she had been unaware of his presence beside her.

And presently he withdrew his hand and turned away.

Two

Strangely enough it was old Gilbert Nason himself who gave Craig the first word of understanding concerning what had occurred during the dinner with the Blounts.

Early the next morning Craig left the floor and returned to his office to find two telephone numbers on his desk.

One was from Marion.

He called her at once. She wished to tell him that she was going out for the afternoon and would not be back in time for dinner. Would she leave orders to have dinner prepared for him or would he take it down town? She might not be home until late—there was some business to be done in connection with the Dramatic Club—the end of the season—the executive had called a meeting.

Her voice was very matter-of-fact, as if his coming home was merely a detail that would have to be placed in its proper setting in the day's routine.

"I don't think I'd like to eat at home unless you are there," he told her. "I've never done it and I don't want to get the habit."

He meant to be pleasant. He meant to tell her that he had forgotten what had occurred the night before, except in so far as he himself was to blame, and that he would find it hard to come to the end of the day without the prospect of finding her waiting for him.

But somehow the meaning he tried to put into his words did not reach her.

"Then you'll not be home for dinner," she said, and the matter was settled.

"What time will you be home?" he asked her.

"I don't know—when I'm through with what I have to do."

There followed a long pause during which Craig sought for something to say. "Well—all right," he fumbled.

There came a sharp click in his ear and he realized she had hung up the receiver. After all, perhaps, he was a sentimental fool... and she had not yet recovered from her mood of the night before.

He hung up the receiver, wondering vaguely what important business of the Dramatic Club could take Marion out early in the afternoon and keep her out till late at night. A moment later he cursed himself inwardly for a soft-hearted fool and turned to the slip of paper on which Gilbert Nason's number had been written.

He found Nason at the office.

"You called me—this is Craig."

"Oh, hello, Craig! Yes, I thought you'd like to try a game of golf this afternoon. Blount was out yesterday and tells me the course at the Country Club is in good shape. I'm keen to get started. How about it?"

"Just the two of us?"

"Yes, just the two of us. Fact is, Craig, I wanted to get in a little chat with you by myself. Over what you told Blount last night."

"So you're going to give me hell, too, eh?" Craig laughed.

He had come to like Gilbert Nason in the months since

he had made himself one of the family and although their ideas did not always coincide exactly, their disagreements were always in the best humour.

"Have you been getting it, eh?"

"Not so much has been said, but—"

Nason laughed. "Oh, my boy, you're young in the game yet. When you've been married well on to thirty years you'll know something about it. But what do you say to a game?"

"I think I need to get out. I'll call for you and run you out. About three, eh?"

"That'll do me fine."

"How's everything down at the works?"

"Very quiet. I don't really expect any trouble. Call for me, then, at three. I feel as if I could get into the eighties to-day."

"I'll be there and I'll give you a run for your money. Are you good for a dollar a stroke?"

"You're on, my boy."

"Sold!" Craig replied and hung up the receiver.

On a strong market, Craig bought another ten thousand bushels of July barley for Claude Charnley and executed a half dozen orders for other firms before the final gong sounded. He took a "stand-up" lunch in a cafe across the street and returned to finish clearing his trades.

At a few minutes before the hour appointed, he drew up before Nason's office and blew his horn. Ten minutes later they were on their way westward through the city to where the Country Club lay beyond the city limits.

Nason made no reference to Blount until they had driven off from the first tee. The two balls had taken a direct line for the flag and Craig lifted his clubs and went off along the fairway with Nason beside him, both feeling that they had made an auspicious beginning in their first game of the year.

Craig took advantage of his opponent's cheerful mood to ask the question that had intrigued him ever since Gilbert Nason had spoken to him over the telephone that morning.

"Well, what's troubling you about our friend, Blount?" Craig asked abruptly.

Nason was not unprepared for the question. "I was just going to speak of it. Well, what do you think of him?"

"Personally, he doesn't appeal to me at all. He reminds me too much of a Bavarian officer to get any sympathy from anyone who has ever met one of the tribe."

"It takes all kinds to make a world—Bavarian colonels as much as British Tommies. But the old boy may not be half bad—his bark is too loud to be dangerous."

"I think it's his bark that I dislike," Craig remarked.

Nason smiled. "I guess you made that pretty plain last night."

"Was it so bad—did I make such an ass of myself as I've been led to believe?"

"You didn't make an ass of yourself at all, to my way of thinking. If you pay too much attention to these damned women, Craig, they'll have you in a mad house before you're full-grown. I don't speak out half of what's in my mind when they're around, but if I do open up once in a while, I leave it and they can lump it if they don't like it. I hope you didn't think I brought you out here to teach you table manners."

"Well, there's some relief in that. Perhaps you're going to set me out for holding Bolshevist opinions about Blount's little world."

For a half dozen paces or so, Nason was silent.

"Well, I've been doing a little thinking—but here I am! Where are you?"

He paused beside his ball and drew his mid-iron from his bag as he spoke.

"I'm about ten yards farther on and a little to the left," Craig said, raising his head to look for his ball.

He stood aside while Nason made his shot.

"Dead on!" Craig cried as the ball flew clean from Nason's stroke.

He walked ahead to where his own ball lay and drove it with as much precision as Nason had shown.

For the next few minutes they were both too much concerned with the positions of the balls to carry on serious discussion on anything else. Their third shots put them both on the green and they halved the hole in five.

They did not return to their discussion until they had driven off from the second tee and had started down the fairway together. This time their positions were farther apart and they walked only a few steps together.

"We're playing in mid-season form, Craig," Nason chuckled.

"I wasn't aware there was such a thing in golf," Craig replied.

But Nason did not argue the point. "I was going to say," he went on, "that I think there are a lot of men, even in the business world, who would be glad to share your views on this dirty mess we call the world—perhaps they do share them—only they don't find much satisfaction in holding a philosophy they can't work. After all, Blount knows what he wants and he knows pretty well how he's going to go after it. That makes it easy for him and makes your ideas a little ridiculous in the eyes of men who are concerned with practical affairs. When he asks you what you intend to do about it, it seems to me you ought to have some sort of answer ready for him."

"I'm just about fed up with the practical men," Craig retorted. "If the best thing practical men can do is to make war and send the youth of the world out to serve as cannon fodder, their practical affairs aren't worth much respect."

"Admit that, Craig. But what are you going to put in the place of what we've got now?"

Craig took a look in the direction in which he hoped to find his ball.

"Let's see—that bunch of old grass there—I guess I'd better get across. Go ahead, I'll talk to you later."

They parted and a few minutes later came to the green together. Craig sank a long putt.

"Down in five!" he said.

A moment later Nason sent his ball into the hole.

"Six!"

Craig set down the score and the two came to the third tee together.

"It's great to get out on a course that's not crowded," Nason remarked, looking about him. "There's not more than a half dozen on the course."

This time their drives lay far apart and they did not meet again until they came to the green. In fact, for the next six holes Craig's form was very erratic and they came to the end of the outward course with Gilbert Nason leading by four strokes. The old man was two holes up, besides, and feeling pretty well satisfied with his showing.

With no one in sight, they sat down for a few minutes at the tenth tee and Nason lit his pipe while Craig smoked a cigarette.

"I've been doing a little thinking on what you said," Craig remarked when he had drawn the first couple of puffs from his cigarette. "You may think me a little stubborn on the matter, but I feel that a man is not called upon to lay down a new programme for society just because he happens to be out of sympathy with the old order."

"What, then?"

"It isn't so much a change in the present order that I'm asking for—or that anyone's asking for, for that matter. If this is the best we can hope for in the world, let's accept it and make the best of it. What I'm trying to get at is the fact that the men who are largely responsible for what we have are apparently satisfied to let it go on. They told us there would have been no war if Germany had not started out to conquer the world. We went out to fight in a war to end war. And yet, with Germany defeated, we are daily hovering on the brink of another war in Europe—a war between nations who were allies only a few months ago. The men who called us out to win world peace are themselves predicting another war in the not-distant future and are already well away on a race for mastery in the air. They called upon us to fight their battles. Why can we not call upon them now to put a stop to the whole dirty business?"

"And in the case of a nation making a war of aggression on another?"

"A nation doesn't do that kind of a thing—as a nation. Its great men—its rich men do it and the others follow the leader as a matter of course. Before another year the people of this country will be split into two camps—that's what Blount wants and that's what he expects. The same will be true in every other country in the world. With the millionaires in control again, the old rivalries will come back and some other August will find our children waiting for the news as we did and counting the hours and making their prayers and bidding their goodbyes and shedding their blood. It will be the same old story all over again. My point is just this: now is the time to stop it—before it is too late. And it is up to our leaders to stop it or one of these days they'll find a world-wide revolution on their hands that will make the past war look like a curtain-raiser to the main show."

"You haven't turned Socialist, Craig?"

"I haven't turned anything. I'm just human and I'm tired of it—damned tired of it—just like millions of others in the world to-day."

Nason was silent for a long time. Then he took his pipe from his mouth suddenly and knocked the ashes out of the bowl.

"Well, let's go on. I'm into your bank account for four dollars already. I'll bet an extra dollar bill I'll make it five at the eighteenth hole."

"You're on!" Craig cried, getting up. "Drive off!"

For nine holes, then, they played golf and left the affairs of nations to look after themselves. When Craig sank his last putt he had reduced Nason's lead in strokes to three and was only two holes down.

Nason did a little mental arithmetic. "That means you owe me one brand new dollar bill, Craig," he said.

"I'll get you on the next flight," Craig replied as he drew a dollar from his pocket and paid it dutifully.

Three

Some perverse trick of Fate caused Craig to turn, as they made their way back to the car, and glance behind him over the course to where a couple of players were walking together down the fairway to the third hole.

It was the girl's jacket, a yellow sleeveless sweater, that caught his eye as he was about to turn away.

He stopped suddenly. "By gosh, that looks like Marion!" he exclaimed before he had time to consider the significance of his statement.

Nason turned as he spoke. "Marion?"

Craig suddenly caught himself up. "It was just the yellow sweater that caught my eye," he said quickly and continued his way with his hand upon Nason's arm for fear the old man might turn and satisfy his curiosity.

"By the way," he said with an enthusiasm that was altogether unwarranted, "I must have you come round with me some time and meet a friend of mine who lives just down the road there a little way. His name is Dyer—Jimmie Dyer. A sergeant of mine overseas—and a very decent sort in his own way."

He did not know why in the world he had asked Nason to visit Jimmie Dyer. On second thought it seemed almost ridiculous. But Gilbert Nason accepted the suggestion immediately.

"Let's do it next time we come out," he said.

"We will, then," Craig replied and the meeting was arranged.

As he took his seat beside Nason in the car, Craig paused long enough to look from one to another of the dozen cars that stood in the parking area.

The fifth car he looked at was Claude Charnley's.

He started his engine and sent the car away with a suddenness that made Nason hold on for dear life as the wheels hit the soft road leading from the club house to the pavement.

And as he drove toward the city he decided it might not be out of place to call Jeannette Bawden and invite himself to supper.

Four

It was after seven o'clock before Craig reached a telephone and called Jeannette.

She was at home—she would be delighted to have him come up for supper—she was having a friend or two —a young man and a young woman—but he must come, anyhow—make it a foursome—they were just sitting down to the table, but they would wait for him if he came at once.

Craig was at the door of Jeannette's apartment ten minutes later. She received him as if they had been friends for years. He noticed that she did not even ask why he was not taking dinner at home. She made it appear that it was the most natural thing in the world for him to invite himself to supper with her.

She led him in and introduced her two friends. They were quite young, both of them, and at first sight Craig could not help wondering just how they had made their way into the affections of Jeannette Bawden.

The girl was not more than twenty-three or twenty-four and looked really younger. She was short, with a pudgy figure and a round head crowned with straight black hair that had been cut very short. Jeannette introduced her as Rose Barron and Craig guessed that she was Jewish. She smoked a cigarette with an air of sophistication that Craig felt sure was lately acquired and sat with her legs crossed in such a way as to invite attention to a pair of very plump knees. It was immediately apparent that she wished to be thought extremely temperamental and perhaps a little eccentric. It provided Craig with a certain amount of amusement to grant her wish in both respects.

The young man was undoubtedly foreign. He had a shock of bushy black hair and a square face that was altogether too serious in one of his age. Craig judged him to be under twenty-five. He caught enough of the unpronounceable name by which Jeannette introduced him to know that it was Russian and decided to let it go at that. Jeannette called him Ivan and

Craig seized upon the name and held it for future use, in case he should ever be called upon to name the young fellow. There was much that was likeable in Ivan. He had the face of a dreamer, the eyes of one who was always seeking. In contrast to the Barron girl, he was quiet, earnest and as simple as a child. And yet, in his dark eyes, there was the smouldering flame of a zealot, the unawakened passion of a fanatic.

"Well, now that we know who we are," Jeannette said after they had chatted a few moments, "come and help me carry in the stuff, Craig. I've decided to get along without any maid from now on. I did my own washing this week just to convince myself that toil is good for the soul."

They had already reached the kitchen as she finished speaking and Craig stepped to the table and let the door swing to behind him.

There was a comical look in Jeannette's face as she turned and looked at him.

"Just try to amuse yourself, Craig," she said in a whisper. "I wouldn't have had them if I had known you were going to be here."

"What's the matter with them?" Craig asked.

"They're just children. But they help me to keep young. But how come you back to your bachelor days so soon?"

Craig tapped her playfully on the shoulder. "I guess Marion felt it was time to show her old man what it really meant to have a home to go to at six o'clock. She went out for dinner."

"Good idea, I say. Here, take this in and set it on the large mat at the farther end of the table. I'm going to make you do the carving."

Craig carried out her orders and she followed immediately with a dish in either hand and bade her two young guests to sit in to the table.

"Craig, I believe you've got sunburned," Jeannette said as she looked at him from the other end of the table.

"Perhaps I have," he replied, wrestling with the joint on the platter before him. "I've been having my first game of golf."

Ivan stirred a little and looked somewhat perplexed.

"You will perhaps think it strange," he said in very even English, "but I never understood the idea behind the game of golf. Of course, there must be some sort of philosophy or some—"

Craig laughed. "It's a pretty fair test of a man's temper, if that's what you mean," Craig remarked.

"Perhaps that is what I mean—I really don't know enough about it to judge. Games—I mean athletic games, of course—have never appealed much to me. I can understand one enjoying a game of chess, for instance."

"I imagine it's much the same in any case," Jeannette offered while Craig was busy with his task. "The idea seems to be to beat the other fellow, if you can."

Ivan turned to her. "That is a very small element in chess," he said. "Of course, there are some who play it with that purpose in mind—undoubtedly—but I find its chief charm in the unlimited number of beautiful situations a player can develop. Besides which, there is a certain inevitability in it. Nothing is decided by chance. Each move you make is according to plan. It is not so. in your game of golf, is it, Mister Forrester?"

Craig wanted to reply, "Not by a damned sight!" but he was afraid Ivan might not appreciate the remark.

"Scarcely—if you had heard Nason swear this afternoon when he sliced into the woods, you would have had a pretty fair idea of how far the execution may fall short of the plan."

Ivan coughed lightly. "That's just it! I don't think I should like the game. There seems to be something disorderly about it."

Rose Barron turned to Jeannette. "Don't you think Ivan is won-n-derful!"

Ivan regarded her in silence as if he wondered whether she really meant what she had said.

"I am not wonderful," he said at last.

"One would certainly never take you for a Bolshevist," Rose retorted.

"One does not have to swear to be a Bolshevist," Ivan told her.

During the course of the meal, Ivan was induced to expound his belief in the new form of government that had come into existence in Russia. He was at great pains to make his exposition clear and he spoke with the precisions of one whose knowledge of English has been gained from much reading. He deplored the lack of authentic news, mildly expressed his conviction that the Russian Soviet would weather the gale, predicted that Russia would rise to a position of first importance in Europe, and then—

"And then?" Craig prompted.

The smouldering fire that lay deep in Ivan's eyes leaped in one bright flash.

"Then... the tide will roll westward over Europe... and soon... the Atlantic will not stop it! America... Canada... we shall all be free!"

Craig wanted to tell Ivan just why the people of Canada and the United States would not embrace the new political creed, but a glance at Jeannette convinced him that Ivan had a staunch ally in his hostess and the prospect of a battle with Jeannette did not appeal to him at the moment.

Besides… Ivan was very young in spite of his unshaken convictions.

He decided to give Rose an opportunity to take a part in the conversation.

"Are you also a disciple of Mr. Trotsky?" he asked her.

She shrugged her shoulders and glanced downward. "I am nothing!" she declared. "Is that not more interesting?"

There was the merest suggestion of an attempt at an accent in her speech, as if she had listened so long to Ivan that she had fallen unconsciously into his manner.

"She is a disciple of the Thing-that-is-not—no matter what it is," Jeannette said, laughing. "Rose bobbed her hair before anyone else in her crowd. Now that they've all followed her example she's going to let it grow. For the same reason she's thinking of cutting cigarettes off her list of daily necessaries."

"I am going to make Ivan marry me before I permit him to live with me, too. I think that will be decidedly original. I know it will shock some of my friends, but—I don't care!"

Ivan colored a little and looked rather helplessly at Craig, who suddenly and irrelevantly remembered the rolled stockings and the plump knees that had been the first things he had really noticed about Rose Barron.

Well… the world was changing, after all… maybe bobbed hair and bare knees were to be taken as signs of the times… but then, he had always thought bobbed hair attractive in Marion…

Five

It was nine o'clock when Rose and Ivan announced their intention of leaving.

Jeannette, by a quick glance and a movement of her lips, conveyed to Craig her desire to have him remain behind for a little while.

When she returned from bidding her two younger guests goodnight at the door, she turned down the lights in the dining room, where they had sat about the table since dinner, and led the way into a smaller room that held a couple of large chairs, heavily upholstered, and a couch with deep cushions.

Jeannette turned on a soft light and drew the window shades. Then she came and stood before Craig where he had stationed himself in the middle of the floor.

"This is *my* place," she said. "My soul and I get in here together—and we seldom admit anyone else."

Craig looked about him. "Just the sort of place I'd imagine you and your soul would make for each other," he said.

Along one wall ran shelves packed with books. The other walls were decorated with odd bits of modern art that aroused no emotion in Craig other than a mild resentment towards the artists who perpetrated them.

"What is this, Jeannette?" he asked, going towards a scarlet cloth that had been hung like a curtain over one corner of a small sectional bookcase.

"Those are the books I really read," she replied.

"I mean this cloth thing," Craig said, lifting one corner of it as he spoke.

"That's a *sari*—a kind of combination skirt and waist and head-dress that the Hindu women wear. I picked it up in Benares when my husband and I were there the first year of our marriage."

But Craig was more interested in the strange patterns that had been worked into the silk, meaningless designs in the Eastern manner. Along the edge small bits of broken mirror glass had been set into the silk at regular intervals of two or three inches.

Jeannette observed him looking closely at the bits of glass.

"They told me those tiny mirrors were for keeping devils away. A devil is supposed to see his reflection and run away. That's why I keep it here. My soul and I need some protection from the devils that beset the world."

Craig smiled. "I once stuck bits of broken looking-glass into the collars of a set of dog harness," he mused.

He glanced over the titles ranged in the top shelf of the case. There were a couple of books by Wells, a novel by Turgenev, Tolstoi's "Anna Karenina," More's "Utopia," a book of essays by Havelock Ellis, a half dozen modern writers whom Craig had never heard of —altogether a strange company to occupy space on a single shelf.

"Sit down just for a minute before you go, Craig. I know how impatient you are to get away, but we've never really had a chat together since we first met."

"We might have had many of them if you hadn't avoided us so persistently," he replied, taking one of the big chairs as he spoke.

Jeannette lit a cigarette and smoked a moment in silence before she spoke again.

"I suppose," she said at last, "we have to choose our friends where we think there is some hope of keeping them—especially when we get on a little in life and get over our schoolday loves. I always think it's a pity we can't keep our friends, in spite of growing differences of opinion."

"You mean you have grown away from us?" Craig asked.

She considered the question a moment. "I'd like to think I had not grown away from you, Craig," she replied. "We never were really great friends—as such things are understood in the world. We have not known each other long enough—nor well enough for that. But I have always felt that we could have been very close friends if—well, if things had been just a little different."

"I'm sorry you seem to think it so impossible now," Craig said quietly.

She flicked the ash from her cigarette into a small tray beside her and raised her eyes to Craig.

"I don't want to be misunderstood, Craig," she said. "I used to be a very good friend of the Nasons. My husband handled Gilbert Nason's legal affairs until the day he went to France. I think they were very good friends. In those days I was a wife. I don't know—now—how I ever contented myself with being merely a wife. I know I am a different person to-day. In the end it may be proven I am wrong. If I am—then, I'm terribly wrong."

"But I don't quite understand, Jeannette."

"If I told you, you would perhaps think I am obsessed by trifles."

"You do me very little credit."

She drew herself up in her chair and sighed deeply.

"Well, I don't know whether Marion has ever told you about our disagreement the last time I called to see her."

"She hasn't told me anything."

"It was foolish, perhaps, but friendships have a way of building on strange and unstable foundations. Marion, I thought, had a great deal of love for me. I know I had for her. But a thing occurred last winter that has made me positively hate the Nasons. Mrs. Nason is a dear old lady in many ways. And I believe I could forgive her, but—well, I'll tell you. Mrs. Nason has been president during the past year of an educational society of some kind or other that the women of the church have organized. I don't know what the functions of the society are, but I do know they meet

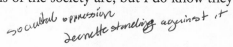
societal oppression
Jeanette standing against it

frequently during the winter months to drink tea and talk over educational problems of one kind or another. They were to have an afternoon of a rather special kind shortly after Christmas and a small committee, with Mrs. Nason as convener, was asked to make all the necessary arrangements. Among other details, it fell to their lot to select a couple of women to do the duties with the tea and the ices. One woman was chosen and when they came to select the second, a member of the committee mentioned the name of an old lady who was the widow of a man who had been one of the most highly respected preachers in the West. Mrs. Nason took the trouble to remind the committee that one of the sons of the woman they were about to honour had unfortunately turned radical and had been one of the strike leaders who were serving terms in the provincial jail for treasonable utterances during the days of the strike. She refused to give her consent to having the mother of a jailbird pour tea for the guests of the society of which she was president. She won her point and another woman was put in her place. Well, I had something to say about it when I next went to see Marion—naturally—and we had words that led her to hint that I would not be welcome in her house unless I changed my views on social matters and learned to keep people in their places. Perhaps I should have overlooked it all and gone back again, but—somehow—I can't, Craig. They are nice people—they have been very considerate of me since my misfortune—I don't know what I should have done without them. Even Gilbert Nason himself was the soul of kindness and thoughtfulness. But one has to make the choice. The Nasons and their kind may be kindly intentioned—they may be generous—they may be considerate—but they are rich and that makes them wrong."

Craig looked a little startled at the vehement manner with which she had expressed herself.

"I mean it, Craig—I mean it—a little more than I've ever meant anything in my life. I begin to realize that I never did mean anything before—I never meant anything with all my life—with all my heart and soul. I used to think I meant things, but I was asleep. It was a dream about things—and I dreamed I meant what I said and what I felt. But I am awake now. I opened my eyes on the night I told you of—the night I spoke to him. And one of the first things I saw clearly was the fact that they took him from me—*they* did—the Nasons of the world, the kindly intentioned men and women who are kind so long as their sense of security is not disturbed, who are generous so long as they are not asked to return what is not their own, who are considerate so long as their comfort is assured. I am coming to think that there is only one hope for the world and that is to kill off all the kindly intentioned ones and let us get on with the business of making the world over."

"And what kind of a world do you want to make out of it?"

She was silent again for a long time. When she spoke at last, her voice was soft as velvet, but with an undertone that seemed to come from the bitterest depths of her heart.

"I would turn the world upside down, if I could," she said, "I would put the Nasons where their pampered daughters and their degenerate sons and their faddist wives would have to work for a starvation wage or go begging."

"I don't see what advantage would come from putting the top on the bottom and the bottom on the top."

"I'm not speaking of advantage. I'm past the place in life where I believe any permanent good can be done for the world as it exists. Religion might have saved it if it hadn't been for the churches. Education might have done something for it if it hadn't been for the colleges. But unless a new day rises in the East—" she pointed toward the Hindu *sari* hanging from the corner of the bookcase—unless a Messiah is born to us, the western world is damned—it is heading straight for its own destruction. And all the mealy-mouthed preachers and teachers in all the sawdust churches and colleges in the world can't save it. My only hope is that those who are down now may have a chance to get up and enjoy the pleasures of life before the end comes."

"And that those who are up may have a chance to get down and enjoy the discomforts, eh?" Craig added.

She nodded her head.

"Don't you think it would be better still if we could bring the two together, somehow?" he asked her.

"Bring the two together? Huh! Try it! If there was any real danger in that, Craig, the few who would be left at the top would simply bring on another war in Europe and we'd get back again to the good old days—just as we are getting back now as quickly as possible."

"Well, I haven't lost all hope—not yet," Craig observed.

It was that thought that remained in his mind as he drove down the street a half hour later and put his car into a garage to have some repair work done on the engine.

And it was that thought that recurred to him again and again as he walked home through the heavy fog that had fallen on the streets.

He hadn't lost hope... not yet...

Six

Crossing a bridge over the Assiniboine, on his way home, Craig paused a moment to study the strange effect of the lights shining through the fog and dimly reflected on the water of the river.

A thousand miles away that river rose. Gathering its waters from mountain and from plain, it flowed steadily eastward, through shining days and nights of gloom, under clear skies and skies of grey—and now under a bridge that stretched like a ghost-span in the hanging mist.

Perhaps… perhaps the world was moving on… through great fogs and heavy nights… but setting ever toward the open sea…

A man came out of the fog, approached him slowly, and stopped beside him to look at the river.

Craig looked at him and saw that he was a giant of a fellow, almost a head taller than himself.

"I've been looking at that for the past hour from the other end of the bridge," he said, pointing to the river.

"Yes?" Craig replied. "I don't often stop to look at things merely because they're beautiful, but I couldn't pass this without—"

"Beautiful?" the stranger said. "Well, I might have thought so once myself. I know better. It's ugly, my friend. Muddy water—stinking sewage—and fog! Just like your God-damned world!"

The stranger walked off and Craig watched him till his towering figure was blurred and lost to sight in the dense fog.

Then he turned away and went home.

CHAPTER IV.

One

MARION SHOWED NO SURPRISE when Craig told her that he had had dinner with Jeannette. He told her of it at breakfast the next morning.

"You tell me about it as if you were reporting your movements to a superior officer," she said.

"Not at all," he replied. "I thought you might be interested in knowing where I was."

She tossed her head and looked at him. "I think the day has passed when a man must give an account of himself at the breakfast table every morning. I could think of people with whom you might have spent the evening more profitably, but one should at least be free to choose one's friends, after all. I suppose Jeannette is still doing her best to bring about a revolution."

Craig smiled. "Well, her views don't coincide exactly with Blount's views. Perhaps she has reasons for feeling a little dissatisfied with the world."

"No doubt she thinks she has. It's quite possible that Lasker Blount might feel dissatisfied with her world if he were forced to live in it."

"I don't think there can be much doubt about it," Craig remarked. "Personally, I don't see very much to choose between them. And that reminds me that you haven't yet forgiven me for speaking as I did the other night at dinner."

He looked at her with a playful chuckle as he spoke.

"I may have seemed a little unreasonable about it," she said, "but I was very tired, to begin with, and your quarrelsome mood was a little too much for me."

"Was I quarrelsome?"

"You were at war with the world and everyone in it," she told him. "It was impolite, to say the very least, and you did surprise me a little with your violent opposition to the work men like Lasker Blount are doing to rebuild the world and make life a little more tolerable than it has been for the past few years."

Craig considered for a moment before he spoke. After all, she did not understand... could not understand. For that matter, he had not married her in the hope that she might understand. He had married her because she was beautiful, because life would be a joy wherever she was, because he had loved her. Why should he wish her to understand something that was not of her world?

"We shall not permit anything of that kind to spoil our happiness, anyhow," he said. "Blount's views don't matter half so much to me right now, with you sitting there in front of me, as they did the other night when I had to look at him instead of you."

And yet, as he went to his work that morning, it was Blount's views that weighed heavily upon his spirit— Blount's and Jeannette's.

He recalled the words the stranger had spoken to him on the bridge. The world... the fog... he hoped, for some reason, that Jeannette and the stranger would never meet...

And then he remembered that although he had told Marion of his meeting with Jeannette, she had said nothing of having been out with Charnley the day before.

Well, perhaps he expected too much of her... a woman has some rights of her own...

Two

On the trading floor he met Charnley who asked him to buy another ten thousand bushels of barley before the close of the market.

"I had my first game of golf yesterday," Craig told him when he had set down the memorandum of the order.

Charnley paused before turning away.

"I'm going out myself one of these days," he said. "What course were you on?"

"The Country Club."

He looked closely at Charnley as he spoke, but the latter gave not the slightest sign of uneasiness under the scrutiny.

"I'll give you a game one of these days," Charnley suggested. "Say the word when you're ready."

Craig watched him as he strode away and mingled with the other traders on the floor.

Then he turned and entered the pit to execute the trades.

Three

The perplexity that had been born of his talk with Jeannette weighed upon him all through the day.

What was to become of the hope that had risen in the heart of mankind? He had felt little disappointed over Blount's attitude. It seemed impossible that a man like Blount could feel anything save the selfish impulses that were prompted by his own greed. But that Jeannette Bawden should have erred so strangely in the opposite direction, that she should contemplate with satisfaction a world in which one class would replace the other without changing the essential nature of the condition itself—that seemed hard to understand. But while he thoroughly disliked Blount, he could not help being attracted by Jeannette. And while he had no patience with Blount's attitude to the world, Jeannette's passion stirred him deeply—she was at least the champion of a class whom the Blounts of the world had persecuted for generations.

"Blount's heart is wrong... and that makes everything wrong," Craig told himself. "Jeannette's heart is right... if it were only possible..."

He felt the need of getting out into the country, away from the stir of the market and the streets, away from faces and voices, where he could find time to think quietly by himself.

At three o'clock he telephoned to Marion and suggested that they have an early dinner in order to go for a motor ride into the country before dark.

"I'd like to take you out to the old farm and show you off to the natives," he told her.

Marion was eager to go. She would have a light dinner prepared when he arrived home. Craig wondered why he should be so inordinately happy at finding her ready to fall in with his mood. He drove home in high spirits.

During a rather hasty meal Marion was her old gay self, full of laughter, almost coquettish toward Craig. Then they got the car out of the garage, and were presently speeding southward along the road that led out of the city. Beyond the limits they took the Pembina Highway and passed through the little French-Canadian settlements with their picturesque old houses and well-kept gardens.

"Of course, Craig," Marion remarked when they were well on their way, "while I am curious to see what kind of girl this Martha of yours has turned out, I don't want you to be disappointed if I fail to find much of interest in her. You said yourself that she was not of our world. If she has been abroad during the war, she has probably developed into a sort of bucolic Jeannette Bawden."

Craig turned his car from the main highway and sent it along a graded road leading to the eastward.

"Without disparaging Jeannette," he replied, "I may say that Martha is not in the least like her. In fact, she is more like you, if a comparison can be made at all. I didn't perhaps do her justice when I said she was not of our world. She—"

"Of course not. You merely wished to tell me that I was quite in a class by myself. That was one of your sentimental days, wasn't it? If I remember right, it was the day you applied first aid to the dog."

Craig glanced at Marion. She was wearing a soft silk frock of blue and looked very young and demure in it. It came to him suddenly how greatly he loved her—and how completely! But he had learned of late not to say too much about it. Marion had never liked him when he was "sentimental."

"I think that was the day," he said. "And I believe I was a bit sentimental, too."

A few minutes later, they turned into an old trail that wound its way among clumps of willow and white poplar to where a group of farm buildings stood in the shelter of a small poplar grove.

Martha had seen the car approaching and had come down the pathway from the house to meet them.

Marion's eyes narrowed as she looked closely at the girl who was approaching them. She walked in a long, swinging stride, as if she had been more used to going about in breeches. She wore a scarlet blouse and a rather short, full skirt of some heavy material the chief virtue of which, Marion thought, was its wearing qualities.

To Craig, however, she was the same Martha he had known in the old days, the Martha who used to run down the same path to meet him coming to see her in the long summer evenings.

He stopped his car beside her.

"I thought you might have forgotten the roundabout way in," Martha greeted him, holding out her hand.

Marion reached across the steering wheel and acknowledged Craig's introduction with her most charming smile.

"Craig has told me so much about the 'little girl on the farm' that I expected to find you in pigtails," Marion laughed.

Craig was relieved to hear his wife laugh. She was in her best mood.

"Drive around that hedge, Craig," Martha directed, "and come into the house by the side door."

Craig did as he was told and Martha went back along the pathway to reach the side of the house by a shorter route.

"Rather pretty, isn't she?" Marion commented. "Of the emotional type, I should judge." She flicked a grain of dust from her sleeve as she spoke.

Martha appeared on the porch at the side of the house and bade them enter. Craig caught a strange, excited light in her eyes as he passed her. Then he looked about him. She had ushered them immediately into her "studio."

Craig could not help wondering why she had not taken them into the house... Was it because she felt more at home where her work was all about her?

The room was a large, square, built-on addition to the house, separate from it on three sides. The walls were mainly windows and there was a skylight in the roof. A better workroom could not be desired. At this time of day, with the low sun pouring in through the west windows, the room was a cube of golden light, and Martha, standing in the middle of the floor with her bright blouse and her tawny hair, seemed to blend with the radiance of the place and give it added color.

"This is where I 'waste my precious time', as Dad puts it," Martha laughed, throwing her hands out, palms upward. "Isn't it wonderfully lighted?"

"It must be ideal for your work," Marion said, her eyes wandering over the objects in the room.

In the centre stood a large table surmounted by a stone slab on which were several heaps of variously coloured clays. Against the wall at one end was a long narrow ledge with wider shelves built under it to hold the paraphernalia of the studio—a few books, much scuffed, a half dozen small pots with countless brushes sticking out of them, a couple of pallets smeared with colours, glasses half full of dirty water, a great miscellany of objects in careless disarray. About the room, without any idea of arrangement, stood pedestals that supported figures in clay, in various stages of completion.

"Any catalogues for sale at the door, Martha?" Craig asked. "This looks like the real thing, doesn't it, Marion?"

"It could be the real thing and I'd be none the wiser," Marion remarked. "Sculpture and modelling are things I know nothing about."

She walked idly over to one of the tiny green clay figures and tapped the top of it with her gloved finger. It felt soft and spongy to the touch and her finger sprang away as if it had been burnt.

Martha glanced oddly at Craig. An unaccountable feeling of uneasiness came over him.

"Show them to us in turn, Martha," he asked. "I am just as ignorant as Marion, you know, but we are both anxious to learn."

The three of them passed from one model to another, Martha giving a word of explanation here and there as they went along.

Her work was unusually delicate, at times almost mystic in its bizarre impressionism. Some of the pieces had been cast in bronze and had received gratifying attention in Paris while she was a student there. She told them of her work, speaking simply, briefly, about herself —almost impersonally, as of someone absent. The masters had spoken encouragingly of her efforts... with lots of hard work... sparing herself nothing... she must arrive. But she was not sure... perhaps she was not sufficiently ambitious...

"You know, I still get immense satisfaction from working with the clay from the bank behind the barn... that's where I first started... do you remember, Craig?"

"I should say I do," he replied, laughing. "Do you remember the day you got so furious with me for teasing you when I found you caked with muck from head to foot? You had gone out to work in the clay after it had rained."

She laughed and looked at Marion who smiled a little patronizingly.

"Gosh, what a temper you had then!" Craig went on. "But it hasn't stopped you from getting what you want, I can see that. Did you work at this between 'drives' over there?"

"Yes, a little, whenever I got a chance. It was a sort of refuge... a sort of retreat from too much reality."

A look, almost of pain, came into her face as she spoke. She turned away and glanced toward Marion where she had paused to look at a frail, spindle-thin piece which Martha had called "Gazelle."

"I think this is beautiful—simply exquisite!" Marion exclaimed. "I suppose I couldn't prevail upon you to sell it?"

Martha flushed slightly and stepped to her side. "No, I couldn't be prevailed upon to sell it, but you may have it. I wanted to give you the one you liked best."

Marion put her arm about the girl's shoulders impulsively. "Oh, my dear! How can I thank you! Now I shall boast to all my friends that I have discovered a genius! It's a perfect beauty!"

Craig came forward and lifted the delicate thing in his hands. It was just like Marion to choose that, he thought. He fumbled for words to express his gratitude, then gave it up and set the piece back again on its pedestal.

"You've certainly surprised me, Martha," he said quietly. "But how on earth did you find time to develop your talent? The war must have almost killed the impulse—you were so close to it."

Martha smiled. "I haven't developed nearly so much as you think. All I have to do is glance at a piece of work by Rodin and despair. One of my old masters in London used to tell me how to become great. He used to say, 'Look once at a beautiful thing and after that live it!' It sounds all right, but it's not so easily done."

They passed along to a little niche in the wall. Here the sunlight seemed suddenly to pierce the shadow and limned two strange figures that had been cast in brown copper. Martha's hand trembled slightly as she turned them about in the light, one after the other.

"These are the best things I have ever done," she said hesitatingly. "I want you to have the one you like best, Craig."

Craig looked at her, then at Marion. He saw that Marion's interest had not been caught.

"This one is *Chrysalis*—this one, *Incarnation*," Martha explained. "The difference is merely a matter of mood. The spirit is the same in both."

They were tenuous, unfolding forms, arresting in their simplicity, quite beyond the power of words to describe—two bold, clear strokes in symbolic impressionism. For an instant Craig felt that he stood in a presence... it was a sensation almost identical with that of the memorable night in France... the night when the hope had been born in him out of the darkness of the world and its sorrow. And then, incongruously enough, his mind turned to Blount... the Machine... the exact antithesis of *Chrysallis*... of *Incarnation*.

"But—but I don't see the sense in this futuristic art —or in any art that requires so much explaining. This must be explained, for I'm quite sure I don't understand it."

Marion spoke as if she not only found it impossible to explain the forms before which they were standing, but as if she questioned the right of an artist to express an idea or an emotion in any form the meaning of which was not clear at first glance.

"I don't think anything but abstract ideas ought to be expressed through this medium, or this form, rather," Martha hastened to say. "I think it's quite true the form is over-used, especially in painting."

Craig was staring, fascinated, at the two figures. He thought they stirred... from within... as if they embodied some elemental principle... some inner life...

"Well, which one do you want, Craig? I declare I never saw you looking so stupid," Marion said, turning away slightly to look again at the *Gazelle* on its disk.

Presently, his eyes upon Martha's face, he chose *Incarnation*.

"I'm glad you took that one," Martha said softly.

"Because you like the other one better?" Marion smiled at her curiously.

"No," Martha replied. "Rather because I don't."

On the way out, they inspected an ironic impression of *Marriage*, shaped somewhat like a toadstool on an altar, which Martha said she was ashamed of, and another called

Reconstruction, a grotesque creature with innumerable hands and no head.

"I think you are ever so clever, Martha. You will let me call you that, won't you, my dear?" Marion asked her sweetly.

At that moment old Peter Lane, Martha's father, appeared in the doorway.

Peter Lane had always lived on a farm. He had always looked upon the city from a distance. He saw the world and its ways through the columns of his newspaper and had ever been of the opinion that the world's ills would cease to exist if every man worked as he worked, with his hands and his body, from early morning till late night, and met his duties as they came to him in their seasons.

He had found some fault with old John Forrester the day he learned that Craig had decided to leave the farm and follow a business career in the city.

"One more gone where he'll have to depend on us to keep him for the rest of his days," was the remark old Peter had made on that occasion.

When they entered the house together, after Craig had introduced Marion to the old man and left her to talk to Martha, the old farmer did not take long to come to the subject that always obsessed his mind whenever he thought of Craig's having deserted his old life for the life of the city.

"You're not thinking of quitting that soft-handed job of yours and getting back to work again like an honest man, are you?" he remarked as he filled his pipe and settled himself for a chat.

"I don't think you'd have me about the place, if you knew I was thinking of coming back," Craig laughed. "I've always had the hunch you were glad to get me out of the country."

"Well, you were a kind of nuisance, but you had the makings of a man in you. I doubt there's little of that left in you by this time, though. You look too damned white and soft to be much good anywhere. If you weren't so overgrown you might get a job as a chorus-man in one of these theatre gangs that travels round the country."

Craig smiled at the old fellow. "What would happen to the country if everyone turned farmer?" he asked in meek self-defense.

"You don't have to work your imagination late hours to figure that out," Peter Lane replied. "We need a few doctors, probably about half what we've got now. I'd kick all the lawyers out to work. The best thing they do is make wars for the rest of us to fight. And there's about one preacher in ten that I'd walk across the road to listen to. I tell you, Craigie, we're never going to have anything but trouble in the world till men get back to working with their hands. They've got to get closer to the soil. When a man gets afraid of his boots getting dirty and when he's careful about a little clay getting on his fingers, he's wrong, all wrong, no matter what there may be about him that looks right. I don't know much about this work Matty is doing in that shop of hers there, and I guess I make fun of it when I oughtn't, but at least she's doing something with her hands, she's making something, she's watching something grow—I don't know just how to say it, but there's something *right* about it. She's going to have a mighty pretty house here and she's going to do it with her own hands instead of buying it in the stores. I feel about it like I feel about drinking your city water. I never take a drink out of your pipes but I want to get back here and have a draught of water out of the well I dug myself. There's more to a drink of water than just something to take when you're thirsty, if you understand me. I made that hole in the ground, I threw out the clay and the gravel a spadeful at a time, and when I got down where I could look up and see the stars in the daytime I struck water. I watched it come out of the gravel and trickle down into the hollow at my feet and I knew it was good water, sweet and cool and pure, and it satisfied something else in me, something that was more than a dry tongue. And that's what your city water doesn't do for me. That's what I mean, Craigie."

From somewhere in Craig's heart rose a thirst like the one Peter Lane described. Was it simply that his heart had warmed to the words that the old man had spoken? Or was it because of something deeper, more elemental? Was it that his heart throbbed with the blood of old John Forrester... the man who had helped to build a nation's highways... the man who had done things with his hands and had gloried in the doing of them?

Marion and Martha came in together and turned the conversation into other channels where it ran until darkness fell.

"I suppose I must tell you when it's time to go home," Marion said, getting up and preparing to leave.

Craig got to his feet reluctantly. "Well, I guess it is getting late," he observed. "One of these days, Peter Lane, I'm going to be out here to stay for a while. I may make a farmer's wife out of Marion yet. Who knows?"

He spoke banteringly and Marion smiled and tossed her head as she looked at Martha. But Peter Lane did not smile.

"Before I go, just give me a drink of water out of that well of yours," Craig added. "Bring me a dipper full—I've been thirsty all evening."

Four

"I suppose it's all right for those who are used to it," Marion commented on the way home that night. "But I don't see what that poor girl sees in burying herself out there, away from everything that's going on in the world."

"I suppose it's all in one's point of view," Craig responded.

And Craig realized that there were some things in life that Marion did not understand... could not understand, in fact...

At first he felt a little impatient with her.

Then he felt sorry for her.

Then he recalled—irrelevantly—a day in summer when he had gone with Martha Lane to pick choke-cherries in a little ravine that ran across the lower end of the farm.

CHAPTER V.

One

DURING THOSE DAYS while Craig talked with Gilbert Nason and Lasker Blount and Jeannette Bawden, and with a host of others whose lack of interest in the re-shaping of the world's affairs was only too apparent, Craig remonstrated mildly in the presence of Marion who gave ear to his protests with a tolerant air that often drove him away to write in his book or talk to himself.

"It's like this, Marion," he would say, "either this thing means one thing or it means another." He squinted oddly through half shut eyes. "Either there is some kind of order in the world—or there is nothing but waste."

At a shrug of impatience from Marion, he lifted his hand.

"No—just listen a moment. You see, we have been led to think that there are things in life worth living for. There is love, for instance—my love for you. I won't be sentimental. But love is something. Beauty is something. Goodness is something. I mean the things in life that we call human—they all mean something to us. They mean everything to us. We were taught to hold them sacred. If they are sacred, then they are worth dying for. Don't you see? And when a man gives his life, it must be because he is helping to buy beauty and goodness and love. He dies because these things would not exist in life if he lived. That's one way of looking at it. Then there is the other way. Perhaps all our ideas of love and goodness and beauty are wrong. We may have been taught what isn't true. Maybe such things are mere weaknesses in our lives. Perhaps we do wrong when we try to be human. Then the whole thing becomes a comedy—a pitiless comedy with God looking on. That would make life one great lie. If these things mean nothing, there's only one thing to do. We might as well slit an artery in our wrists and end it. Why suffer for the good if there is no good? If we thought that—really thought it—and believed it—there wouldn't be a man or a woman alive in another generation. But we don't think it. We go on living—we want to live because we believe these things are true and mean what we think they mean. Well, then, we've all got to believe it. We've all got to work together for what's really worth while. We've all got to do our bit, wherever we can, and however we can. That was the principle we went on when we were at the front. Some could fight and others couldn't. All right—we left the others at home to do what we hadn't time to do. Now, when we're through—when we've done what we could— if we find they're not willing to go on with the work, what does it mean? Don't you see? It means that someone is lying down on his job. It means that we won't be driven out to fight another war. We'll let the big fellows fight it out by themselves."

He paused and considered a while. Of course, the "big fellows" wouldn't fight it out among themselves... and they wouldn't be left to do the fighting... a new call would bring out the manhood of the nation again as it had done in the past... or would it? Would the young men of the world grow tired of fighting over issues concerning which they knew little or nothing? Would the women of the world grow weary of sending their sons into the battle line? Would Marion send her son... when she had one to send?

"Do you want your son—our son—when he comes—and when he grows to be a young man—do you want him to be called away from his life's work and be slaughtered—or sent home maimed for life?"

Marion looked up from the book she was trying to read.

"There'll be time enough to discuss that when we have a son to send," she replied.

"I know—but just suppose, for the sake of the thing we're discussing—"

"You mean the thing you're discussing, of course," she retorted.

He drew a deep breath and got to his feet. He strolled to the other side of the library where they were sitting and leaned against a bookcase. He applied a match to his pipe that had gone out during his talk to Marion. He stood for a long time blowing the smoke from his lips and watching it ascend in pale blue clouds towards the ceiling.

Resting on the bookcase where he had set it the day after his visit to the farm, was the little figure that Martha had given him to take home.

Incarnation!

Something that had been put into flesh!

There *was* something... the fight was *not* for nothing... life was not wrong... love, beauty, the good things, the human things... they were right...

He turned suddenly and looked at Marion.

She had been for him the embodiment of all these things. Was she settling down into the unromantic routine of her new life, forgetful of everything in the world but the fulfilment of her duties as a wife?

For a moment he seemed to see in her the embodiment of the world as he was coming to know it now after two years of vain hoping. When he had seen her first, after his return from France, he had looked upon her as one of the younger generation who would carry the torch forward and plant it where it would light the way that civilization must march—onward and upward to the goal that only youth can see in visions.

As he looked at her now he realized that a change had come upon her. She was beautiful as ever. Her hair held the same mysterious lights. But she was in repose, she was relaxed, she was luxuriating in her own security.

He suddenly remembered that she had not sung to him for weeks. It was as if the youth in her had suddenly become dormant. He saw her as she would be in the years to come, if the world went back to its old ways. He saw her as an old woman, with wrinkled hands and lustreless eyes, beset with fears, broken by sadness, a futile, helpless old mother, trying to be brave in her day of trial... knitting grey wool... nodding over her clicking needles...

And all because she had chosen the easy way... the way of forgetting...

He was suddenly overcome by the thought of what she could do with her youth... and she and others like her in the world... if they would only remember... now...

He spoke abruptly, sharply.

"Marion!"

She started suddenly and lifted her face to the light. Her eyes were flashing with anger.

"When you get into these moods of yours, I could just hate you!" she declared as she got to her feet and tossed her book on the table.

"Marion, dear, I—"

"I mean it! I stayed at home to-night because I thought we might spend the evening together pleasantly. But you begin by lecturing me till I'm positively weary and end by frightening me half to death. You've simply spoiled my evening. And I didn't tell you that I refused an invitation to go

out with friends who would have been polite, at least. I shall
know better next time."

He tried once more to offer some sort of apology, but she
turned angrily and went to her room.

Craig followed to the door of the library and called to her
as she flew upstairs, but she made no response.

Well... he had done it again... just when he thought he
might stir her to some interest in the thing that was perplexing him...

It would probably take two or three days to restore good
feeling again... two or three days during which she would
taunt him with references to Charnley... she had done so
frequently of late, when she had been annoyed with him...

Damn Charnley...

At any rate, she was not cold... she knew how to become
angry when she was crossed... that gave to their squabbles
an alleviating flavour of comedy...

Two

It was this thought that he carried over into his thinking
about the world in which he lived during the next few weeks.

So long as there was unrest... so long as the world was
astir... so long as people were active, even if they were
active only in protest, they would remain vital, at least. In
moments of stress, people thought about things... they did
things. What they thought might be wrong... what they did
might be destructive... but there was a living power in it
with only the need of direction...

When the world was dead, as in the old days, the dema-
gogues found their opportunity. While the people slept, the
war-lords, sitting apart, planned the world's destruction...

And during the weeks that followed, Craig's mind had

little opportunity to sink into lethargy. Day after day, Gilbert Nason called him by telephone or asked him to the house while he told him of the crisis that was approaching in his relations with his men at the factory.

By the middle of June the men had actually gone on strike and Nason confessed himself unable to handle the problem alone. He called Lasker Blount to his aid. His "experiment" had been a failure.

Blount's mind was very clear on the situation. The disturbance was simply another demonstration on the part of the "reds" whom a long suffering people still permitted to remain in the country because a spineless government refused to take issue with the workers of the country. With a strong government in power, the whole question could be settled in a week. He—Lasker Blount—would give every man and woman in the country twenty-four hours to say where they stood. And those who didn't like the country could get to hell out of it!

That was Lasker Blount.

But wherever Blount's name was mentioned, another name was almost invariably coupled with it. It was the name of a man who had come to the city during the past year and had already proven himself a dangerous menace to the public peace. He had harangued street audiences in Market Square and had come out boldly for direct action on the part of the labouring classes. He had preached the Gospel of Hate to his hearers and had called upon them to rise in revolt against an existence that had become intolerable. He had been heard to blaspheme in his sermons to the mob. He was without Christian principle or ethical motive—an undesirable who should never have been permitted to enter the country in the first place.

They called the man Amer.

Once again the threat of a general strike was discussed freely in the streets. And gradually it came to be recognized that the fight was between Blount and Amer.

And when the tension had reached its height, Craig met Jeannette Bawden on the street.

She greeted him with a smile, then stood looking at him without speaking, her eyes glowing with strange light.

"It's coming," she said in a quiet undertone that neverthe-less betrayed her excitement.

"Looks as if we're going to have a flurry, anyhow," Craig admitted.

"A flurry!" she chuckled. "I don't mean this little affair of Nason's. That's out of his hands now. His little experi-ment burst like a toy balloon. But the sentiment has spread. The other crowd has called a meeting to-morrow night at the Fort Garry. Let them meet—their bankers and their preachers and the rest of the lot. We're holding our own meetings. The thing is growing. It will take a little time—perhaps a year. This time everything will be organized from coast to coast. A little flurry here and there will serve to keep the fire burning. The worst thing possible now would be for Gilbert Nason to throw up his hands and sur-render to his men. That would settle it. The men would go back to work again and everything would be serene. We've got to keep life in the thing all along the line. When we're ready—everything will stop at once!"

"There'll be nothing left to do then but turn the thing over and the New Day will be here," Craig smiled.

She became serious. "Don't make fun of me, Craig," she said. "We've either got to have it happen like that or—"

She hesitated. "Well—or what?"

"Or it would be better if humanity and civilization were wiped off the face of the earth! This can't go on indefinitely.

Take your choice."

She was gone before he had an opportunity to tell her what his choice would be, were he forced to choose.

Did he know? Was life, then, intolerable... unlivable? Would it be better perhaps, to wipe it all out... blot out the record of humanity... make it as clean as the back of your hand... and begin all over again?

A half dozen sparrows fluttered up from before him as he made his way across the street. They reminded him of the early morning when he had gone to the window and put his head out to find the air filled with birds...

The memory brought with it the new hopes that had been born in his heart at the time.

After all, the only intolerable life was a life without hope...

As he entered his office the telephone rang. To his "Hello!" Gilbert Nason replied in a voice that had lately lost its old time ring of confidence.

"I've got to get out, Craig," he said. "My nerve is gone. I didn't sleep a wink last night. Come and take me out for a round of golf as soon as you can get away."

By three o'clock they were on their way to the club. Craig purposely avoided any reference to Nason's problem on the way out and they went round the course without discussing anything more important than their luck on the greens.

As soon as they were settled in the car, however, Nason broke forth.

"You see," he said, as if they had been discussing the problem all afternoon, "the thing has got out of my hands. Jeannette Bawden used to twit me about my little experiment— that's what she called the factory. Well, it was an experiment. I admit it. I thought it was possible to carry on an enterprise without paying any attention to labour unions and such like. A contented workman wants no union to stand back of him. If he is getting all he wants, he should be satisfied. And I believe my men were satisfied with the treatment they were getting. They have been getting better wages than any workmen in their trade in the country. They got their share of the dividends at the end of the year in the form of a bonus. The books were open to inspection by their own representatives. We dealt with each other in the open and I never heard a kick from any of them. I only laid down one condition and that was that they should have no truck with unions. In fact, I didn't deny them the right to join a union if they wanted to, but I resolved that any differences between us should be settled without interference from the outside. Just why they should have gone back on their original understanding with me and made their demands now is what I don't understand. I know things haven't been going so well for me. They can't expect to get money if we can't sell the goods. And all the unions in the world won't pay them wartime wages if there is no market for the product of their labour. You see, that's where these fellows get unreasonable. What good will it do them now to force union regulations on a business that has been going along for the past seven or eight years without a hitch? What good will it do them to make me recognize their union if I have to close down the works the next day? Why, damn it, there's neither rhyme nor reason to the thing."

"Why not recognize the union and have it settled without any more trouble?" Craig asked. "It can't hurt you to—"

"And knuckle under to the professional agitators who started the trouble? If it was simply a matter of giving in to my own men, the case would be a simple one. Even then I'd be outraging my own sense of fair play. The principle of the thing would be broken. I'd be forced to put the business in the same class with all the other enterprises in the country. I'd have to face the same troubles as they are called on to face every year or so. Besides—why, I'd lose my interest in the thing. Haven't I got enough to do with union officials in the dozen and one other things I'm tied up to, without having to spend the best part of my life dickering with them in a business I made for myself and nursed like a child till it reached a place where it could stand on its feet? I tell you, Craig, this little factory of mine has been something more than a business for me. I am losing money in it—have been losing money in it for more than a year now. But I'm ready to go on losing money indefinitely, just so long as I prove to some of my skeptical friends that the thing I started out to do can be done. I mean, that a factory can be run by the men who are employed and by the man who owns it and that outsiders can be told to stay out where they belong."

"Of course," Craig commented, "if it can't be done that way, it's worth while finding that out, too."

Nason looked at him quickly. "What do you mean?"

Craig smiled without returning the look. "I made up my mind not to be drawn into any discussion this afternoon," he said, "and here I'm falling right into it with both eyes open."

Nason laughed. "I made up my mind to the same thing, exactly," he said, "but I forgot myself. I've put it out of mind till to-morrow night's meeting. I'll tell you what. I feel like talking to someone that's got a human streak in him and can talk about something besides strikes and ultimatums and arbitration and lockouts. What do you say to paying a visit to that sergeant friend of yours—you remember?"

"You mean Jimmy Dyer?"

"I don't remember what you called him. You said he lived along here somewhere."

"We'll do that. We'll take a look at Jimmy's garden. I feel a little guilty about Jimmy. I haven't been out to see him since last summer and I promised to call on him again when the garden was in full bloom. We'll come to the street along here somewhere—if I can pick it out."

A few minutes later they turned down a side street and stopped before the little cottage where Craig had visited Jimmy Dyer almost a year before.

Three

Millie Dyer met them at the door and ushered them into the tidy little room where Craig had once sat with a glass of fruit punch in his hands and chatted with Jimmy Dyer about his garden.

Craig introduced Nason and was on the point of asking for Jimmie when a strange feeling seized him and checked the enquiry before it had left his lips.

There was something in Millie Dyer's manner, in the quiet seriousness of her face, in the resigned attitude with which she sat in her chair and faced them and waited for them to speak... could it be that Jimmy Dyer... much can happen in a year... was Millie Dyer alone in the world?

Craig wrenched himself free from the fears that obsessed him and spoke in a friendly tone.

"Thought it was time I was getting round to see you," he said. "I've thought often of you and Jimmy and the kids—how are they all?"

She lowered her head slightly and for a moment was intent upon her hands folded in her lap.

"I—I thought you—you knew," she said quietly.

Then it was true. Craig felt as if a cold iron had been thrust into his heart.

"Why—my God! nothing has happened?"

Millie Dyer nodded her head slowly and Craig saw that her eyes had filled with tears.

He got up from his chair and went beside her. Laying a hand on her shoulder, he stood for some time without being able to speak.

At last the words came slowly, jerkily, brokenly.

"Why—I didn't know—I should have come before—but—"

"I can understand," she said. "It's all right. It was sudden—unexpected. He came back with a weak heart —poison gas did it. He never had much to say about it. He wouldn't admit it. But it—something just gave way very suddenly and—he went in a few hours."

"How long ago?" he asked her.

She made an effort to control her sobbing.

"Just after Christmas."

Gilbert Nason leaned forward in his chair and spoke softly to Craig. "Maybe there's something we could do — some way we could help."

Millie Dyer looked up quickly and sat for a moment without speaking. With an impatient gesture she brushed the tears from her eyes as if to get a better look at the man who had spoken.

"You are probably trying to be kind," she said suddenly.

She paused again, her eyes resting on Nason, and tucked away a loose strand of hair that had fallen over her forehead. Into her eyes had leaped the flame that Craig had seen hidden there months before.

"You are probably trying to be kind," she repeated. "And you have called on me with the Captain and I don't want to offend you. I wouldn't. But there isn't anything you can do—you or anyone else. And there's no way you can help. There's a lot of women left alone in the world—lots of them right here in this city—and some of them might take help if you offered it to them. Some of them can't help themselves.

But I can. Jimmy Dyer never took charity from anyone and he wouldn't want his wife to take it from anyone, either. No, Mr. Nason, there are some of us who are strong enough in body to go out and work for our children and strong enough in mind, too, to do a little thinking for ourselves. Somewhere I read of what one woman made her mind up to do when she got word that her husband had been killed. She was going out to take the life of some warmaker—take it with her own hands. And that's what the men who make war are driving us to do. They will force the women to make war on those who made war for us. We'll go out and find the men who sit in upholstered chairs and play the game of politics and business and move the Jimmy Dyers of the world about on the checker board like so many bits of wood. We'll find them. They killed our men. We'll kill them. What else have we to do? We'll dog their steps. We'll make them afraid to go out unattended. They'll be afraid to touch food or water for fear of being poisoned. There'll be ways, and ways—and ways! But we'll stop it—we'll stop it! We'll bring no more sons into the world for them to feed to cannons. We'll send no more husbands out behind brass bands to spill their blood in the field. We kept the homes—the gardens—the flowers... the poppy beds..."

She paused as her voice broke.

Craig patted her gently on the shoulder. He could not speak to her. There was nothing to say.

Suddenly she got to her feet.

"But I am forgetting myself," she said quietly. "You have been very kind to call. If you'll stay just a moment I'll make a cup of tea."

Craig was about to protest, but Gilbert Nason spoke up at once.

"I don't know of anything I'd like better right now," he

said heartily. "Send in the children and let us talk to them while you're making it. Only don't go to any trouble about it. Just a cup of tea."

Millie Dyer disappeared into the kitchen and in a moment came back with her two boys, one on either side of her, and presented them to the visitors.

The boys came forward shyly and took the hands extended toward them and Craig and Nason drew them between their knees and talked to them while their mother went back to the kitchen.

"I know you," the older boy said to Craig. "You came here with Daddy last summer. You're the captain."

Gilbert Nason chattered freely to both of them about a score of things dear to the boy mind, dogs and aeroplanes, Charlie Chaplin and Mutt and Jeff, marbles and automobiles...

And Craig listened with growing admiration for the old man... there was something good in a man who could talk to children like that...

Four

As they drove home, half an hour later, it seemed to Craig as if he had suddenly been lifted into another world.

It was Millie Dyer's world... the world where women suffered and were coming to the end of their patience... the world where they were even now resolving to suffer no more the terrible hurts of man's mis-rule...

And beside him, Gilbert Nason talked on in a ceaseless monotone that irritated him and challenged all his resistance to keep from getting angry...

"Of course, the little woman is right... and she's a pretty little thing... a great pair of eyes... but what can a woman do, no matter how she tries... no matter how wrought up she gets over it? After all, it's a practical world... It's a world where things have to be done, not talked about..."

"We'll wake up one of these days to find the Millie Dyers doing things," Craig ventured to prophesy, "unless we do something ourselves before they get started."

For some time Gilbert Nason was silent.

At last he stirred uneasily in his seat.

"Well, Craig... I'm ready... I'm ready to do whatever can be done... and I believe there are lots of men just as ready as I am... if... "

"If the Blounts of the world were all killed off," Craig interrupted. "I am beginning to believe there's a place in the world to-day for a few professional assassins."

"Don't forget the meeting at the Fort Garry tomorrow night!" Nason reminded him.

Five

While they sat at the table that night, Craig told Marion of the visit he and her father had paid to Millie Dyer that afternoon.

"I think it would be a nice thing if you'd take a run out there one of these days, Marion," he suggested. "I'll take you out in the car any afternoon you—"

"I don't think it's at all necessary," she interrupted him. "I wouldn't know what to say to the woman. We have nothing in common."

"You might find something in common."

She evaded the suggestion.

"It puzzles me to know just what you see in people of that type, anyhow," she remarked. "After all, people do use a little discretion in such things."

Six

"Millie Dyer!"

The name recurred to Craig continually during the next day. And every time he thought of it, his imagination dwelt on the thousands of Millie Dyers the world over... Millie Dyers whose poppy beds were being left to die...

It was this thought that harassed him as he drove his car to the hotel that evening at about six o'clock and found a line of other cars standing in close formation on both sides of the street.

"I can't help looking at all this as Millie Dyer might look at it," Craig said to Gilbert Nason as they stepped from the car and started up the flight of stone steps to the hotel entrance. "A quarter of a million dollars in automobiles lined up along the curbs!"

Nason hurried up the steps without looking behind him.

"Sentiment is all right in its place, my boy," he replied. "But if we stopped to sentimentalize over every automobile we met in the streets we'd never get a day's work done."

Craig followed Nason into the large rotunda that was already crowded with men. Almost at once his eyes fell upon the bulky form of Lasker Blount standing in the centre of a group of men whose personal appearance pronounced them to be men of position in the community. There were a few old men, keen old chaps whose words came quickly and whose gestures might have been copied from the stage—so true they were to type. There were a number of young men who stood together in noisy groups apart from the older men. But the middle-aged men were in the majority—well-dressed, aggressive men who were in the habit of taking life seriously though they knew how to laugh at one another's jokes, men who represented fully three-quarters of the business ability of the city and carried themselves with the confident air of successful executors.

Many of Craig's business associates were there. He caught sight of Sharples and was making toward him when he recognized Claude Charnley approaching the broker from another direction and stopped. Somehow he was in no mood to meet Charnley. He heard his name called and turned to find Croker beckoning to him.

"And how's the Magpie?" Croker greeted him. "Still doing the act of a voice crying in the wilderness?"

Craig shook hands with him and dug him playfully in the ribs.

"Still croaking," he observed.

"I'm rather surprised to find you fraternizing with the monied class, Forrester," Croker told him. "Had a sort of hunch you were going over to the Bolshies when I last talked to you. Another case of 'when a man marries,' is it?"

"I should think there's just as much room for me here as for an old Ishmael like you," Craig replied.

"There's room for everybody—provided he doesn't show too much red in his eye. We're here because we believe the world is in a pretty rotten shape and isn't going to get much better right away. That lets me in. The only place I break with the rest of them is that I don't think it ever has been much better."

Already the men were moving into the large dining-room that had been reserved for the occasion and Craig took Croker's arm and led him along with the crowd.

"Let's get in and be among those present," he said.

They found a table directly in front of the speaker's table and remained standing while the crowd distributed itself about the room. Presently the doors were closed and a sharp tinkle of a knife against a glass brought an immediate hush upon the assembly. The chairman spoke a half dozen words that escaped Craig who at the moment was listening to a whispered remark from Croker. Another voice, sonorous and almost pompous, rose from beside the chairman and the men bowed their heads while a blessing was asked.

Craig heard the voice and lifted his eyes slowly till they rested on the face of the man who besought the Almighty to bless the food and to make His spirit to shine upon them while they reasoned together. It was the Reverend George Bentley.

There followed a noisy shuffling of chairs and the room was again filled with chatter and loud laughing.

Craig and Croker together studied the faces of the men who sat at the speaker's table. The chairman was a prominent citizen whose services to the Empire, in times of peace, had been rewarded by the conferring of a knighthood. Sir Henry Wilton had had a brilliant career in the profession of law and had dabbled a little in politics where he had stood as the champion of orthodoxy and tradition. He had been somewhat too religious in his utterances from the public platform, the more so since his gifts to righteous causes had never exceeded the expectations of those who sought them. Beside him sat Lasker Blount—and beside Blount, Gilbert Nason.

For some reason Craig resented seeing Nason sitting in a place that identified him with Wilton and Blount. Nason was not of their kind. Accident and circumstance had made him a man of business. In reality he was a man of sentiment.

But Croker, growling beside him, drew his attention away from the head table.

"Nice little picture, this," Croker observed. "No garlicky

nobodies in this crowd. These boys don't dream dreams in garrets. These are the city's respectable citizens... the men God has blessed... the men who used to slap Tom Jones and Bill Smith on the back when they were going out to fight... "

"A lot of these fellows went out to fight, too," Craig protested.

"Sure they did... sure they did. But I haven't seen them fraternizing with Jones and Smith since they came back. And I haven't heard of either Tom or Bill getting an invitation to this little party, either. Sir Harry up there wouldn't approve of that. Neither would Kaiser Blount... But it isn't so long ago...

Craig did not hear what Croker went on to say. His mind was busy with the details of a picture that had suddenly risen before him... a road in Flanders... a night of pitchy darkness with rain falling... mud and more mud in endless miles... and the stench of death in the wet air...

And later, in their billet... men, drunkenly weary, dropping down anywhere... anywhere... and sleeping in their soggy uniforms.

Had these men forgotten those nights? Or did they still remember... hoping they might now find some way... some brotherly way... to settle their differences?

Seven

Sir Henry rose in his place and bowed graciously before the applause that greeted him.

He spoke briefly, but eloquently, of the purpose for which the meeting had been called. His expression of gratitude to the men who had called the gathering was gracefully turned and evoked another round of applause. Nothing was clearer to his mind than that the community—perhaps the whole nation—would be called upon, before the end of the summer, to fight for its very existence. It had been known for some time that money from Germany and from Russia was being used to foster the spirit of discontent in the country, to make our victory, so dearly bought, no less horrible than defeat. He was pleased to introduce Mr. Lasker Blount, on his first public appearance in the city, and congratulated the business men of the city on having added to their number a man whose experience in the settlement of disputes induced by salaried agitators had been so wide and so eminently successful. He called upon Mr. Blount.

Craig could not bring himself to join in the applause that greeted Lasker Blount when he rose to speak. He cut the end from a fresh cigar and applied a match while Blount laboured through an after-dinner story by way of catching the attention of his hearers. It appeared that two Irishmen, one of whom had turned Socialist, were having an argument over the principle of the equal distribution of property... One of them, the Socialist, had two pigs...

Craig closed his mind to the wandering details of the anecdote... In the presence of Lasker Blount his sense of humour failed him utterly...

He drew his knife from his pocket and trimmed off another quarter of an inch from his cigar. While he waited, he struck another match and applied it quite unnecessarily to the glowing end. Then he held the burning match in his fingers and watched it until the laughter that followed the story died and a hush of expectancy fell upon the crowd waiting now for Blount to get on with his address.

With the first word that broke upon the hush, Craig dropped the burning match into a cup and sat up to listen.

For more than half an hour Blount reviewed the unsettled conditions in Europe, that seething cauldron of unrest and near-anarchy. He described the famine horrors of contemporary Russia with its women and its children starving in the ditches. He pictured a beaten Germany, facing national collapse and bankruptcy, preyed upon by radicals whose only desire was to establish themselves in control of the government and bring utter ruin to the German republic as they had done to Russia. He spoke in great detail of the radical menace in England, working through the trades unions for the overthrow of authority and perpetrating every kind of outrage against law and order. Wherever there was disruption and upheaval he saw it in the work of long-haired propagandists who were the paid servants of Lenin and Trotsky.

Finally he turned to Canada. He had made a careful study of the situation as it existed between Halifax and Vancouver. He had unassailable proof for everything he was about to say. There was a nation-wide conspiracy, financed, as he had said, by aliens who sought the downfall of western civilization and the overthrow of the Christian religion.

"Bunk!" whispered Croker.

But Craig did not reply. He was not so much interested in what Blount was saying as he was in the effect his words was having on the men seated around the tables.

Blount regretted to say that not a few of the men who had fought for King and Country in the Great War were among the most outspoken opponents of the present order. Men whose records in the trenches might have been above reproach, but whose actions in the approaching crisis were nothing short of a disgrace to the colours they bore. What was the matter with men who would fight for a country and then enlist on the side of the power that was bent on its destruction? We had the greatest country in the world right here if we only made good our opportunity. If there were those who enjoyed the freedom, the material blessings, the unbroken peace of the Land of the Maple, but who nevertheless found nothing in it worthy of their love, let them "get to hell out of it!"

The phrase had become famous… it had made Lasker Blount famous.

It was greeted with cheers and loud clapping of hands.

"Oh, my God!" Croker muttered aloud.

Craig suddenly realized that his fingers were closed in a tight grip that made the veins stand out on the back of his hands. Was it possible that intelligent men were ready to swallow whole the sophistries of a man whose whole argument was little more than a fatuous defence of an arrogant feudalism?

Blount's voice had risen almost to shouting pitch. He would find these men, he would make a blacklist, he would bring their leaders out and herd them into boxcars, he would run them down to the seaboard and ship them back to where they came from like so much livestock in a cattle ship. He would make a second round-up of the men who peddled seditious literature, he would herd them to the public barber shops and have their hair cut, he would take them to the public baths and duck them one by one until they swore allegiance with their last gasp, then he would put them to work in road gangs without pay for a year.

Craig thought suddenly of Ivan.

For the rest, the men and women who were merely looking for a little excitement, he would run them like rats to their holes and give them their choice between working for honest livings and doing flunkey service for honest workmen. And if the business men of the city found the task unpleasant, he would be pleased to do it himself—he had no friends among them.

"This is one of the best shows I've been to since before the war," Croker remarked.

But Craig was finding it almost impossible to control his rising anger.

"I'm going to get out to the air in a few minutes," he whispered to Croker.

But Croker put a restraining hand on his arm.

"Let's see it through, Cap," he said, "He's just about run down."

And, indeed, a moment later, Blount wound up with a flourish and took his seat. Sir Henry suggested hastily that there was time left for a full and free discussion before they proceeded to the business of appointing a citizen's committee to co-operate with the civic and provincial authorities and to invoke the aid of the federal government, if necessary, to prevent a crisis.

For more than half an hour, then, Sir Henry had all he could do to keep some semblance of order. He named one after another from those who leaped to their feet at every opportunity, all resolved to add their word to what the chief speaker of the evening had said.

And on each occasion, one little man who seemed to be sitting apart from the others, lifted his thin voice to address Sir Henry in an effort to gain a hearing. When he had failed to win the chairman's favour he sat down only to pop up again at the next opportunity. After three or four abortive attempts to express himself, he became the centre of interest of half the crowd and Croker turned to Craig again.

"Who let that in?" he asked.

"Let him speak," Craig replied.

The words were no sooner out of his mouth than the little fellow was on his feet again, the last speaker having just taken his seat.

"Let him speak!" Craig cried aloud as the chairman wavered in his decision. "Let him speak!"

His cry was taken up by half a dozen others and Sir Henry lifted his hand toward the insistent one as a signal to say whatever he had to say.

"I 'aven't much to s'y," the little man said in an accent that was strongly cockney. "But w'at I wants to know is, 'ose Weedin' country is this? Is it 'is?" He pointed to Blount as he asked the question. "Is it yours?" He waved a thin arm over the men seated at the tables. "An' if it is, 'ow'd you come by it?"

"We fought for it, brother!" came a voice from the other side of the room. "Did you?"

The question was taken up immediately by voices coming from every part of the room so that the speaker found it impossible to proceed until order was restored.

"No—I didn't. Did 'e?" The speaker pointed to Blount again.

The question brought forth a storm of boos and cries of "order! Throw him out!" until Sir Henry finally gained control once more.

"Unless this discussion is conducted in a becoming manner, we shall have to declare it at an end and proceed with other business," he said abruptly.

Suddenly the Reverend George Bentley rose in his place. "We are forgetting that we have asked God's blessing on this meeting," he reminded them. "Let us ask it again!"

He lifted his hand and bowed his head. It was a bold stroke. The muttering ceased immediately and Bentley's voice came clear and strong as he prayed once more for God's guidance.

"What a damned mockery!" Craig muttered.

Bentley had no more than pronounced his "Amen!"

when another voice spoke out, a voice that was as clear as the voice of the man who had prayed—and much stronger.

Every eye in the room turned to look at the massive frame of a man who stood in a small balcony that had been occupied by an orchestra earlier in the evening.

"Good God!" Croker exclaimed. "It's Amer!"

Craig turned in his chair and let his eyes rest for a moment on the giant figure that stood above them.

A faint memory leaped within him… that towering frame… the huge shoulders… the massive head…

It was the stranger who had spoken to him in the fog.

Eight

"I am the Uninvited Guest!" Amer said after he had addressed the chairman. "You cried down the last speaker because he was not a soldier. I am a soldier with a record I am not ashamed of. I came here through a side door because I wasn't good enough to be invited to your tables."

A murmur of protest grew until Amer's voice was almost drowned in the confusion.

"Let me speak!" he bellowed above the din.

The noise subsided momentarily under the terrific power of the man's voice.

"I came here to see if the man you listened to would speak one truth that would give a gleam of hope to the luckless nobodies who sweat for you and reap starvation for reward. I listened to every word—and every word was a lie. He has told you that their leaders are paid—"

The confusion had grown again until Amer was shouting to make himself heard. A shuffling of chairs indicated that some of the men were preparing to oust the intruder by physical means. Craig looked round in time to see two or three getting to their feet and moving toward the doors.

But the Reverend George Bentley came to the rescue once more. In a loud voice he struck up the first notes of "God Save the King." Others joined at once and in a moment the whole crowd had taken up the song.

In his place in the balcony, Amer stood at attention until they had reached the end of the anthem. Then he spoke again.

"He has told you... "

Bentley's voice led off once more and the song was repeated.

Once more, Amer waited till the last note was sung. Once more, too, he started to speak.

But the song was begun again in a lusty chorus that swelled more loudly than ever.

Craig stood with his eyes on Amer... felt an insane rage rise in his heart as he thought of the brutal unfairness of the men who were prostituting a sacred song... looked once at the grinning face of Lasker Blount and wished he were close enough to strike it...

When the song was begun for the fourth time, he saw a look of fury leap into Amer's face... saw him leap over the edge of the balcony and feared he was going to leap down... then he saw him open his mouth to speak.

But the crowd saw Amer's final attempt to make himself heard and raised their voices to drown the words.

Amer looked down at them, smiled faintly, then turned slowly and stepped to the door at the back of the balcony. Once more he turned and looked at them all... then opened the door and disappeared.

In a fury he could not control, Craig lifted the chair beside which he was standing and brought it crashing to splinters on the floor.

"Damned blasphemy!" he cried. "Damned blasphemy! Let me out!"

The song was ended as he spoke and men on either side stood aghast as he strode to the door and went out without casting a glance behind him.

Nine

Outside, he strode across the street to where his car was standing in the shadow of trees that lined the avenue.

As he took his seat in the car, he glanced back once toward the hotel and saw the tall figure of Amer emerge from the shadows at the side of the hotel and join a woman who stood waiting for him in the street.

The woman was Jeannette Bawden...

CHAPTER VI.

One

THE NEXT AFTERNOON, Craig sat in Sharples' private office on the fifth floor of the Grain Exchange. He and Sharples were listening to Claude Charnley outlining his position in the market.

Since Charnley had begun buying July barley, the price had advanced from a dollar and sixty-four cents a bushel till it held firm now around a dollar seventy. That day the market had closed at a dollar seventy and one-eighth. During the first half of June, the coarse grain market in general had shown a tendency toward higher prices with only an occasional "break" caused by profit-taking that in no way had affected the strong undertone. Charnley had taken his share of the profits on a rising market, but had followed each sale by adding to his holdings when he saw that the price recovered almost immediately after every temporary slump.

By the middle of June, Charnley was "long" more than a million bushels.

During the past week, however, Craig had begun to feel a change in what the traders call "sentiment." Reports from the grain producing areas of the United States were more optimistic than they had been during the first few days of summer. The countries of Europe were recovering slowly and their recovery was beginning to show itself in the production of grain. Countries like Poland and Roumania were already forecasting a yield representing an increase of fifty per cent. over the previous year. Czecho-Slovakia, whose total output of barley for the past five years had not been as much as spoken of in the foreign market news, promised a crop of thirty million bushels of barley. The Canadian crop alone would be probably ten million bushels in excess of the previous year and well above its average for the five years following the outbreak of the war.

"It's time to get out," Craig had told Charnley a half dozen times during the past ten days.

And so they had met to talk it over.

Charnley was for holding on till the middle of July.

"It has held firm now since the end of March," he argued. "Barley was selling around a dollar forty-five then. My God, if I'd packed up a half million bushels or so then when I had the hunch—I'd have cleaned up—"

"If we had the list of closing prices for the next month," Craig said, "we'd be millionaires, if we could keep it a secret. The trouble with trading in futures is that you can't do it in the past."

"Magpie," Charnley said, "if we switch this million bushels into October and add another to it all we'll have to do is sit tight and watch the market rise. Will you come in with us?"

Craig glanced at Sharples' desk littered with reports and telegrams. Absent-mindedly he was working out a little problem in geometry involving an ink bottle, a paper weight, and the ash tray into which Sharples was just at that moment knocking the ashes from the end of his cigar.

"Come in with whom?" he asked quietly.

"With Sharples and me. Among us we have enough capital to swing a real trade in barley and if my hunch is right—"

"I never gamble," Craig interrupted. "You know that, Charnley."

There was a note of impatience in his voice as he spoke. It was not so much that he had been asked to depart from his habit of conducting a strictly legitimate business in the export trade and to enter a venture of a purely speculative nature. The suggestion had come to him many times, from men who had won fortunes in the pit and had tried to prove to Craig how easily he might do the same. But Charnley had made the suggestion—he had made it once or twice before—and the memory of a talk he had once had with Marion about it was still fresh in his mind.

In fact, during those days when it seemed so easy to find new grounds for disagreement with Marion, it was only with the greatest difficulty that Craig kept his personal affairs and his business interests separate. He had never permitted himself to become a victim of any unreasonable jealousy and he harboured no suspicions, and yet, he had never felt quite comfortable over his discovery that Marion had spent an afternoon on the golf course with Charnley and had said nothing about it at the time nor at any time subsequently. Perhaps it was his determination to keep suspicion and jealousy out of his heart that caused him to appear more than ordinarily friendly in his relations with Charnley whenever they met on the floor of the trading-room.

It was precisely this phase of the situation that occupied his mind as he squinted at the articles on the top of Sharples desk.

"I know you never gamble, old man," Charnley replied, "and I'm not asking you to gamble. I'm inviting you to take part in a legitimate deal that is as sure a thing as any deal in the grain business can be."

Craig disliked, horribly, Charnley's use of the familiar "old man."

"How do you make out it's no gamble?" he asked abruptly.

Charnley moved uneasily. "If it comes to that, everything in the business is a gamble, Magpie. The farmer is the biggest gambler in the whole system. We gamble on the price fluctuations. He gambles on the weather for about ninety days out of the year and then has to gamble on the price as well when he comes to market his stuff. I don't get your argument at all. I've never heard you object to farming on the basis that it was pure speculation."

Craig busied himself again with the ink bottle and the paper weight. "It's funny how a lot of you fellows can see your own side of a question so damn clearly," he said slowly, "and are blind as bats when you look at the other side of it. The farmer can't help taking the chance that he takes. His chances are part of the conditions under which he works. But he puts his back into the work he does and gives the world something when he is through."

Suddenly he got to his feet and walked to the window, then turned quickly and stretched his arms above his head.

"What's the use of arguing about something that's as plain as hair on a dog's back, Charnley?" he said. "You know what I mean. I know what you mean. Let it go at that and save words. What's going to be done with your million bushels of July barley?"

"That's the point," Sharples said. "We want to know your opinion of the market, Magpie. Charnley and I have disagreed and we've just about decided to take your verdict."

Craig folded his arms and leaned back against the corner of the window. "I don't see what there is to disagree over on that question," he said. "The market has hit the top for this year. It closed at seventy to-day—seventy and one-eighth. It was there a week ago. It looks firm, but it's beginning to show pressure. The old days when a couple of millionaires could corner the market and control it are gone forever. What's a million bushels in the world's supply of barley? We'll have fifty or sixty millions in Canada alone this year. They'll have two hundred millions in the States. Japan will grow another hundred millions. There'll be another five hundred millions in Europe—probably about nine hundred million bushels of barley in this year's crop. Now, then, what can one man do when that crop gets moving? What can a group of men do? They've just got to sit and take the thing as it comes. You think your buying has had the effect of bulling the market. Go ahead and match your buying powers against the optimistic reports coming in from all over the world. We are going to feel the effects before another week—two weeks at the latest. One of these days we'll get another report on the crops in France and Spain. Then watch 'er sink! If you want my opinion, that's it. Take your profits now while the market holds. If the break catches you, you'll find yourself out of luck."

They argued the point for another hour, at the end of which time Charnley had decided to get rid of half his holdings at once and test the strength of the market.

Craig returned to his office with Charnley's orders to sell a hundred thousand bushels the following day.

As he opened the door he looked in to find Martha Lane sitting in his chair, her hands folded on the desk before her.

Two

Martha smiled up at him without speaking and waited until he had come in and closed the door behind him.

"Well, how on earth did you find your way into this corner?" he asked her as he walked to the desk and set down the papers he carried in his hand.

"I've learned to find what I look for, sir," she replied, getting up and giving him her hand. "And now that I've found you out, you might just tell me, if you can, just how you manage to exist in a box like this with nothing around you but a lot of other boxes and men going in and out of them all day long."

Craig led her back to the chair and made her sit down again.

"I suppose you lived in a box yourself—with other boxes around you—while you were studying in London and—"

"I didn't live," she said.

"I guess that's my answer, too, if you must have one," he replied.

"Of course," she went on, "I didn't pretend to live like that—I didn't try. I lived in a world of my own that was as large as the world outside. Larger. That's one thing that can be said in favour of the kind of thing I have been trying to do for the past few years. When you are dreaming beautiful things... or trying to, at least... you are rarely conscious of the limits set to your physical existence."

"That explains how easy it is for artists to starve to death in a garret," he observed.

"I never got to that stage," she replied. "I'm afraid my appetite was always much too good, and is yet, to justify any hopes I may ever have had of being a great artist."

He was silent for a moment as he looked at her. "Of course," he said at last, "you don't see the whole thing here, either. To begin with, I'm rarely in the office except for a few hours in the afternoon. The floor is a very much bigger place to move around in and there's a great deal more life to it. But the real point is that a man here lives just as much in another world as an artist does. All day long we are in constant touch with the principal commercial centres in practically every country in the world. This morning I bought fifty thousand bushels of rye that will be ground into flour for bread to feed a few hungry mouths in Bessarabia where the rye crop was about two million bushels short last year."

"Then you really are doing something," she replied. "I had an idea this was some sort of a well-regulated and highly respectable gambling den."

For the next fifteen minutes he explained to her the difference between dealing in "futures" on a purely speculative basis and trading for purposes of export.

"After all of which," she said, when he was through, "I know just about as much as when I came in. No amount of telling will ever make clear to me how a man can buy and sell what he hasn't got and never expects to have. It's as clear as mud."

"Well—anyhow—what brought you here?" he said, finally. "This kind of thing doesn't happen without some dark reason behind it."

"There is a dark reason," she said. "Craigie, I'm in trouble."

As she spoke there was a funny twinkle in her eye that served to offset the disquieting effect of her announcement.

"Well, out with it!" he said.

"I'm going to put on an exhibit in the fall."

"Where does the trouble come in?"

"Trouble enough. I've decided to bring it on early in the season—not later than the last week in October. That means there is a lot of work to do between now and then. I've got to get a suitable place and go about arranging the thousand and one details that belong to a venture of that kind."

"And you want me to help you, eh?"

"Who else? You see..."

She talked for more than half an hour of the things she would have to do during the next four months if her plans were realized in a way that would reflect credit on her work and command at least the respect of those to whom she wished to make her appeal.

"And now, with the whole scheme outlined," she said, finally, "what do you think about it?"

"It looks good!" he said with genuine enthusiasm. "There is one point you haven't mentioned, however."

"That is?"

"You are quite sure you can awaken enough interest in the thing to make it worth your while. It would be a disappointment—"

"I've thought about that, Craigie. I thought about it for weeks before I decided to come to you with my plans. I think we'll find enough interest to put it over. You see… well, things are not the same as they were before the war. If it were not for the war… I don't know that I should have had the courage to go through with it. But there has been an awakening… people who never saw anything in art before have found in it an expression of something within them… something that was born within them during those terrible days. I'm sure of it. Look at the new interest in poetry, for example, that sprang up almost at once. Men like to sing songs when they march to fight. I think the spirit has been carried over… I think it is there… waiting for new forms… and perhaps…"

She paused.

"I hope you're right, girl," Craig said quietly. "I've tried to keep my faith in something like that myself… something a little different, perhaps, but very much the same, too… I hope you're right… "

"I think it's worth the effort, anyhow," she said.

"It is… it is! he said, decisively. "Let's give it a try."

She got up and gave him her hand once more. He reached out and took both of them and folded them between his own.

"Marty, old kid, we'll put it over!" he said, "Just for old times' sake, eh?"

"Thanks, Craigie—awfully! I didn't really believe... I felt I had to have someone else tell me it would be worth while... before I would let myself believe it... and I thought of you. I used to settle a lot of things that way... I guess it's the old habit creeping back again."

He looked at her while she spoke and felt a delicious stirring of an old time tenderness that he had all but forgotten.

"Marty... it was a good habit, that. Too bad good habits have to be broken as we get on... But we'll work together on this. I'll have a lot of time to myself soon. Marion is going to the lake for the summer with her mother and I'll have very little to occupy my time in the evenings. By the way, won't you come up to the house for supper with us?"

"Not to-night," she replied, and then, as if she feared she might have rejected the invitation too abruptly, added, "You won't mind if I don't... just this time?"

As she spoke the telephone rang suddenly and Craig turned to answer it. Marion had called to tell him that she was with her mother and that he should come there for dinner instead of going home.

He hung up the receiver and returned to Martha who was preparing to leave the office.

"Well, when are we to get started on the big show?" he asked. "When will you be in again?"

"I want to get some things done at once," she replied. "There is the problem of finding some place suitable."

"That's right. Get that attended to at once. I'll look around and have a few suggestions to make to you by the time you come in again. When will that be?"

"I must get in next week... probably a week from to-day.

They went out of the office together and Craig left her at the elevator.

As he bade her goodbye, Claude Charnley swung down the corridor and stepped into the elevator with her.

Craig watched the elevator drop out of sight, then turned and went back to the office. For a moment he stood and looked from his window. Two sparrows were fluttering noisily around a nest they had built in a niche of the wall almost within reach of Craig's hand. He turned and opening a drawer in his desk took a handful of wheat from a small bagful he had taken from the sampling room more than a month before, when the sparrows had first begun to build their nest. Opening the window, he spread the wheat on the stone sill, then closed the window again.

And as he watched the birds come down and pick at the grains shining like old gold in the afternoon sunlight, he remembered the look Charnley had given him as he stepped into the elevator.

Something in the look nettled him unreasonably...

Three

When Craig arrived at the Nason home, he found Mrs. Nason busy with preparations for dinner.

"Where's everybody?" he asked as he looked about him and saw that Mrs. Nason was alone.

"Gilbert hasn't come home yet," she said. "I think Dick is in the library reading. Marion went up to her room about half an hour ago. You'd better run up and see her. I don't think she's feeling just up to the mark."

He ran upstairs immediately and slowly opened the door of the room that had been Marion's before she had married. Craig had always loved the room. There was so much about it that was just Marion and nothing else.

She was lying across her bed as he looked in, her arms raised and her head pillowed in her hands. Her eyes were closed and he stepped quietly into the room and shut the door noiselessly behind him.

At the side of the bed he knelt and put his arms about her gently as he stooped to kiss her. Before his lips touched hers, however, she opened her eyes and turned her head to one side.

His kiss fell upon her cheek as she brought her hands from behind her head and let them fall on the bed beside her. She closed her eyes again and lay motionless, her breast rising and falling slowly to her breathing.

"You're not feeling well?" he asked her.

She stirred a little, with a gesture of impatience.

"I'm feeling all right," she replied.

As she spoke she sat up slowly and brushed her hair from her forehead.

He stood before her a moment, looking at her, then caught her head between his hands and held her face so that he could look at it.

"Why didn't you tell me you weren't quite up to snuff? I'd have come home early."

"There's nothing wrong with me—nothing," she told him.

She took his hands from her head, got to her feet and pushed him to one side as she made her way to the dresser where she began to comb her hair without speaking.

Craig sat down on a chair near the head of the bed and watched her for a moment in silence. Marion could create an atmosphere about herself when she was out of sorts. Craig resolved to ignore her mood, if indeed it were a mood, and trust to a lucky turn in the conversation to help bring her out of the dumps.

"Martha Lane was in to see me this afternoon" he announced. "She has decided to put on an art exhibit... her own work... some time early next fall."

She turned on him suddenly. "You might just as well know now that you simply annoy me by trying to talk to me," she said.

"Well... what have I done now?" he asked. "It seems to me that I do very little these days without—"

He paused abruptly. He had not meant to show any impatience. When she did not reply, he got up and moved slowly toward the door.

When he was half way across the room she spoke again.

"I should think you would have a little consideration for those around you even if you have none for yourself," she stormed, and Craig turned to find her facing him, her hands clenched at her side, her eyes flashing.

"I'm still at a loss to know what it's all about, Marion," he replied.

"I am referring to your mad action last night at the Fort Garry," she went on. "You did not tell me anything about it when you came home—"

"It was so unpleasant, I didn't wish to—"

"You might have known I should hear of it sooner or later."

"To tell the truth, I tried to put the whole affair out of my mind—and would have done so, probably, if you hadn't brought it up again. I didn't think you would be interested."

"Interested? Good heavens? Do you think it is no concern of mine that you are being talked about today for what you did last night? Do you think it does not interest me when at least half a dozen of my friends call me up to tell me how completely you forgot yourself?"

For a moment a kind of reckless fury seized him.

"Well... damn your friends! If a friend of mine tried to

criticize you in my hearing, how long do you think he'd last? I'm not even interested in what your gossipy old females have to say about anything I do. When you want to talk to me quietly about what I did, or why I did it, I'll be glad to discuss it with you. In the meantime I prefer to say nothing about it."

He turned quickly, opened the door, and went downstairs. In the library he found Dick buried in a book.

"Hello, Dick!" he greeted the youth as he made his way to a chair and sat down.

Dick glanced up and laid his book aside. He yawned and stretched his arms above his head. "Took my last night out before going to the lake," he said sleepily, "and I haven't got over it yet."

"A night out seems to be a very necessary thing in your life, Dicky, my boy," Craig remarked as he took a cigarette from his case and put a match to it.

"Well… one man's idea of what's necessary doesn't have to always correspond with another's. It's largely a matter of point of view, I suppose. If an experience is sufficiently pleasant to contemplate, I usually get it, if I can, whether I think it necessary or not. Last night, for example, Bud Frawley and I had dinner in an apartment with two sisters… very interesting girls…"

He went into a long description of how he had spent the previous evening and how he had crept in by way of the back door when he arrived home long after midnight.

"Just what do you find interesting in women of that sort Dick?" Craig asked him when he had finished his account.

Dick was silent for a few moments before he replied. Finally, he seemed to have found an answer to the question.

"I think my chief interest in them… lies in the fact… in the fact that they are the last of a long line of degenerates. You see, their father was the illegitimate son of a French count and a peasant woman of Picardy. It seems... "

Craig did not follow the story any farther. His mind turned upon the strange prospect of a nation's youth whose chief interest in life was found where Dicky Nason found his... Or was it true that the youth of to-day were all like Dicky? There were some left... he was sure of it... some in whose hearts burned the old flame of idealism that had leaped high in his own heart when he was twenty. Dicky was not truly representative... Besides, even he had better stuff in him that he admitted... he was merely playing the role of the professional youth of the day.

Well... there was, after all, a professional youth... and somehow... in a vague, intangible way... the youth of the nation was not what it was...

Perhaps he was already growing old fashioned... he remembered that Vicky Howard had told him so...

And then he remembered that he had left Marion alone in her room. Perhaps he had been a little unkind. After all, the differences they were having were over questions more or less abstract... Or were they?

At any rate... such things must not come between them... people who had loved each other were sometimes driven apart by just such things...

He got up from his chair in the middle of Dicky's discourse on youth's right to choose its own pleasures, and hurried back to Marion's room without apologizing for his abrupt departure.

One of them would have to make the first move and he knew Marion would not be the one to make it.

Four

He stood with his back to the door he had just closed and looked at Marion who was sitting on the chair near the bed manicuring her finger nails.

"Marion," he said, "this kind of thing isn't going to help either of us. It's going to hurt us both. Ultimately, it's going to kill something that we can never bring back to life again. That would be terrible. Listen. Forgive me for speaking so harshly a few minutes ago. I try not to be hasty, but sometimes my bad temper gets the better of me. I guess that's what happened at the hotel last night. But I think you would have been tempted to lose your temper, too, if you had seen and heard what I did. I can stand anything but rank unfairness and injustice. I'll tell you all about it when we get home tonight. Just let us forget it now and have nothing unpleasant. After all, we do love each other... and there's nothing in the world I wouldn't do for you."

"Then you can prove it by being a little more reasonable in the opposition you show to the men who are doing all they can to make the world fit to live in," she replied in a voice that was coldly deliberate. "I simply don't know how I'm going to face some of my friends and apologize for you when—"

Craig strove to take a humorous view of the situation.

"Send them around to me, dear, and let me do the apologizing. I'd like to see just how they would take an apology from me."

"If you mean what you say," she retorted, "you will take the step yourself and not wait for anyone to come to you."

"Lord, woman... go out and hunt them up?"

She got up from her chair and lifted her eyes till they met his.

"I'm in earnest about this," she told him. "I simply cannot go on living with a man whose only desire in life seems to be to break down and destroy everything that's worth while."

Craig winced a little before the charge, but he checked the words that sprang unbidden to his lips.

"The committee that was appointed last night," she went on, "the committee of business men who are going to organize to protect decent people from these ranting foreigners in the north end will meet to-night. Father has invited them to meet here in the library after dinner. They represent the men you insulted publicly last night. The least you can do is to go to them and admit you lost your temper... do something... say something that will make them understand."

Craig considered a moment.

"I suppose Blount will be one of the number," he commented quietly.

"I don't know... it doesn't matter. If you meant what you said when you told me you would do anything for me, you will do what I ask."

"It's a little humiliating."

He felt ridiculously like a schoolboy as he stood before her and admitted he would find it difficult to carry out her wishes.

"It cannot possibly be more humiliating than to have one's friends call one on the telephone... one after another... "

Why did she mention her friends again?

"Marion," he said, looking at her with a cold directness he had never shown her before, "there is a limit to a man's patience in such things. I have come up here to tell you that we must not let things of this kind stand between us. You insist on bringing them back and placing them squarely between us in a way that makes it impossible for me to remove them. If an apology to that rotter, Blount, would restore our happiness and make our love for each other the simple, big thing it ought to be, I'd do it. I'd apologize and be damned to him! But it wouldn't. It might make you happier, but it would change me... I can't tell you just how... but you wouldn't be the same to me after I had done it. Now, what do you want me to do about it?"

She returned his steady gaze.

"I have told you what I want you to do about it," she replied.

A look of pain swept over Craig's face. He turned and placed his hand on the door-knob.

"I'll think about it," he said.

He opened the door and went out.

In the hall below, he met Gilbert Nason who had just come home for dinner.

Five

Thanks to Gilbert Nason, the dinner went off without unpleasantness of any kind. The old man had long since learned to sense the moods of his women folk and was a practised hand at avoiding unnecessary domestic disturbances. One glance at Marion as she took her place beside Craig at the table, and an exchange of glances with his wife, and Gilbert Nason set himself quietly to the task of serving the dinner, doing his best to carry on a conversation with Craig as he carved the roast.

"Looks as if Wilson is going to have no part whatever in the campaign in the South... The Republicans are out for blood... and it looks to me like a walkover. This man, Harding, that carried the Republican convention is evidently going to make the League the main issue of the fight... I don't see where it will have a chance... Looks as if the American people are being lambasted by men like Borah and Johnson until they're scared stiff of sitting down to the same table with other nations of the world unless they're permitted to ask the blessing and then carve the joint... and serve it, too... They'll live to see their mistake... lots of them will. The greatest opportunity a nation ever had... You serve the potatoes, Marion, please... Too bad Wilson had to go under just when the world needed him most... A sort of dreamer, in his way, but... That looks a little rare for you, mother. Better let Craig have it... The world might be a better place if there was more room for the dreamers... You don't want meat, Dick... This will be for you, then, Marion... After all, I suppose, it's a practical world. The practical men seem to be able to make themselves heard, at any rate. I wonder what kind of man they'll put out to lead the Democrats... With the right kind of a man, there might be a chance... even yet..."

"Am I going to be left out of it, Gilbert?" Mrs. Nason asked with her eyes on her husband's plate.

"What... eh? Well, a man can't settle world problems and serve roast beef at the same time..."

"Roast lamb, Gilbert," his wife corrected him.

"So it is! Well... there. Now let us get along. I have to meet that committee in less than an hour. I wish you had been on that committee, Craig. I need some moral support against those old hard-heads like Lasker Blount. Give them their way and they'd settle every strike with a squad of soldiers... For that matter, there's no reason why you shouldn't sit in, anyhow, and smoke a cigar with us. The discussion will be general, and very quiet."

Gilbert Nason was unwittingly making Craig's position harder to bear.

"I don't think there would be much gained in having me sit in with a bunch of men whose opinions are so entirely opposed to my own," Craig replied quietly.

"Forget that, Craig, my boy," Nason advised.

"The trouble seems to be just there," Craig remarked. "I find it impossible to forget it. If it were a purely personal matter it would be entirely different."

Mrs. Nason sensed the unpleasant possibilities in the conversation and hastened to interrupt it before it went too far.

"Since we're going to the lake tomorrow, Gilbert, perhaps Craig would prefer to spend the evening with Marion. He won't—"

"Not at all, Mother," Marion spoke up. "I'm going to help you get some things together. Craig won't mind a bit. Besides, Vicky and Claude said they might be around this evening for a few moments to bid goodbye. There's no reason why Craig cannot go with Daddy."

It was the first time Marion had spoken since she had come to the table and Craig observed that her voice was more than ordinarily pleasant—a little extravagantly so, perhaps.

"There is still the reason that I might prefer spending the evening with you," Craig ventured.

Marion chose not to reply.

But some time later, when Mrs. Nason had succeeded in turning the conversation into other lines, Marion spoke again, this time in an undertone that Craig alone heard.

"If you do not go, I shall," she said.

Six

Claude Charnley came a little after nine, and with him, Victoria Howard.

Craig thought he had never seen her looking so—well, so soft. He could think of no other word that expressed what he felt. As she came into the house with Charnley and stood in the hall where Marion and Mrs. Nason had met her, her face seemed rounder, her eyes larger and more liquid, her whole manner more clinging than ever.

"I asked Claude to bring me over," she told Mrs. Nason, "because I felt so blue."

"What about, dear girl?" Mrs. Nason inquired.

"Really nothing, I guess. Sometimes I... Well, I just can't help weeping. I... I wept for two whole hours this evening."

The prospect of spending the evening within sound of Vicky's voice was intolerable to Craig after what had happened between him and Marion. He withdrew as politely as he could and went out to stroll about the grounds where the gardener had been at work since the early days of spring.

The air was very soft with a scent of newly broken buds and fresh green leaves. Presently he found himself at the side of the house where an old bench had been placed among the trees.

Above him, as he sat on the bench, voices came from the open window of the library where Nason and his companions had been in session since eight o'clock.

He was unable to distinguish many words until the voice of Lasker Blount presently broke forth.

"What Streeter says," Blount boomed, "is true as far as it goes. I agree with him that any public meeting of the kind Nason suggests would be difficult to handle. We had to resort to heroic measures to quiet one man last night. If that one man should run in a hundred of his irreconcilable friends from the north end we'd have a free fight."

Craig realized Blount's reference was to Amer.

"Heroic measures?" he thought and smiled to himself.

In his heart, Craig was convinced that Lasker Blount was a coward—morally and physically.

"The real point is," Blount went on, "that we take the wrong view of the function of the general public when we think of them as a tribunal before whom we must plead our case. The public can be used to much better advantage. Our first step should be to prepare them so that, when the break comes, if it does, they'll be ready to throw themselves into the fight on the side of law and order. No strike has ever been won without the sympathy of the public. Where would we be to-day if we had lost the sympathy of the people during the war?"

There followed a few minutes of discussion by other members of the committee whose voices were little more than a murmer compared with Blount's voice.

Presently there was a general stirring and Craig knew that the men were preparing to leave. He could not help feeling relieved that he had remained quietly apart during the discussion. His difference with Marion could be settled between them—as it should be settled.

Suddenly the sound of Marion's voice startled him. She was speaking to the men in the library. He listened for a moment, but was unable to make out what she was saying.

She could have spoken only a few words, however, for Blount made himself heard almost at once.

"The beautiful wife of our fighting Captain," he said, and Craig had an image of him stalking across the floor to greet her in his characteristically effusive manner.

And then, in a moment, he realized that she had taken her cue from Blount and was speaking of what had occurred the night before.

He got to his feet and listened. He could make out only a word here and there.

"... the Fort Garry... forgot himself... give the impression... hoped they would overlook..."

Craig left his place by the rustic bench and made his way hastily to the front of the house...

Seven

"And so I know you will not condemn too harshly what was merely a flash of impatience. I thought he was here himself, but he must have gone for a walk. I know he intended to be back in time to meet you and speak for himself."

Marion stood in the doorway of the library, with Lasker Blount beside her, and faced the men who were preparing to leave.

"If our wives all paid as much attention to what their husbands say and do," Blount observed with a smile, "what a well-regulated world we would have. But here's the Captain himself."

As he spoke Craig stepped out of the hall and presented himself at the side of Marion.

She looked up at him and essayed a smile.

"Why, Craig, I thought you had gone walking somewhere," she said. "I looked all over the house for you."

"I'm sorry," he replied.

"Nothing to regret, Captain," Blount assured him in his best manner. "Your wife has spoken for you."

It was clear that even Blount was aware that Marion's speech had not been given with Craig's full assent. He was doing what little he could to pass the whole thing off as a joke among friends.

"I overheard something of what she said," Craig replied, "and I am sure my wife has spoken with the best intentions in the world. She does not know that she has placed me in a very awkward position."

"Let's forget it, Captain," Blount suggested affably.

"Unfortunately, I cannot," Craig said, his eyes searching Blount's. "I feel too intensely about it to forget it so easily, Mr. Blount. I may be placing you in an unpleasant position now, but I feel that I must explain myself so that we shall understand each other in the future, if we have not done so in the past. I have done all I can to keep my faith in the men who are in control of the affairs of this country. You are at least representative of the class. But after what happened last night, I am forced to tell you that my faith is gone. For two years the people who suffered during the war have been looking to you and others like you to prove yourselves worthy of their trust. They did not all expect a new world in a day, but they did expect you to show your will to prepare the way for a new world. Instead, you have gone back to the old ways, the selfish ways, the ways you travelled in the days before the war. You are doing everything in your power to force the people back into the old ways. If it will make anyone feel better for me to apologize for losing my temper last night, I'm ready to do so and I do it gladly. It hurt my own self-respect more than it offended you. But I must tell you, in all honesty and self-respect, that I shall not sit again, as I sat last night, listening to what I know to be untrue, without demanding an apology for the insult to my own intelligence."

"You speak rather strongly, Captain Forrester, for a man who has just expressed regret for losing his temper," Blount remarked.

"A man can hold his temper, Mr. Blount, and yet speak the truth—and speak it strongly, too," Craig replied.

"Perhaps you do not realize that what you have just said implies that I was guilty of mis-statement in my address last night."

"I think I understand it very well," Craig said quietly. "And I think you understand it."

Lasker Blount turned to Gilbert Nason. His face was a shade paler. His lower jaw trembled slightly as he spoke. "If you don't mind, Nason, I'll be going," he said in a shaking voice.

"I think you are simply mad!" Marion muttered, then turned and fled into another part of the house.

There followed a few moments of intense silence while Blount moved into the hall, followed by Nason, and received his hat and coat. When he was ready to leave, he turned to Craig again.

"You will do well, sir, to attend carefully to what you have to say in public after this. It would be very unfortunate for your friends if you formed the habit of forgetting yourself as you did last night—and as you have done tonight. Goodnight, Nason. Goodnight, gentlemen."

Craig did not attempt to say anything in reply as Blount went to the door with Nason and passed out.

He stood in his place in the wide doorway until Nason returned and laid a hand on his arm.

"Craig, my boy," he said, "you've made a bad enemy, I'm afraid."

"He'd be a damned sight worse as a friend!" Craig declared.

And once again he returned to the old bench at the side of the house and sat down in the gathering dusk.

Eight

It was there that Gilbert Nason found him half an hour later, after the men were all gone.

"Well, my boy," he said as he sat down beside Craig, "you've set off a fire-cracker. I've been wondering how long it would be before you set the match to it. I've been expect-ing it for some time. And in a human way, of course, you're right. I feel just as you feel about it. Lots of us do. But what's to be done? When men like Lasker Blount get hold of things—at least they seem to know what they want to do."

Mrs. Nason called from the house.

"I guess we'd better go in," he said. "They may need us to give them a hand."

They found Mrs. Nason with Charnley and Vicky Howard in the drawing-room.

"Do go up and get Marion to come down," she said to Craig when she got an opportunity of speaking to him alone.

Craig went into the hall and made his way upstairs with a heavy sense of impending disaster. He arrived at Marion's door and opened it slowly. She was lying across her bed in the same attitude he had found her in before dinner.

He closed the door behind him and stood looking at her for a moment.

"Your mother wants you to come down for a few minutes before we go," he said.

His voice was not quite so affectionate now... He was waiting to see just how she would respond...

She got to her feet and stood before him, a cold smile lift-ing one corner of her mouth. When she spoke, her words came slowly, deliberately, each a dagger-point of cold steel.

"I shall go down when you have left the house. Don't wait for me to go home with you. I am not going. I shall stay here to-night. I have been convinced for some time of the folly I committed when I married you. I have known from the first that I married you simply because I thought you loved me—not because of any love I ever had for you. Now I know your love for me means nothing at all when it stands in the way of your own selfish pride. Now, please go!"

Craig steadied himself. His eyes narrowed, closed, then opened again.

"I'll go... Marion. I don't quite know what you mean... I know I do love you... that is my pride... has been my pride... And you'll come home... I know you will... I'll be waiting till you do... Tell them I've gone home... any excuse will do. I'll just slip out."

He stole downstairs and got his hat and coat without attracting attention from anyone in the drawing-room. Turning to leave by the back way, he encountered Mrs. Nason in the kitchen where she had gone to prepare a light lunch for her guests.

She looked up as he entered and an expression of pained surprise clouded her countenance.

"Why, Craig, what's the matter?"

He stood before her, unable to speak.

She put her hand on his arm. "Don't permit anything to happen between you, Craig," she whispered. "It'll be all right by morning. Don't forget to draw strength from the Source of All Power, Craig. God—"

"God!" he interrupted her, his eyes narrowed to mere slits as he looked at her. "God—yes—God! There are some things I want to tell Him if... if I ever see Him!"

He moved slowly past her and went out.

Nine

Late into the night Craig sat alone in his library and waited, starting at every sound that came to him from without.

At long intervals he wrote in his book, broken fragments of sentences that had little coherence, short periods that ended before his thought was completed.

"If God lives..."

Before him, on his desk, stood the two little figures that Martha Lane had given him and Marion on their visit to the farm.

"Love..." He wrote the word slowly... then wrote it again.

He began another line. "I must know..."

He closed the book and leaned forward with his arms folded across it.

His mind wandered drowsily from one thing to another... Blount... the bridge and the fog in which he had first seen Amer... October barley... Marion... always he came back to her as she had stood before him in her room...

He would have to draw some money from the bank to give her tomorrow before she left for the lake...

And there was the matter of the broken chair at the Fort Garry... he had intended to pay for that...

PART THREE | THE MADMAN

CHAPTER I.

One

THE FOLLOWING MORNING, on a market that continued to show considerable strength in spite of the heavy offerings with which Craig and Sharples attacked it, Charnley's holdings were reduced by fully one half.

In the few minutes while Craig waited for his report of errors from the clearing-house, he worked with a pencil on a small pad and made an estimate of Charnley's profits.

"Probably about thirty thousand dollars on the day's sales," he said to himself finally. "Not bad pickings."

The door opened and Charnley himself came into the office.

"Well, I still think we're making a mistake," he said as he came and stood before Craig's window with his hands thrust into his trousers pockets. "We gave them a half million bushels to-day and the market closed a cent and a half up. Your hunch cost me something over five thousand dollars to-day."

As he spoke, Sharples entered the office, cigar in mouth, and seated himself on one corner of Craig's desk.

He looked at Charnley.

"Well, satisfied with your day's work?" he asked.

"He's kicking on his losses," Craig put in.

Sharples took his cigar from his mouth and grinned at Charnley.

"Charnley, you're just a plain hog," he said. "You've cleaned up over twenty-five thousand today and the market looks good for thirty or forty more. You're going to get out of this deal sixty thousand to the good. Isn't that enough for the time you've been working on it?"

Charnley turned on them. "Enough? Nothing's enough! What the devil do you think I'm in this game for? I'm not grousing on what I've made out of it. But I followed the advice you fellows handed out and I knew I was wrong. The market is good for another ten cents between now and the end of July."

Craig turned quickly in his chair. "Then why in God's name do you come to us for your advice? Why not try someone who has the same hunch as yourself? As far as I'm concerned, you can take your trades to them as well."

Sharples leaned over and put a hand on Craig's shoulder. "Easy—easy, Magpie! You're nervous or something this morning."

Craig settled back in his chair and turned half way round to Sharples. "Perhaps—perhaps I am," he admitted. "Well, what do you want us to do with the rest of the stuff to-morrow?"

Charnley turned from the window at the question. "Don't lose your head with me, Magpie," he said, "just because I happen to differ with you on the market. I came to you for advice because I thought you could give it to me. I still think so and I'm ready to act as the two of you advise."

There was an air of almost patronage in Charnley's attitude as he spoke. Craig felt it at once, though Sharples was probably quite unaware of it. What moved Craig most was the conviction that Charnley's patronizing manner was not wholly the result of his success in the market. There are achievements in life that affect a man more subtly than a sudden run of good luck in business.

"Then my advice is—sell!" Sharples suggested. "Where do you stand, Magpie?"

"I haven't changed my mind since yesterday," Craig replied.

"Compromise with me to the extent of one day," Charnley begged. "Let 'er ride to-morrow and I'll give you the orders for the day after."

"That suits me," Sharples said and getting up, started for the door. "I've got to get back to the office."

"So long," Charnley said, almost in a tone of dismissal, and Sharples went out.

The moment the door was closed, Charnley turned to Craig.

"Of course it's no affair of mine, old man," he said, in the same patronizing manner, "but you've been off color for some time. I hope the market isn't getting you already. A man is supposed to be good for about ten years in the pit—"

"I'm good for the rest of my life here," Craig interrupted. "And I'm feeling as fit as I have any time since I came back from France. But—"

He drew his watch from his pocket.

"I've got to get down to the station," he said quickly. "The folks are going to the lake."

He didn't say "Marion" and he didn't say "my wife." Something, perhaps it was merely the presence of Charnley, prompted him to speak impersonally of Marion. Perhaps it was because he had waited all day for a telephone message from her—waited in vain. The fact that Mrs. Nason had telephoned before noon helped very little—when he had asked for Marion his mother-in-law had explained that she had gone out for a moment but that they were both expecting him to be at the train.

Charnley went to the door as Craig got up and prepared to leave the office.

"By the way," he said, and again Craig felt the patronizing air with which he spoke, "I wish you'd say goodbye to

Marion and her mother for me. I was going down, but—tell them I'll try to get down to the lake and spend a week-end with them before long."

Craig recalled the day Charnley had given him a message to deliver to Marion—a reminder that she was to play a game of golf with him before the end of the week. He remembered, too, that Charnley's manner on that occasion had stung him to anger. Always his proprietary bearing toward Marion had made Craig want to fight.

Now, however, he felt something that was not unlike humiliation... humiliation touched with sadness and a sense of loss...

Two

He found Gilbert Nason first when he made his way through the crowd in the large waiting-room at the station.

"Here—give me a hand with this stuff," the old man called as soon as he caught sight of Craig.

A couple of porters were lugging bundles across the floor followed by Nason himself, struggling under a load that was making the old man sweat from his exertions. Craig took the heaviest of the bundles and followed the porters.

A few minutes later they joined the women who were standing at the foot of the flight of steps leading from the waiting-room to the train platform above.

Mrs. Nason greeted Craig effusively, then turned and talked to her husband, leaving Craig to Marion.

He took an envelope from his pocket.

"You'll probably need some money while you're down there," he said, giving her the envelope. "If this isn't enough let me know when you run short."

She took the envelope and folding it, tucked it into her handbag without speaking.

Craig placed himself between her and her parents and stooped toward her.

"Shall I come down to see you when I feel like it, or shall I wait till you ask me to come?" he murmured.

"When you feel like it—naturally," she replied coolly.

"That isn't the kind of answer I want," he told her quietly…"You must want me to come or—"

"We must go," she said, a little more loudly so that her mother heard.

"Yes, dear," Mrs. Nason responded. "Good bye, Craig. And both of you get down on Saturday. We'll have a lot of things for you to do. One of you really should have come down with us to-day. But we know how busy you are. Don't fail to come on Saturday. Good bye."

She kissed her husband and gave her cheek to Craig as she spoke. Nason put his arm about Marion and kissed her, then pushed her gently toward Craig.

With his arms circling her shoulders, Craig drew her to him and held her a moment with his lips close to her ear.

"Marion—Marion," he whispered.

But she turned her cheek to him without speaking and drew away from him to join her mother waiting for her at the foot of the steps.

Together Craig and Nason stood and waved their hands to the two women as they mounted the stairs and disappeared.

"Well, it'll be great for them to get away from the hot streets," Nason remarked as they turned to make their way out of the station. "Comes to that, it doesn't do man any harm to have his wife leave him for a while. He'll think more of her when she gets back. Eh?"

"Maybe." Craig replied.

Three

During the days that followed, Craig's thoughts were all of Marion and the ugly prospect of further and more serious disagreement between them.

He sought in himself for some explanation of the coldness that had crept into their relations. He called himself to task for having failed to keep his home life separate from that other life, the life he was trying to live in the world outside. After all, a man could have his own views with regard to the world and society without permitting them to interfere with his personal life. The hope in a man's heart for a better day and a better world was one thing, but the love of a man for his mate was another.

Perhaps he had not been quite just to her. The fact that he had been spoken of disparagingly by her friends was something that caused him little anxiety, but such things were important to a woman, especially to a woman raised as Marion had been raised, in an atmosphere of respectability and refinement. He had not been kindly enough, he had been too outspoken in the presence of the people whose esteem she wished most ardently to keep, he had permitted his impulses to master him when a little self-control might have saved the day for both of them.

And yet, somewhere in the world, hopes that had been born amid the cries and curses of dying men must be kept bright. Even if it were left to one voice to speak out and keep others from forgetting, well—the voice must speak!

With Europe in chaos, with the American people kicking the League of Nations about like the political football it had become, what an opporunity for Canada, the young country just raised to the dignity of nationhood, the land of youthful promise and fresh idealism—what an opportunity to make herself known to the rest of the world as the champion of a Cause that had already been all but forgotten!

And in the streets men talked of prohibition and "home-brew" and the unreasonable prices demanded by "bootleggers" for their wares!

Four

For the first night after Marion's departure, Craig accepted Nason's invitation to stay with him. But after that, he found it impossible. The old man was much too deliberate in his manner of avoiding any reference to the difference that had sprung up between him and Marion. Once when Craig had made an effort to bring it into their conversation Nason had brushed it aside with a wave of his hand.

"Let it settle itself, my boy," he had said. "I have had my differences—we all have them with the womenfolk in the house. But it turns out all right in the end."

Craig demurred. "The truth is," he protested, "these things don't turn out all right in the end. It doesn't take long to destroy the fresh bloom of a woman's love—or a man's, either."

Nason laughed. "That goes, sooner or later, anyhow, Craig. A man can't expect to feel his pulses leap every time he meets the woman he has been married to for twenty-five years. Marriage is a practical affair after all—and a compromise, like all other practical affairs. You'll be going down with me, next Saturday, of course?"

"I might as well," Craig replied. "That reminds me that I forgot to tell Marion that Charnley would be down to see them."

Thereafter they made no reference to wives.

In his own house, Craig found it increasingly difficult to spend the long evenings alone. There were too many things to remind him of Marion and their evenings together, many of which had been surpassingly happy, now that he came to think about them. Besides, with the strike assuming a more serious aspect daily, there were crowds in the streets at night and a general air of expectancy that was apparent the moment one left the purely residential sections and wandered into the business area. The tension made Craig restless.

On the third evening after Marion had left for the lakes, Craig lingered downtown after he had eaten dinner at a restaurant, and lighting his cigar, made his way north along Main Street till he reached the section occupied, for the most part, by pawn-shops and second-hand clothing stores. Presently he found himself following a crowd that led him down a side street to a little square with trees on four sides and a large platform in one corner of the enclosure.

Craig was reminded again of the meeting he had attended in the Fort Garry. Here, in Victoria Park where the radicals of the city had been wont to hold forth during the long summer evenings, the men were of a very different sort. They had come with their wives and had crowded without ceremony into the little park to await the speeches from the platform. Craig could not help observing the glances that were thrown in his direction. His clothes, his bearing, even the cigar he smoked proclaimed him a stranger among them, as much a stranger as had been the little wizened Cockney who had found his way somehow into the dining-room at the Fort Garry. He was probably just as welcome.

And yet, Craig could not help feeling that here, among these ill-clad malcontents, was something more human, more idealistic, too, than among those others who had gone to hear Blount cry his alarms. There, where the Blounts of the world flourished, life was a complicated thing and a man like Nason was without the strength to follow the dictates of his own conscience. Here, among Amer's people, life must be a simple thing. There was so little to lose. A man might speak and act as the mood prompted him without being afraid of the consequences.

But the speaker had got to his feet and was taking his hat off as he moved to the front of the platform.

Craig set himself to listen, and waited till the applause died away.

It was a strange sort of speech, that. The man spoke with a studied deliberateness that seemed strangely out of place before such an audience. For nearly half an hour Craig waited in vain for something impassioned, something burning, to fall from the lips of the speaker. At the end of that time the man took his seat while the crowd applauded mildly.

At once a second speaker left his chair at the back of the platform and stepped toward the crowd.

The applause that had been little more than respectful before, broke forth from the crowd like a storm.

"Ho, Tuttle," someone called from the back of the crowd and the cry was taken up—"Ho, Tuttle! There's Tuttle! Give 'em hell Tuttle!"

Throughout the confusion the man called Tuttle stood with his hands folded across an ample stomach, his face beaming as he looked about over the crowd and lifted his eyebrows as he recognized one after another of his friends.

As soon as the confusion had died down sufficiently, Tuttle spoke in a voice that was vibrant with emotion. It was very evidently the voice of a practised speaker and the man himself was a born actor. He had a trick of brushing his hair from his forehead with a gesture that was almost angry.

The expression in his face changed as suddenly as the tone of his voice which he lifted in fiery protest or lowered in deep appeal as he paced from one side of the platform to the other or leaned far out and stretched his arms over the heads of those who stood nearest him.

For some time Craig could not attend to anything Tuttle was saying. His whole interest centered in the man himself and in the very obvious methods he employed to excite the passions of his hearers. Presently, however, the words of the speaker began to take on meaning. He was speaking to "the people"—telling them of "the strength of the people"—calling upon them to uphold the "rights of the people." He directed their attention to the "bosses" of industry—proclaimed a "war to end wage slavery"—swept his hair back angrily and cursed "the system!"

About Craig, the crowd, men and women alike, were carried away by Tuttle's fiery eloquence. They broke into cheers when he told them that, unless the strike were settled and "settled right," there wouldn't be a wheel turning on any railroad between Halifax and Vancouver, there wouldn't be a bushel of wheat moved from an elevator between the Great Lakes and the Rockies. They knew what they could do—the workers knew! They could put out the lights, they could turn off the water, they could produce a milk famine, they could—Craig felt his anger rise as it had risen while he sat listening to Blount!

An appeal was made for funds to help support the families of the strikers and a dozen hats were passed through the crowd while Tuttle led them in the singing of a half comic parody set to the tune of *Let a Little Sunshine In*. When the money was brought forward and dumped out of the hats into a leather bag on the platform, Tuttle got to his knees and made an obvious pretense of counting the money while the crowd continued singing. Then, clutching the bag in his hands, he lifted it—slowly, shakingly, as if the task of lifting it was almost too much for him—until he had raised it as high as his chin. For a moment he struggled with it, the veins standing out in his neck and at his temples, his whole frame trembling from the exertion. Then he lowered it quickly as the song came to an end.

Another storm of applause broke about Craig.

Was it possible that these people were blind to the hypocrisy of the man? Could they not see that Tuttle was no more than a mountebank, a demagogue, a cheap actor whose insincerity was stamped upon his very countenance?

As Tuttle went to his seat, cheers broke from the crowd once again and continued till he was obliged to rise and bow several times in grateful acknowledgment of their acclaim.

Suddenly, from somewhere back of the platform, a man scrambled up and was helped to his feet by two of the men who occupied places beside Tuttle.

The evening was well spent and the first dusk made it difficult to distinguish the man's face clearly. But there could be no mistake about the newcomer. His huge frame lifted itself till he looked like a colossus in the waning twilight.

"Amer!"

The name fell from Craig's lips with something of awe in his voice as he spoke it. There was something so overpowering about the man's presence! The sheer brute force of him! The mountain-like stolidity of the man as he stood unmoving and unmoved while the mob thundered beneath him.

All at once the din ceased. Amer lifted his hand.

"I have heard him speak—your little Christ!"

His voice was a shattering blast!

"I have heard him speak—your little Christ! I have heard your cheers! He promised you power—and you cheered.

He promised you comforts bought with money—and you cheered. He stamped and fumed and sputtered in curses—and you cheered. Now you give your cheers to me. I fling them back!"

A hush of death fell upon the crowd. Craig saw Tuttle squirm uneasily in his seat.

"A raging tempest sweeps the nations of the earth into chaos—and your little preacher bids you look on a tempest in a teacup! The curtain has risen on the drama of civilization—and he invites you to a Punch and Judy show! The flesh of millions has been ripped and torn and left to rot under a stinking sky—and he would have you turn off the light in the home of some little puppet on the other side of the river.

For fifteen minutes, Amer stood like a giant, swaying only a little as he spoke, his voice thundering across the crowded square, his stern face set like a mask of rage! He heaped scorn upon their petty squabbles, he cursed their Tuttles for charlatans who offered cheap balm for their bruises he' unfolded a vision of a world in agony, of a civilization in the throes of death, of a humanity whom God has forsaken!

And Craig, his head lifted above the crowd, felt his pulses quicken and his blood leap. With muscles taut and breath indrawn, he listened to every word—listenend until the voice suddenly ceased and Amer turned away.

Then he shouted aloud... he beat his palms together... shouted again and continued to clap his hands... and presently knew that the applause around him had died away and that he was prolonging it alone!

He looked about him. Two or three faces were grinning at him out of the crowd. Behind him a movement had started toward the gates. The crowd was going home. He looked toward the platform. Tuttle was standing in the center, where Amer had stood only a few moments before, talking excitedly with a dozen or more who had clambered up from the crowd.

Where was Amer? A reckless desire to reach the place where he had last seen him seized Craig. He pressed forward... out of the way!... dug his elbows into any who pushed in upon him from the sides... pulled others from before him... reached the platform and mounted it.

Crossing the platform quickly, he looked about him at the faces of the men... remembered that he had only to look once about him for the towering frame of the man... leaped down at the back of the platform and plunged through the trees where shadows had already begun to close.

Vaulting the fence, he came into the dusk-dimmed street swarming with men and women going home.

But nowhere could he catch a glimpse of anyone who might be taken for the man called Amer.

Five

When he reached his office the following morning, Craig took the telephone and gave the operator Jeannette Bawden's number. There was no response. He waited a few minutes and called it again. A moment later he was informed that the telephone had been taken out.

He hung up the receiver with a feeling that something mysterious had occurred in Jeannette's life. He decided to drive around to her apartment as soon as the market closed and make a call on her in person.

When he returnd to his office at the close of the market, he found Martha Lane awaiting him. She had come to town early that morning and had been busy on the preliminary arrangements for her exhibit.

He had been talking to Martha for less than five minutes when the telephone rang and Jeannette Bawden greeted him.

He told her at once of having heard Amer and of his efforts to get into touch with her earlier in the day.

Then she told him of a change in her plans—she had taken an apartment in another part of the city—she had been thinking of having him up—she had seen in the papers that Marion and her mother had gone to their summer home—she wanted to know if he would come up for dinner that evening—she had a surprise in store for him, but she couldn't keep the secret—Amer would be there, too!

"But I have already invited a young lady to dine with me," Craig replied.

"Bring her along—if you think she'll fit," Jeannette suggested.

"That's right—I think she will," Craig responded. "I'll accept for her and take the responsibility."

He winked at Martha as he spoke.

It was arranged. They were to be at Jeannette's apartment by seven. They would have the whole evening without disturbance of any kind.

Craig hung up the receiver and smiled at Martha.

"That gives us the whole afternoon to ourselves," he remarked. He thought Martha looked extremely well in her early summer frock. "By golly, Marty, I'd like a ride into the country. This weather—"

She looked at him with mild reproof in her eyes.

"Mister Man, I came to town to-day because I had work to do. Let's get at it."

He looked up at her from under his heavy eyebrows. "You used to call me out to play... I guess it's the old habit coming back on me."

She smiled. "Perhaps, if you help me between now and dinner-time, I'll let you drive me home."

"Let's go," he said.

Six

After four furiously busy hours, they came to Jeannette Bawden's new apartment and were met at the door by Jeannette herself, smiling and radiant.

"Why, you live right across the road from a friend of mine," Craig told her. "Do you know Charnley—Claude Charnley?"

"I've met him—at the Nasons' once."

"He lives in the block directly opposite," Craig repeated. "But, Lord—this is Martha Lane, Jeannette. Nice girl from the farm. We went to school together before we grew up. I've told her all about you."

Jeannette put an arm affectionately about Martha's waist and the three went together into the living-room at the end of the narrow hall.

As they stepped into the room, Amer got up from a chair where he had been sitting with a book in his hands and a large pipe with a curved stem hanging from his mouth.

"Well," Jeannette said, "This is Craig—and this is Martha Lane. If you would like a more formal introduction, I'll try it all over again."

But none was necessary. Craig had looked forward all afternoon to meeting Amer and had told Martha what he could about him. They shook hands and after a few moment's chat, followed Jeannette through a large doorway into the dining-room where the table was already set.

At close range, Amer presented very little of the effect he produced at a distance. He was still giant-like in stature, with a huge head set on the broadest pair of shoulders Craig had ever seen. His arms and hands were powerful and his chest both high and deep.

But his face was almost sad in repose. His eyes were deep and dark under brows that were actually shaggy. His lips were full and the chin broad and very square. Craig could not help feeling that Amer would be a formidable opponent in a struggle, but he was won by the softness in the man's eyes and the depth of affection in his voice whenever he spoke, especially when he spoke to Jeannette.

It was not long before Craig brought the conversation around to the meeting in Victoria Park the night before. A moment later, he referred to the meeting in the Fort Garry. Presently Amer's voice became less casual in tone. He lifted his shoulders and drew himself closer to the table.

"They feed on lies, Forrester—all of them," he said, "It doesn't matter—the bosses or the wage-earners—all alike. Let someone play up to their vanity, tell them stories that will make them laugh or cry, pat them on the back and make reckless promises—and the rest is easy. Blount is a liar of the first order, but he's no worse than Tuttle. They both want the fight to go on. They both do all they can to advertise it. They both know they would have nothing to do if the fight was settled. Politics! Mob idols—that's what they are, the politicians. The thinker, the dreamer, the idealist—there's no place for him in the world. Who leads the crowd? The man without conscience and without self-respect who can feed them on the pap they want, the man who can rouse their hatred by fabricating falsehoods, the man who can lead them through the streets with banners that bear lies in red letters, the man who can herd them into election booths and pay them for their votes, the man who can raise a cry of outraged national honour and lead them into trenches of mud—they're the leaders Forrester, the men we're asking to give us a better world to live in. All liars! We never hear of the men who have the vision. As a rule they don't survive it. They get it when they starve in a garret with the rats, or when they lose their dearest friend and live on with a broken heart, or when they lie half way between life and death under an open sky, or when they leap out into the night and plunge forward where the ground is being blown up under their feet. The few who come back to the world and tell what they saw are howled down by the politicians."

"Or sung down," Craig put in.

"They're called madmen—their dreams have left them crazed! I'm mad. You—Jeannette has told me something about you—you're mad, Forrester, mad!"

And so it went on, till presently the meal was finished and the two men took their talk with them into the living-room while Jeannette and Martha sat at the table and chatted pleasantly over their cigarettes.

"Let's do the dishes," Martha suggested, finally. "We can visit each other just as well in the kitchen."

"I think I shall like you very well, Martha," Jeannette said in a low velvet voice that was rendered almost inaudible by the sound of the men's voices coming from the other room.

Seven

A little less than two hours later, Martha got up from the chair where she had been sitting opposite Jeannette in the kitchen.

"I think I'll remind Craig that I have a long trip home yet," she said.

The dishes had been disposed of long since and the two had been sitting where they could talk over the hundred little personal things that women delight in when they are alone.

Jeannette got up suddenly and put her arms impulsively about Martha.

"I think I'll tell you," she said, quite irrelevantly.

Martha looked at her, perplexed.

"Tell me?" she said.

"I've wanted someone—someone I could tell my secret to," Jeannette continued, and Martha noticed that her eyes were bright with tears as she spoke. "You must know from what I've told you that—that life is very dear to me these days."

Martha understood. "I'm very glad," she said.

"I loved him from the first night I told you of, when I heard him speak in Market Square. When I met him I told him so. It is very easy to tell it to a man like him. He came to see me the next night—and he has been with me ever since. We had to take another apartment, but—"

Martha drew her arms about the woman. "Jeannette, Jeannette," she whispered.

"You must tell Craig for me," Jeannette said. "He may not understand—quite. Men are more conventional. Amer wanted to marry me, but I couldn't—I couldn't become— just a wife. Some day, perhaps, when we have proven each other—no, that has been done already. But we may marry—I'm not thinking of that—life doesn't offer such happiness to many women. You can never know it till you have loved with all your body and soul."

Martha's eyes dropped suddenly. "I did once," she said, "and it has taken years to kill it."

"I knew it—I knew it!" Jeannette exclaimed. "You loved— *him*?"

She inclined her head toward the living-room where Craig's voice had risen just then in reply to something

Amer had said.

"We mustn't speak of it," Martha said.

She turned away suddenly and hurried ahead of Jeannette to join the men in the front room.

"Craig," she reminded him, "are you going to hold out all night?"

He sprang to his feet and looked at his watch.

"By Jove!" he exclaimed and vanished into the hall.

He returned immediately with his hat and coat and stood awaiting further orders from Martha.

A few minutes later the four of them stood at the door, bidding good night and promising one another a second evening together just as soon as it could be arranged.

Craig opened the door and stepped into the hall where he waited while Jeannette took Martha in her arms and kissed her goodbye. When she had given the kiss she paused with her arms still encircling Martha and looked over the girl's shoulder at Craig.

"Craig Forrester," she said in her deepest, softest voice, "what a terrible fool you've been!"

Eight

And Craig, guiding the car along the country road leading southward from the city, thought much of what Jeannette Bawden had said.

"Just what did Jeannette mean by that remark of hers?" he asked when they had left the lights of the city far behind them.

"I'm sure I don't know," Martha said in a low voice.

"And I don't know," he replied.

But he knew he had lied... he thought he had lied convincingly.

"I suppose we can all be fools on occasion," Martha observed.

And Craig was suddenly aware of a warm presence beside him and fell into a deep, deep silence.

CHAPTER II.

One

BEFORE THE END of the first week in July Sharples and Craig had disposed of the last bushel of Charnley's barley on a market that had held firm throughout the whole operation.

"Just under ninety thousand dollars," Charnley confessed in Sharples' office when the latter ventured to ask him how he had come out of the transaction. "And I would have gone over the hundred thousand mark if I had held that first half million for another week."

"Well," Sharples commented, "ninety thousand dollars is a lot of money. I don't see what better luck a man would want than that."

"Luck? You've been long enough in this game, Sharples, to know that the amount of money a man makes, or loses, for that matter, doesn't really mean anything. The first deal I made was in flax. After waiting for two months and pyramiding my profits, I came out of the market a little over twenty-one hundred dollars to the good. The next day the market took another jump of two cents. The loss of that two cents a bushel that I might have made if I'd stayed in another twenty-four hours hurt more than the discovery that there was no Santa Claus."

"In other words, Charnley," Sharples remarked, half jocularly, "you're just a young hog."

"I've never seen you throwing away any chances," Charnley retorted.

"And I don't think you will. But you don't hear me kicking about what I haven't got. When I'm out of a deal I put it behind me and do my best to forget it. If a man gives too much thought to what has happened in the past, even if he's been in luck, he's going to get cold feet sooner or later. If he can't take his losses like his winnings, if he can't roll them all together and put them out of mind, he shouldn't be in the game at all. A good gambler starts every day as if it was his first."

"Well... maybe so... maybe so, Sharples," Charnley mused.

"I was short a half million wheat once. I'd put over fifty thousand in the bank under my wife's name for a drawing account. I had another fifty thousand in government bonds. I had a hundred lots of real estate worth another hundred thousand. And I had a little over twenty thousand cash in my own name at the bank. Altogether, I was worth well up to a quarter of a million. As I say, I was short a half million in May wheat. I took a run to Chicago. When I went round to the Board of Trade the next morning wheat had taken a jump of a cent and a half. I sold a hundred thousand more. The next day I came back to Minneapolis. The market had gone up another two cents. I sold another hundred and fifty. When I got back home I hit the market with two hundred and fifty more during the next three days and kept the price where it was. In two weeks the price went up eight cents. I had to put up margins amounting to more than a hundred thousand dollars. Before I covered the real estate was gone, the bonds were cleaned out, I had wiped out my credit at the bank, and my wife had forty cents left in her account. Besides, I owed the clearing-house more than nine thousand dollars."

"Good God!" Charnley exclaimed.

"That's not all," Sharples went on. "Inside forty-eight hours the market turned and went back in a week to where it started from. When I told my wife it had gone back and she realized we would have been nearly half a million to the good if we could have hung on for another two days, she just sat down and laughed. I laughed, too. A man can shed tears over a little bad luck, but when it goes against you like that, there's nothing left to do but laugh—laugh or jump into the river."

"The Fickle Dame has never played any such tricks on me," Charnley remarked.

"You'll never know whether you are a good gambler or a poor sport till she does," Sharples replied. "And it's worth more than money to find out."

Two

With confidence born of success, Charnley resolved upon a bolder enterprise, this time in October barley.

Fortune had smiled on him during the weeks of May and June. The operations that had been so successful for Charnley had been carried through on a market that had been consistently firm. The crop of the previous year had been far below the average. During the period over which Charnley had done his trading there had been an active foreign demand with only a small visible supply to meet it. As a result, the market had advanced several cents between the day on which he had sold his last bushel and the last day of July when deliveries were called for.

From the early days of June, however, reports from the prairies were consistently favourable and the promise of a large crop had depressed the market. During July the sentiment had been overwhelmingly "bearish." The Fordyce people, heaviest exporters of barley in the Exchange, were having their innings after a long fight with the "bulls" who had made them sweat for every bushel of barley they had bought for July delivery. During the last days of July, old man Fordyce himself had thrown himself into the fight to stem the rising tide before his orders were filled.

With October barley losing from a cent to three cents every day, however, Fordyce walked about the floor of the trading room with a grin on his face that betrayed his complete satisfaction with the trend of the market. Trailing behind him, watching every move he made, were a score of smaller traders who looked to Fordyce to lead them to fortune before the end of the summer.

"Go short in October barley!" was the motto.

One heard it in the corridors and in the elevators, even in the streets outside the building. It had become a sort of slogan among the office boys and messengers wherever they met in the halls or flitted about among the traders on the floor.

"Go short in October barley!"

Three

By the middle of August Charnley had not ventured to make more than half a dozen small trades. Both Craig and Sharples sensitive to each day's fluctuation in the prices, warned him to keep clear and Charnley had taken the warning without protest.

"You can't fight the Fordyce gang single-handed," Craig told him time after time. "Wait till they've had their turn. It's coming to them anyhow. They haven't done much more than follow the market down its natural trend. Keep your eye on Cartwright. I don't think he has a thousand October barley on his books altogether."

Jim Cartwright was the most consistent "bull" in the market. Daily he wandered about the floor, testing the market's weakness by making a bid for fifty or a hundred thousand bushels at an advance on the market only to have the bid taken up by one of his own brokers.

Toward the middle of the month, Craig called Charnley aside as he stood at the entrance to the board room.

"Look for a change," he said quietly. "They've struck bottom."

He didn't tell Charnley that he had orders in his pocket to buy a hundred thousand bushels of October barley for Cartwright—and to buy it at the market price.

Four

Three days later, with the price of barley steady at a dollar and sixty-two cents, Craig bought two hundred thousand bushels on Charnley's account.

The following Friday, he added another hundred thousand at a dollar sixty-one and three-quarters.

The market closed that day at a dollar sixty-one and a half.

Charnley gave Craig a check for twelve hundred and fifty dollars to cover his loss in margins.

And for more than a week the market held firm around a dollar and sixty-one cents, advancing or declining an eighth of a cent on offerings of small lots by "scalpers."

The "dog days" had set in.

Five

During the week of Marion's absence, Craig spent much of his time helping Martha Lane perfect her arrangements for the exhibit which she had decided to hold in the first week of October.

They had gone together to visit Amer and Jeannette whenever possible and the four had spent glorious evenings in Jeannette's apartment, the two men talking over the latest developments in the strike, but more particularly in the world at large where Amer saw nothing but a consistent effort on the part of the leaders on both sides of the Atlantic to swing back into the old lines and surrender the destiny of the human race once more to the diplomats who met to play their age-old game behind closed curtains.

"The only recovery in the world is just where we had some hope life was extinct," Amer declared. "Stinnes exploits Germany. England will be in control of the world's oil in another five years. The United States has the world's gold and is buying the soul of every small country in the world with her national loans. All preparing on a vast scale for a trade war that will culminate in another holocaust. Give them another ten years to get ready, Forrester. Then set another fire-cracker off in Sarajevo and the preachers will be in the streets once more calling upon the youth of the world to die in defence of an outraged humanity."

Craig found himself struggling against the admission. In his mind was the memory of the Millie Dyers of the world, the wives whose husbands had gone.

"They will not give their sons, Amer... they will not!" he protested.

They would not...

Jeannette and Martha took sides as it pleased them, now with Craig, now with Amer—but almost invariably in agreement between themselves.

Concerning Marion, Craig was almost in despair.

He had gone down with Gilbert Nason every Saturday and had stayed over until late Sunday evening. He had brought along books and magazines and boxes of candy—like a bashful young lover courting the attentions of his lady-love.

He had hoped... he had tried every art... he had done his utmost to please her...

One night in particular, the last Saturday in July, he had tried a plan that he had worked out with almost foolish faith in the outcome.

Vicky Howard had gone down to spend the week-end and Croker had been invited as well. There was a moon and a lake of glass. The shore line was like a pattern cut from black paper and stretched along the edge of the lake in the moonlight. The islands were like dumb monsters asleep under the stars.

He had induced Marion to come with him and they had stolen away in the shadows that covered the path leading down the hill to the side of the lake. There he had lifted her in his arms and had set her in a canoe. Silently he had pushed the frail craft into the lake and had threaded his way among the islands till they had come to a rounded bay lined with tall reeds. Sliding the nose of the canoe into the sandy shore, he had stepped out and lifted her once more in his arms. Carrying her to the top of a shouldering rock, he had found a place all mossy under the branches of a tall tamarac and had set her down. He had carried a cushion from the canoe and laid it in place for her head. Then he had sat on the moss beside her and talked.

He had told her of his loneliness without her... of the hopes that had been born in him during the black, rain-drenched nights in Flanders... of how she had come to him as the fulfillment of much that he had dreamed... of how he still hoped... and wanted her to help him keep faith in his better self... of how her beauty and love and passion had made him proud... and of how he wanted her still... wanted her with all his life and all his strength and all his hope in the world that was to be...

He had leaned above her to put his lips to hers.

But Marion had fallen asleep...

Six

During the last week in August he received a brief letter from Marion telling him that she was planning a house party for the end of the week. She wanted him to get into touch with the "crowd." Crocker and Charnley and Ayers, Vicky Howard and the Frawley girl. She urged him particularly to invite Martha Lane to come along, too, and make the party complete.

The next day Martha telephoned him from Jeannette's apartment. He gave her the invitation that had come from Marion.

"I'll go," she said promptly, "if you want me."

"If I want you? Of course I want you."

"Then yours be the responsibility," she replied.

Nason joined them at the station on Friday evening and took Martha into his care from the moment he was introduced to her. He confessed a lay interest in art and insisted on her telling him all about her exhibit. The telling occupied the time of the entire trip to Minaki and when they got down and were met by Marion and Dickie, the old man led the way with Martha to where the launch awaited them at the landing below the hill.

Later, from the lake, they saw the cottage perched on the bluff, its porches gaily decked in bright streamers of bunting that fluttered and shone in the light of the westering sun. Gilbert Nason, unusually hilarious, led a cheer as they rounded the point and came into full view of the cottage and a moment later Mrs. Nason appeared on the front porch and waved her hand to them.

Everybody was in gay spirits. The cool breeze from the lake, fragrant with spruce and tamarac, was particularly exhilarating to people from the hot streets of the city. And the prospect of two whole days and nights with nothing to do but romp in the open was actually exciting. By the time they sat down to the table—a table brightly decorated and lighted by candles that stood in a double row down the centre—the contagion of gaiety had spread even to Dickie who had seated himself beside Martha without having made any apology for the preference.

Craig had never seen a company so thoroughly satisfied with themselves and with the world they lived in. Marion was more like herself than she had been for months. Even Croker's jibes at things in general were tempered with rare good humour that invoked almost boisterous laughter from Gilbert Nason, beside whom he sat. Ayers forgot his Oxford manner and argued with Miss Frawley about the legitimate degree of interest a professional nurse might show in her male patients. Charnley found his chief delight in chaffing Vicky Howard—and she her chief delight in encouraging it.

In an incredible short time, it seemed, the meal was over and the men went to the porch to smoke their cigars while the ladies set the house to order.

Presently Mrs. Nason came out to announce that the girls had decided on a bon-fire on the beach and a swim by moonlight.

"That means we'll have to get out now and drag the wood down," Nason said.

The men fell in with the idea at once and for fully half an hour scrambled among Nason's supply of old clothes until all were dressed for the woods. Then followed an hour or more of clambering over rocks and through underbrush in search of fuel for the beach fire, loud calls for help from someone who had found a log too heavy to handle alone, smothered imprecations where a barked shin rewarded undue eagerness, and above all the voice of Gilbert Nason exhorting them like a foreman of a railway gang.

But the pile was built, a great heap of logs and dried sticks and broken limbs and not a little driftwood that Ayers and Dickie had brought by boat from a couple of nearby islands.

When the men returned to the cottage they found the ladies already in their bathing suits and sitting about with wraps thrown about them.

"Hurry, hurry," Marion admonished them. "The moon will be up in an hour and we want to light the fire while it's dark."

The men scattered into the rooms and emerged in a few minutes in their bathing suits ready for the beach.

It had grown quite dark by the time the company had left the house and headed by Gilbert Nason, who carried an improvised torch to light the way, made a gay procession along the narrow path that led to the sandy shore where the wood had been heaped.

While Nason set his torch to the pile, they arranged themselves in line for a "snake-dance" and for some minutes leaped about the mounting flames like savages on an island in the South Seas. When they could dance no longer they flung themselves on the warm sands and watched the white sparks go up like snowflakes lifted by the wind and carried out over the smooth surface of the lake. When the roar of the flames had died down sufficiently, Nason regaled them with an old pioneer song of some twenty verses that told the tragic story of a reckless hero of the plains. Ayers was inveigled into contributing an Indian legend spun out of waterfalls and moonlight and the love of an Indian maiden.

And then, suddenly, the moon came up...

While Nason and Mrs. Nason and Dickie sat together on the shore and gathered the burning embers into the centre of the fire, the others raced into the water and struck out towards a small island that lay steeped in moonlight a few hundred yards from shore.

Half way to the island, Marion suggested that they swim around it and back to their starting point without pausing to rest. Croker was the only one to protest, but by the time they had reached the island he was still going strong and scorned Ayers' suggestion that they put in to shore and rest before returning.

They were rounding the farthest point of the island when Marion spoke to Craig for the first time since they had left the shore.

"Craig, dear, I think Vicky is having trouble," she said. "She's falling behind. "You'd better wait for her."

Craig dropped back and waited for Vicky to come up with him.

"How are you coming?" he asked her.

For a moment she did not answer.

"I—I think—maybe I'd better rest—just a little—if you'll wait," she said finally.

Craig called to the others and led the way to the shore of the island followed by Vicky. When he had lifted himself out of the water he put his hand down and pulled the girl up beside him on a rounded rock covered with moss.

She sank down beside him with a sigh and wiped the water from her shoulders shining in the moonlight. For some moments they sat together in silence, their eyes on the water in which strange shadows moved like great fish sailing by in opalescent light. The stillness about them was broken only by the voices of the swimmers returning to shore.

Douglas Durkin

"Well," Craig enquired at last, "are you good for it now?"

She moved so that her shoulder touched him ever so lightly.

"I suppose I could go... I wasn't really very tired... but don't let's go... not just yet."

She spoke softly in odd little bursts of words, as if she was about to cease speaking after each phrase.

Craig looked at her, her round face, her soft lips, and her eyes that seemed twice their natural size in the pale light.

"You'll be getting cold," he warned her.

"No... I don't think so. Anyhow... I like it here... the shadows and the moonlight and... and everything."

She paused a moment and turned her eyes up to him.

"Do you know that... you have never... we have not been together since the last time we were down here?"

"Since the last time we were here?" Craig replied. "Why—"

"Oh, I mean really together... alone... so we could talk. You know, I liked you that night."

Craig fortified himself by chuckling, "Now, Vicky, Vicky— you know your weakness. This moonlight isn't good for you. What's more, it's time we were on our way. They'll be wondering what has happened."

She was silent for some time following the mild rebuke and Craig got to his feet and stood before her, waiting.

"Don't go yet," she urged. "People don't wonder about such things nowadays. They used to... before the war... but not now. They take some things for granted... And, anyhow... I don't care if they do wonder. If I could be with you... they could wonder all they liked."

"Why, Vicky!" Craig exclaimed.

She got to her feet and started towards the water. At the edge of the rock she paused and turned to him, her soft, round body gleaming in the moonlight.

"Oh, you are so stupid!" she said. "You don't seem to understand."

He stood on the edge of the rock beside her, ready to plunge into the water.

"I may be stupid, Vicky," he admitted. "But a man is always safer if he's a little stupid."

She caught him by the arms with her two hands and turned him about till he faced her. "It's because you are so… so safe… that I could almost hate you. You knew I cared for you… a year ago. I do now… in spite of her. And there isn't one in the crowd who doesn't know how little she cares for you. If you weren't so hopelessly stupid… and so hopelessly old-fashioned…"

Craig winced a little, as if from some physical hurt.

"Just a minute, Vicky," he said. "You say everyone knows that—that Marion doesn't care for me?"

"A woman can't be in love with more than one man at a time," she retorted.

He put out his hand to catch her by the shoulder, but she slipped away from him and plunged into the water.

He waited till she came to the surface, then stood for a moment and watched her as she struck out along the side of the island and gained the open water of the lake.

Then he sprang over the edge of the rock and followed.

Seven

Craig did not speak with Vicky Howard again that night.

If it were true that Marion loved someone else, where was the need of talking to Vicky? Or to anyone else? Love is the centre of life. If love be taken away… what is there left of life? The centre gone… only the edges… the broken fragments of a circle that can never be closed…

He did his best to enter the spirit of fun-making that prevailed about the beach fire for more than an hour after the swimmers had returned. But he could not free himself from the feeling that these figures dancing about the dying fire were only ghost-forms—moths, perhaps, that fluttered crazily in the red glow of the embers.

If it were true that Marion loved someone else...

Mrs. Nason had made coffee over the fire and served it in the open while the others sat round in a circle. Craig sat with his cup in his hands, his eyes on a little heap of glowing ash near the centre of the bed of live coals. He watched it whiten and fall apart as if old age and decay had overtaken it in the few short moments since he had first seen it.

If it were true...

"What makes you so terribly dull?" It was Marion herself who asked the question. She had come and sat down on the sand beside him to drink her coffee. Before he could reply, a burst of laughter came from the other side of the fire where Charnley had picked up Vicky Howard in his arms and had improvised a scene in which a hero had rescued a wretched maiden who had been at the mercy of a wild beast, who was Ayers. Vicky clung with her plump arms about Charnley's neck until he finally collapsed on the sand—Vicky still clinging to him.

"Your heroine is a little heavy, Claude!" Marion cried above the laughter.

"She should be built more like you," Vicky retorted as she sat up and gave Marion a vicious look.

But the sound of Vicky's voice only brought again to Craig's mind the words she had spoken to him before leaping into the water.

If it were true... It couldn't be true...

Walking home at midnight along the little path that led

through interwoven moonlight and shadow, Craig found Martha Lane beside him.

"I have had quite a nice chat with Dickie," she told him.

"I noticed," he replied.

"Dickie has been writing a short story this summer," she went on. "All about a youth of twenty who had an affair with a woman of forty and twenty years later had another affair with a girl of twenty only to find that the girl was the daughter of the woman he had known twenty years before—and his own daughter, besides."

"He's running true to form," Craig responded.

"The boy has something in him, Craig," Martha observed in defense of Dickie. "He has creative ability of a kind, but he has never been touched by the sense of the heroic in life. That's what has happened to most of the boys who were just too young to fight and just too old to usher in the next generation. The world will have to wait for a new crop."

But Craig's mind was obsessed... the world was somehow out of reach... its Dickies and its lost ideals and its shallow mockeries...

One thing mattered... only one. He must get back to the centre of things... he must not lose his grip there...

Perhaps it would be best to speak to Marion... to tell her what Vicky had said...

If it were true... Marion would tell him... she was like that.

She had told him, that night in her room in the Nason home, that she did not love him. She had hinted something to that effect, at least. But she had been angry then. She could not have meant it, in her heart.

If it were true... it wasn't true... it couldn't be true...

And from the lake, as he lay awake that night struggling against the doubts that assailed him, there came intermittently the wilderness cry of a loon.

CHAPTER III.

One

ON A GREY DAY in the latter part of September, Croker met Ayers on the street.

"Have you seen our friend, Forrester, lately?" Croker asked.

Ayers had seen him just once since they had all been together at the lake.

"I was just wondering what you thought about him," Croker continued. "Which way are you heading? Good—I'll go along a couple of blocks with you. I've just been over to the Grain Exchange... had a talk with him. They call him The Magpie over there... but you knew that. Christened him that one day for a joke... because he never had anything to say... the way they call a [******] Snowball. He sort of turned the joke on them, though, when he got married. Turned out he could talk about as much as any of them... only he talked mostly about serious things. Well, I wish you could see him and tell me what you think. Something's happened there, Ayers, something inside... deep down. He's gone back to his old silences again. Doesn't talk any more about things. I've seen him every few days in the last month and I tell you he's got to get out... got to get away somewhere. They don't last long in the pit... a lot of them don't. But he was strong... looked good for a lifetime at any business. He looks good yet, in a way. Big, husky, hear him above the whole pitful when he makes a trade. But he's not there... something's eating at him. He used to take my little jokes... you know what I mean. Just yesterday he asked me, 'Croker, where's it all going to end?' I know what he meant. I told him it would all end like the road that led out of the city and dwindled to a prairie trail and finally became a squirrel track and ran up a tree. He used to smile at things like that. He didn't smile yesterday. He turned on me... slowly. 'No,' he said, 'there's more to it than that, Croker. There's something—something that lasts.' And then he was silent again. I talked... just gabbled along for an hour. But I don't think he heard anything I said... not that it mattered. Here's where I leave you. Come up to the office some day and we'll go out to lunch together. Maybe you'll be able to make him talk. Seems to me if he could only talk he'd feel better. Looks like that to me. Call me up!"

Two

From the upper edge of the pit, Craig watched the milling mass of traders scrambling beneath him.

After a steady advance in the price of barley during the first three weeks in September, the market had suddenly collapsed in a week to a dollar and sixty-two cents—the price at which Craig and Sharples had bought heavily on Charnley's orders. The head of a large firm of exporters who had found himself in difficulties a year before on account of limited shipping facilities at the head of the lake, had manœuvred shrewdly during the inactive days of July and August. He had acquired control of fully three-quarters of the tonnage available for the shipping of the fall crop. By the latter part of September, exporters began to foresee the possibility of having a number of contracts on their hands which they could not meet. A desire on the part of the "longs" to get rid of their holdings began to show itself in the market and the downward trend had continued for more than a week before a firmer undertone began to be felt.

Cartwright, who was holding several million bushels, was the steadying influence that came into the market just when the Fordyce interests and their followers began to feel that they had routed the enemy. On the last Monday in September, after a slight break at the opening of the market, Cartwright gave Craig orders to buy a million bushels at a dollar and sixty-two cents. Fordyce and his men hurled their offerings only to have them taken up as soon as they were put on the market. At the end of the day, however, Craig had not been able to buy more than five hundred thousand bushels at the figure Cartwright had mentioned.

The two forces were evidently deadlocked. They would remain so until someone with large holdings on either side or the other gave up the struggle.

Charnley, after watching the struggle for days without taking any active part in it, set himself, through Craig and Sharples, to assist Cartwright in holding the enemy.

As Craig watched struggling traders in the pit beneath him, he had in mind the words that Charnley had spoken to him outside the doorway to the trading-room a few minutes before the opening of the market.

"Take all you can get at sixty-one and a half," Charnley had told him.

The first trade had been made at an eighth of a cent above a dollar and sixty-two, the price it had closed at the day before. From that it moved up a cent and a half, then dropped slowly back till it hovered at an eighth below sixty-two.

Craig stood and listened to the chorus of discordant voices without moving a muscle in his face. Occasionally he narrowed his eyes slowly, frequently he glanced suddenly from one side to the other as someone attempted to undersell the market.

Slowly the price moved down—an eighth at a time—small trades that may have been mere feelers put out by Fordyce's men.

"Sell October barley at sixty-one and three-quarters!"

Someone at Craig's elbow shouted into his ear. But he did not as much as turn to see who was making the offer.

"Sixty-one and five-eighths!"

But Craig appeared not to hear the voice.

Finally it came—a voice from the opposite side of the circle. "Sell October at a half!"

For the first time that morning, Craig's voice broke from him in a roar.

"Sold! Sold!"

Suddenly he became the center of attack. A dozen men rushed upon him at once from all sides.

"Sell at a half! Sell at a half!"

Card in hand, Craig picked the traders out one at a time and scribbled down the record of each transaction in the midst of the din. He spoke no word, he made scarcely a gesture. Occasionally he swept one arm out before him as if he were gathering in the barley with his hand. Let them come! He was there to take their offerings and hold the market even if he had to do it single-handed. Gradually, however, the storm subsided. A couple of Cartwright's men came into the fight and in less than ten minutes the offerings had all been taken up and the price remained at a dollar and sixty-one and a half.

As a result of those ten minutes, however, Craig had bought one hundred and sixty thousand bushels of barley for Claude Charnley. Altogether, since the beginning of the "deal" in October barley, he had bought four hundred and sixty thousand bushels.

That day the market closed at a dollar sixty-one and a half. Charnley had incurred a loss on his previous holdings of a quarter of a cent a bushel—about seven hundred and fifty dollars.

While Craig was still busy with his clearing sheets, Charnley put his head in at the door.

"Any time you want a check for margins let me know," he said.

"All right," Craig replied. "I'll carry it for a few days, till the market steadies down."

And when Charnley withdrew, Craig wrote a check for seven hundred and fifty dollars and took it up to the clearing house with his returns.

Three

Craig talked to Jeannette Bawden on the day before the opening of Martha Lane's exhibit. They were standing together in a hall in the Board of Trade Building where Martha had worked every day for the past week to arrange her display.

"This has kept me going, Jeannette," he said, "this and my work in the pit. For the last month... or more. A man can't fight his own doubts, but he can fight doubt in another. She wouldn't have gone through with this if we hadn't fought her. Now... I'm glad."

What Craig said was true. At the last moment, Martha was ready to give up the whole undertaking. The strike had spread and had threatened to extend into a general walk-out in sympathy with the original strikers. But Amer had told her not to give up. He was doing his best, night and day, to prevent the strike reaching a crisis at a season of the year when there was the least possible likelihood of the workers winning. He hoped he might succeed.

A more difficult obstacle to the enterprise was the discouraging response Martha met among those to whom she had hoped to make her strongest appeal. It was this, in particular, that Craig had fought against. Day after day, he forgot his own struggle in his fight to keep Martha from giving up hope.

He had not given up his own struggle. Jeannette had watched him closely during those days and had talked to him a little about Marion. She could not tell him that his doubts were without foundation, that Marion was as much in love with him as he was with her. She knew better. She had seen Marion emerging from the apartment house across the street and was well aware that she had gone there to see Claude Charnley. But she feared Craig, feared what might happen if he knew. And she did everything in her power to delay the hour of discovery.

"When we used to make a run across ground that had been mined," Craig went on, "we used to keep our eyes on the spot we were making for to get under cover. When the ground under us began to come up where the mines were set off. it was a good thing to be able to keep your mind fixed on something. When the world begins to go to pieces under your feet, it's a good thing to have one little hold... like this... anything to keep you from getting panicky."

"What are you going to do next week—when this is past?" Jeannette asked him.

"Well... there'll still be my work... there'll still be... why, what are you talking about? There'll be everything again... it's all coming out right. You'll see."

"Let's hope Martha's show will come out right," Jeannette replied. "That's what matters just now."

She was telling him to keep his eyes on the objective before him... turning his mind away from the ground that was breaking under his feet.

"That's right... that's right. Here she comes."

As he spoke, Martha emerged from a small closet into which she had gone to dress for luncheon. She wore a gay little touque that sat at an impudent angle on her head and a loose-fitting autumn jacket of tan suede over a skirt of rough wool.

"Let's go," she said smiling at them. "Even genius eats— when it can."

Four

About the middle of the following afternoon, Martha was rewarded by the first flutter of interest on the part of the public.

The women drifted in idly in pairs, carrying an air of having nothing better to do. There was an occasional group of three or four, lorgnetted and ostentatiously scrutinizing, bearing ponderously the stamp of the connoisseur and the critic. Later two or three swarms descended, winding up an afternoon tea with "something smart and out of the ordinary."

In the evening the men came, some from sincere and intelligent interest, some from curiosity, some to catch a glimpse of Martha, who was rumoured beautiful.

Martha, a little pale, but flawless in her poise, received them at the door, with Jeannette close by giving out the simple little catalogues they had prepared.

What caught the eye immediately was the striking contrast between Martha and Jeannette Bawden. Martha's bronze hair and delicate skin were set off by a long, simple Russian gown of black and flame colour. Jeannette's costume was equally simple and vivid, and presented her in all her rich, challenging beauty. The men caught their breath as they passed the two. The women wondered.

Gilbert Nason, eager to count himself among the patrons of art, "especially in a new country where appreciation of things artistic was likely to prove disappointing to the artist," had gone to no little trouble to place the affair on a proper footing. It was largely because of Nason's efforts that Sir Henry Wilton had consented to give the exhibit his distinguished patronage.

"The thing ought to be done right, Craig," Nason had declared. "The girl deserves it."

He had made up a little party—the Blounts—the Streeters—Marion and Craig—himself and wife—and had swept into the hall a few minutes after the arrival of Sir Henry and Lady Wilton.

The prospect was highly pleasing—the thing had been "done right"—and Nason felt a little proud of the part he had played in making it a success.

Craig, for his part, had taken Nason's advice and had met Blount and his wife with every outward appearance of having forgotten the differences that had come between them. Marion, pleased with the change that had apparently come over Craig, was almost demonstrative.

"I never saw you look so well, Craig," she declared as they entered the hall. "You are positively stunning!"

Craig put his hand on her arm and felt his heart throb as he looked at her.

"You are more beautiful than ever," he told her.

A moment later, he came upon Jeannette and left Marion while he spoke to her.

"It's going well," he said.

"I'm glad you came—I mean both of you," she replied with a glance toward Marion where she stood talking with the Blounts. "They have ignored me, of course, but I don't mind that."

Craig leaned toward her.

"Don't shut them out," he pleaded. "I told you everything would turn out right in the end. It has... it's already turning out right. Some day we'll understand."

And when he went back to join the group, Jeannette saw Marion extend her hand to him as she turned and met him with a smile.

Five

The evening was half spent before Craig found an opportunity to speak with Marion.

He found her talking with two substantially built matrons who had been standing before a delicately modelled figure that Martha had named "Fragment." It was a slender figure of a girl poised on her toes with her head thrown backward and her tiny breasts lifted in a movement of abandon.

"It's very... very eloquent," one of the women commented. "But I cannot understand why you should call it by that name—Fragment."

Martha smiled, a little sadly. "I named it that... as an afterthought," she said. "I had intended calling it 'Love.'"

"Oh, I think it should have been called 'Love'! That would have been most appropriate."

"No," Martha observed, and the smile had died from her face, "not quite. I didn't... somehow, I missed the feeling I tried for. It wouldn't just come out for me. I gave it up finally and changed the name of it."

The point was very evidently lost on the two who were listening to her explanation.

The lines of self-righteousness deepened about the mouth of the woman who had remained silent while her companion was exclaiming over the figure. She spoke as Craig came up with them.

"I think your work is very pretty—very sweet, indeed. Miss Lane," she observed. "I'm Mrs. Ogletree... you may not know. There's one thing about it, however, that I find difficulty in explaining... I mean in work of this kind taken generally, of course. I do think too much lewdness is perpetrated in the name of art, especially in sculpture. Why on earth must so much of the figure be exposed... can you tell me that? It seems to me that very graceful effects could be achieved with drapes and... and wreathes, for example. I have a perfectly beautiful piece at home... 'The Three Graces'... draped... very gracefully." Mrs. Ogletree tittered suddenly and dropped her voice as she moved a little closer to Martha. "I confess I wouldn't want my husband to run around unescorted in a place like this."

Her companion responded with a titter.

Mrs. Ogletree grew suddenly grave. "But speaking quite seriously," she went on, "I think there are instincts, especially in men, that are roused by a display of this kind—instincts that would be better if they were discouraged."

She ended with a sweeping look about her and drew her chin in slightly toward her neck, revealing, Craig noticed, a mole from which three long hairs protruded conspicuously.

Neither Mrs. Ogletree nor her companion had seen Jeannette Bawden, who had descended suddenly upon the group and had heard the good woman's comment.

"As I know men," Jeannette remarked with a smile, "I'd think it a gratifying service on the part of art if it would rouse even that—in some men."

Mrs. Ogletree gave her an uncomprehending stare and moved on with her companion.

Six

Gilbert Nason was not alone in his efforts to "do the right thing." He found ready support in his wife and Marion, who, as soon as the exhibit had been pronounced a success, arranged an afternoon affair at which Martha Lane could meet the "best people" in town.

The last afternoon of the exhibit was chosen and invitations sent to more than a hundred of the city's elite. Martha left Jeannette Bawden in charge of the exhibit and attended Mrs. Nason's function mainly out of gratitude to her hostess, and especially to Gilbert Nason, for the interest they had shown in her work.

Martha would have been more comfortable if Marion had not taken complete possession of her the moment she entered the house.

"I discovered her!" Marion declared to all her friends and Martha could do nothing but submit with a smile.

She would have preferred being "discovered" by someone else, if, indeed, the process had been necessary at all. Not that Marion failed in graciousness or in the genuineness of her enthusiasm. But contact with Marion was something that Martha instinctively wished to avoid. Every time they met, an old hurt opened in the heart of Martha Lane—the hurt that reminded her of a hope long dead.

But the affair was a tremendous success, nevertheless, and Martha had many reasons for feeling glad she had gone. Not least among the many was a rumour that reached her ears to the effect that one of her best pieces of work, a bronze *Bacchante*, had attracted the attention of a man who was ready to make her a handsome offer for it.

Martha's first impulse was to laugh at the suggestion that her work should be taken seriously after such a brief introduction to the public. But the rumour persisted. She was told about it at least a dozen times during the afternoon and warmly congratulated, though no one seemed to know where the offer was to come from.

She determined to mention it to Marion.

"Of course it's true, my dear," Marion assured her. "Why in the world shouldn't it be true?"

For a moment Martha was silent. Then the full significance of the event dawned suddenly upon her.

"Oh... I must tell... "

She paused abruptly... It was Craig Forrester to whom she wanted to run with the good news!

Marion waited. "To whom?" she prompted. "Mrs. Bawden already knows about it, I'm quite sure. You have become very close friends, haven't you? I should think she would have told you."

Martha turned to find Marion's eyes searching her strangely.

"My dear old Daddy will positively weep when he hears about it," Martha replied. "He's very sentimental where my work is concerned."

Marion smiled. "I adore sentimental old people!" she exclaimed.

Seven

The announcement did not disturb Jeannette Bawden.

"You knew about it before," Martha accused her, "and you have been keeping it a secret from me."

"To tell you the truth, I did hear about it—yesterday," Jeannette replied. "But things like that make good secrets. I'm never sure about promises that come from men who have enough money to pay five thousand dollars for a bronze."

"Five thousand dollars!" Martha exclaimed.

Jeannette started. "I thought you knew. Didn't they tell you how much?"

"They didn't mention the price, naturally," Martha replied, "And it *would* have been a little out of place. I'm terribly curious to know where the offer is coming from."

"Don't be. Curiosity and enthusiasm are nearly always lost in affairs of this kind. I have my own idea about it, but horses wouldn't drag it out of me."

Eight

At home that evening, Craig suggested that it would be fitting for them to visit Martha on the last evening of the exhibit.

"I agree with you," Marion said, "but I have a meeting of the Dramatic Club executive to-night that may keep me out quite late. I have been with Martha all afternoon—she must have met at least fifty—yes, more—of the nicest people in town. I wish you would go down. You can explain to her why I did not go with you."

Craig threw himself into his chair, disappointed, a little perplexed.

"When did you know about the executive meeting?" he asked.

"I have known about it for some time. Why do you ask?"

"I really don't know. I had rather counted on having you come along, that was all. I'll call for you and drive you home?"

"No. I'm not sure just when we'll be through—and we may have to go down to the theatre for a while after the meeting. Don't bother about me. There's always somebody with a car—I expect Claude will be there."

Claude! There it was again. The old doubt... the old suspicion raised its head in spite of his efforts to keep it down... and just when he thought he had mastered it.

"Then I'll drive you down," he said.

There was a note in his voice that made her turn suddenly and face him.

"I thought we had put that all behind us," she said. "I have no objection to your driving me down. And I have none to your calling for me to take me home, if it were convenient for me. But when you make your suggestions in that tone, I simply will not listen to them. If you don't mind, I'll go down on a street car. I'll be leaving too late for you to wait for me anyhow."

She left him abruptly and went to her room.

What had he said? What had there been in the tone of voice with which he had made the suggestion?

Then, suddenly, he realized that whatever his voice had betrayed, there had been black suspicion in his heart.

Well... the fight was back upon him again... all to be gone through again... days of it, perhaps... and all because he had not known enough to keep silent when his heart was not right...

Nine

He waited till half past eight hoping that Marion might yet decide to come down from her room and permit him to drive her to the executive meeting. When she did not come, he put on his coat and went out.

At the doorway of the exhibit room, a half hour later, Martha met him. A little red spot on either cheek spread in a quick flare to her throat as she took his proffered hands.

"There's news... goods news, Craigie!" she exclaimed. "I

have a prospective purchaser... I don't know who, but he wants to buy my *Bacchante*... Jeannette says he will pay me five thousand dollars for it." She became suddenly pensive. "I only hope it's someone that's possible... someone who understands, at least."

Craig put her two hands together between his own and patted them affectionately. "I'm glad, Marty, glad." He looked at her strangely. "Marty," he said slowly, "someone ought to love you. I've never seen you so beautiful as you are to-night. I don't believe I ever really saw you before."

She withdrew her hands almost as if she were afraid of him... afraid of the look in his eyes and the sound of his voice...

Rose Barron suddenly threw herself between them.

"H'lo, Captain Forrester! You remember me, don't you? We met one night at dinner—Jeannette's place."

Craig remembered.

"Ivan is here, too. He's dumb—can't talk—hasn't said a word since he came into the hall. Don't you like this?"

Craig stared at her as if he didn't quite comprehend.

"This is the beginning," she went on. "We're going to have our own art. We're going to have studios and artists and models and a bohemian quarter and everything. Aren't we, Miss Lane?"

Martha took the girl's arm and the three walked together down the long room to where Ivan stood before a figure of a dancing satyr. He was staring fixedly at the figure and did not hear them as they came up. But when they had come quite close, Martha saw him lift a hand and lightly touch a hoof of the exquisite creature. His touch was furtive as if the action had been prompted by some inner urge. And when Rose spoke to him, he started as if he had been caught doing what he knew had been forbidden.

The look in his face as he turned to them was the look of a child. It brought the tears suddenly to Martha's eyes—tears of understanding and gratitude.

Rose saw the look in the boy's face and turned to Craig.

"Don't you think Ivan is won-n-derful!" she said. "I love him!"

A moment later they found Jeannette. She was in a fit of depression.

"It's partly because we have come to the end of one of the happiest months in my life," she explained to Craig when he pressed her to account for her mood. "We have worked together on this and have been very happy. Now it's over."

"There will be other work for us," Martha said consolingly. "Besides, we have come together now and who can tell what we may do in the future?"

Jeannette got to her feet from where she had been sitting and glanced toward the door.

"It's the future that I'm thinking of," she said. "I haven't told you." Her eyes were still on the doorway. "There come Blount and Nason and a half dozen of your patrons, Martha."

They prepared to go and meet the visitors, but Craig laid a hand on Jeannette's arm to restrain her.

"Has anything happened?" he asked her.

"I don't know," she said quietly. "I'm expecting Amer in a few minutes. He has been with the strike committee all day. As a result of those disturbances in Market Square last week, the mayor has forbidden street assemblies of any kind until the strike has been settled. The strike committee received notice last night. Tuttle has been doing his best to get the men to defy the mayor's orders, and Amer has been fighting it out with him. He telephoned me at six o'clock. The situation didn't look promising when he spoke to me. He may come in any moment now, however, and then we'll know. But here comes our friends. Duty calls."

Jeannette herself was the most gracious of them all when Nason came down upon them in his breeziest manner and drew Blount with him into the group.

"Here we are!" he announced. "Came along to congratulate you on a most successful exhibition." He was talking to Martha. "Fact is, you've got us all talking art—yes, and believing in it, too by golly. More real artists who dress like human beings and less of the longhaired variety who talk a lot of bunk about psychoanalysis and free love, eh, Blount?"

Blount was eager to add his word of approval. "I believe art is one of the main hopes of our civilization," he remarked. "And I think we ought to do all we can to bring local talent to the fore. If we could get the people interested in this sort of thing, we might get their minds off things that don't concern them. We can't all be business men and we can't all be politicians and we can't all be artists, but we all have our place and we ought to keep it. If we all filled our place as well as you, Miss Lane, the world would be a very much better place to live in."

Jeannette found Craig's toe and stepped on it.

"I might tell you now," Blount went on, "there is a little matter of interest to you, Miss Lane... it is of interest to us all, I think... a matter, in fact, that is the excuse for our making this personal call at so late an hour. We are waiting for the arrival of Mrs. Nason and Mrs. Blount before we... before we speak of it. They ought to be along any moment. You will permit us to look around once more while we wait, I am sure."

Martha smiled in reply and invited them to spend the time as they wished while they waited.

And as they moved away, the tall form of Amer appeared in the dim light of the doorway.

Jeannette and Craig saw him at the same moment. His heavy brows had fallen so low that his eyes were almost hidden. In his face was the look of a man who has been through torment.

Craig turned, after a glance at Amer, and met Jeannette's eyes.

A look of pain swept over her face. They knew that Amer had lost the fight.

Ten

Craig started across the floor to meet Amer, but Jeannette was already hurrying toward him where he stood in the doorway. When Jeannette reached him he put out a hand and remained, unmoving, with his eyes shifting slowly from Craig to the group at the other end of the long room. Even when Craig came and stood before him, waiting for him to speak, he held his silence, his eyes fixed upon Blount and Nason where they stood on either side of Martha before the bronze *Bacchante*.

"Tell us," Jeannette urged.

He turned his eyes to them as if he had not seen them before. A faint smile touched his lips.

"My dear... I have failed," he said with infinite sadness in his voice.

She did not speak in reply. She took his great hand and pressed it between her two soft, white hands, then drew back a little as Craig stepped closer.

"It may not mean so much... in the end," Craig ventured.

Amer looked at him for a moment before he spoke. "It means..." He paused. "It means... much. Let's get out of here... I must breathe."

"We can't go yet, dear," Jeannette told him. "Martha has to wait... she has sold—"

"Then we'll wait," Amer replied. "Here, Forrester... let me go down with you... Don't run away from me."

Together the three walked down the full length of the long room and came at last to the group in the centre of which stood Martha Lane talking to Nason and Blount.

Martha looked up as Jeannette joined the group. At the same moment, Lasker Blount raised his eyes and encountered those of Amer who had paused on the outskirts of the little circle with his hand on Craig's arm. For a moment the two men eyed each other without speaking. Presently Nason turned his face toward Amer and in a moment every eye in the group was trained upon the man who had entered so silently that none except Craig and Jeannette had seen him.

When the atmosphere was most tense, Gilbert Nason made a brave attempt to relieve it.

"Ah—Amer," he greeted him affably, "I—we hardly expected to find you here."

Amer smiled. "You wouldn't," he replied. "You wouldn't expect to see a Nobody in an art gallery."

Nason coughed lightly. "I wouldn't say that—I wouldn't say that."

"I know you wouldn't," Amer retorted. "You wouldn't say anything that was in such bad taste. But you think it. I haven't come here to look at these." He swept his arm about him to indicate Martha's work. "They are all beautiful... and I'd like nothing better than to spend an evening with them. I feel the need of it. But I came here... because I have no place to go... because I am an outcast... because these are my friends. I have thought you a fair-minded man, Mr. Nason, and a man of good intentions. You will be sorry to know that the people I have been working with have decided to pay no respect to your mayor's orders. Our friend, Tuttle, will issue a general invitation to-morrow for a public demonstration to take place the following day. You will be sorry to hear that. I am sorry to have to tell you. We are sorry for very different reasons."

"We are all sorry," Blount put in.

Amer turned slowly and looked at Blount.

"It would be in bad taste for me to call you a liar, Mr. Blount, particularly in a place of this kind. But it is equally in bad taste for you to lie."

"I believe the ladies have come," Nason said quickly.

All eyes turned toward the door where Mrs. Nason had just entered, followed by Mrs. Blount and three or four other women in evening wraps.

"Come away," Jeannette whispered to Amer, and together the two moved a little apart as Mrs. Nason approached.

Eleven

Mrs. Nason put her arm about Martha in an affectionate embrace.

"I hope we have not kept you all waiting," she said.

"Not at all," Martha replied, and Craig observed that her voice was tense with excitement.

"We are ready, Gilbert," Mrs. Nason announced after a few moments of animated conversation that followed the arrival of the ladies.

Nason nodded and then stepped towards Martha, his face beaming as he looked at her.

He stood for a moment looking at her, then turned and faced Blount.

"Don't you think you ought to do this, Blount?" he said. "I don't know that I'm quite equal to it."

"Go ahead, go ahead!" Blount smiled. "I'll help you out if you get stuck."

Nason turned again to Martha and gave her his most engaging smile.

"We have all agreed that your work is worthy of some practical recognition," he said.

A hush had fallen upon the others as they stood about listening to Nason's voice, their eyes upon Martha's face.

"We have not seen anything like this from one of our own... of ourselves, one might say," Nason resumed with a somewhat pompously inclusive sweep of his arms. "Now that we have found you out and know what you can do, we have made up our minds that you shall stay with us, not run away to some eastern metropolis as so many of our other artists have done. To come to the point at once, Miss Martha, we have picked one piece—this beautiful figure before which we stand—and have decided to make you an offer for it. We should have enquired, perhaps, and found out whether your *Bacchante* was—whether you would be willing to part with it, before we ventured to make you an offer."

He paused to give Martha time to reply.

She raised her eyes and hesitated a moment, not knowing just how to express what was in her mind.

"I'm sure," she said slowly, "I would be very ungrateful if I refused to consider anything so—so gratifying as an offer for a piece of my work."

"Then, to speak plainly and briefly," Nason continued, "I have been asked to inform you that one of our most distinguished citizens will be proud to make *Bacchante* his personal property, if you will be pleased to regard this, which he gives you in return, as expressing only in part the high regard we have for the work and for the artist who wrought it."

It was very evident that he had memorized the exact words in which he presented his offer. As he concluded, he drew an envelope from his breast pocket and handed it to Martha who took it with trembling fingers and held it for a moment while the silence grew tense about her.

Lifting the flap of the envelope slowly, she drew out a folded slip of pale blue paper and opened it.

It was a cheque for five thousand dollars. The name at the bottom was that of Lasker Blount.

For a moment Martha stood looking at the signature, her hands trembling uncontrollably, the tears starting to her eyes.

She turned and found Craig beside her.

"Craigie," she said, almost in a whisper and showed him the cheque.

Mr. Blount," Nason said, turning and placing his hand on the bronze figure behind him, "I envy you the possession of so handsome an example of the work of one of our own artists."

A brief round of applause broke from the group as Nason bowed and stepped aside to give place to Blount who came forward as the applause died and took his position beside Martha.

"Speech, Blount!" Nason called.

Blount smiled, turned to look at the bronze figure behind him, then shifted his eyes to Martha.

"I am sure you would be better pleased to hear from the little lady whose fingers worked many long hours before her dreams finally took shape in the beautiful image we have before us and which I shall be very proud to own. I must not forget, however, that I have not yet received the artist's acceptance of my humble offer. Realizing that we are a practical people and that art, if it is to have any real place in our modern life, must have its practical application, I wish to convince Miss Lane of the utmost sincerity of my inten-

Capitalism @
its finest destruction of
art

tions with regard to her work. I have no intention of placing the figure, much as I prize it personally, in an obscure corner of my own home and leaving it there to be forgotten. I have determined, in short, to do my little part towards making her work known throughout the country. To that end, I have consulted with my good friend, Mr. Nason, and have learned that small replicas of the figure can be made from metal sufficiently inexpensive to justify my having a few thousand of them struck off and distributed among the customers of my company for use as paper weights. The figure will remain the same except that it will be in miniature with stamped lettering along—"

He paused abruptly as he felt a hand upon his arm. He turned to find Craig Forrester confronting him, the check Nason had presented to Martha crumpled and clutched in his fingers.

"You have said enough... you have said enough!" Craig told him. "Don't you see what you are doing?"

On one arm he held Martha who seemed to have grown suddenly too weak to stand alone.

From some distance away came Jeannette's cry as she rushed in to relieve Craig of his burden.

And slowly, from where he had been standing apart, Amer moved down upon the group, his two arms held before him like those of a wrestler coming to meet his opponent. He was moving toward Lasker Blount, whose face had grown suddenly white at the sight of the great shoulders stooped forward and the spreading arms.

Craig, with a glance at Amer, leaped to Blount's side.

"Go away... go away!" he said in a voice that was tense from terror. "Go away... go away!"

But Blount only moved back a step, his eyes still upon Amer.

Craig turned suddenly and stood before Amer. "Amer...
Amer! For God's sake, Amer! There are women here! Amer!"

Amer paused... lifted his shoulders slowly... let his arms
fall at his sides... drew a deep breath... and smiled.

"Tell them to get out," he said. "Let them go... and take
their women with them."

With Nason's help, Craig cleared the room of all but
Martha and Jeannette and Amer.

Blount was the last to go. At the door he paused a
moment and turned upon Craig.

"Forrester," he said, "your wife and your wife's people
save you. I hope you will not forget that. As for this other...
this beast you call your friend... he is doomed."

"Get out!" Craig ordered. "We wouldn't wipe our feet
on you."

Twelve

An hour later, the four friends were together in Jeannette's
apartment.

Jeannette and Martha had talked and wept and talked
again—and had ended it all by laughing. Amer and Craig
had remained silent through it all.

Presently, however, the two men found themselves alone.

"Well, my friend," Amer said, "there you are! I heard
Blount's words when he halted at the door. He spoke the
truth. I'm doomed. Blount knows I'm dangerous. He likes
Tuttle's methods better. There will be a parade... a demonstration... a fight in the streets. The public imagination will
be fired for a day or two. The strike will be settled, the men
will go back to work, and Blount will be happy again. That's
the way the Blounts work everywhere... and that's the way
the people are taught to forget their indignation. And so

we'll go on… we'll go on till the Blounts begin to disagree among themselves. Then they'll put the Tuttles behind the bars and conscript the males who are physically fit… and the next war will be on. There'll be the same old sermons and the same old appeals and the same old vague promises… only a new slogan or two… then millions of weeping women and fatherless children."

"I believe… " Craig began, then paused. "I believe… " he began again, "I believe… "

He seemed to have lost his power to speak.

At last he broke out… angrily. "I believe the women… the women who are mothers… I believe they will remember… they will make it impossible."

As he spoke, he had an image of Millie Dyer sitting in her little cottage… the tears in her eyes… her voice broken… her face tense with rage.

Amer got up from where he had been sitting. "Let us go out… I must get out under the stars. The women will be glad to be left alone for a little while. We can talk better by ourselves."

A moment later they were on the street where Craig's car was standing at the curb before the apartment house.

They seated themselves and Craig prepared to start the engine.

Suddenly from across the street came the sound of a voice singing. Craig leaned from the side of the car and listened. A song had just ended and a burst of applause followed.

"Wait a minute," Craig said. "Let's listen."

A moment later the notes of a piano came to them from a window in the apartment house that stood on the opposite side of the street.

Then the voice came again!

"Dear one, the world is waiting for the sunrise,
Every rose is heavy with dew—"

Craig did not wait for the song to end. He stepped down from his car and started across the street.

"Wait for me," he said as he hurried away.

A few moments later he knocked at the door of Charnley's apartment. There was a sudden hush within and then Charnley opened the door. As he did so, Craig put his foot against it and held it.

"Will you tell Marion that I have called for her," he said in a voice that was totally void of expression.

"Sure, old man," Charnley replied.

As he turned away to get Marion, Craig glanced into the apartment. Half a dozen men and women were lounging about in various stages of intoxication.

In a few moments, Marion presented herself alone at the doorway, dressed and ready to leave.

"Good night, all!" she cried as she passed into the hall.

Craig followed her till they reached the main entrance. Then he laid a hand on her shoulder.

"Wait a minute," he said.

He looked at her, coldly, silently.

"Marion," he said, "you have never lied to me. Did you lie to me to-night when you told me you were going out to a meeting of the executive?"

Her face was pale as she heard his question.

"I am not going to answer to you for every move I make," she evaded.

He dropped his hand.

"Very well," he said. "You have answered my question."

When they reached the car, Amer offered to get out, but Craig urged him to stay. They drove off, no word coming from either Marion or Craig as the car sped down one street after another, across the bridge where Craig had first met Amer in the fog, and finally came to the street on which stood Gilbert Nason's home.

"You will take me to mother's, please," Marion said.

"As you wish," Craig replied and sent the car around the corner.

Thirteen

"Stay with me... stay with me," Craig pleaded as he returned to the car from escorting Marion to Nason's door.

Then for more than an hour they drove along a road that followed the river westward from the city—drove till they found a bridge that brought them to the north side of the river and a long stretch of pavement that brought them back into the city again.

It was long after midnight when they arrived at the corner of Main Street and Portage Avenue. Since they had left Marion, Craig had not spoken a word. Amer had talked a little... quietly, at long intervals... talked about the beauty of the night with the starlight touching the autumn leaves with a ghostly silver glow. Amer knew what was in his friend's mind... and what was heavy on his heart. He had talked it all over with Jeannette many times. They had wondered just what would happen when Craig discovered the truth. They had promised each other to stand by him. Now that the moment had come, Amer found it impossible to do anything.

And so he talked of the night... and the stars... and the eerie light on the leaves...

As he put his car around the corner and started southward along the street in the general direction of home, a woman with a drunken companion reeled across the street in front of the car.

Automatically, with an instinct born of long experience, he brought the car to a stand within a few inches of the woman. In the glare of the head-lights she turned to look at him, her leering face twisted into a silly grin.

It was the face of Millie Dyer...

Amer heard a groan from the man beside him—a deep groan of pain such as he had heard in the battlefield when a man had been hit by a bullet.

He waited till the man and woman moved out of the way. Then he put his hand on Craig's arm.

"Let me take the wheel," he said quietly.

Without protest, Craig sat gazing before him while Amer got down and came round to the other side of the car. Then he moved into Amer's place while the latter climbed into the seat and started the car.

No word passed between them until they reached the street in front of Craig's house.

"I'll go in and stay with you to-night," Amer said quietly. "We can telephone the girls."

He helped Craig out of the car and put a hand on his arm as they started up the walk to the house.

But Craig shook the hand from his arm with a gesture of impatience and walked erect, like a soldier on duty, along the narrow pathway to the small porch that framed the doorway. He drew his latch-key from his pocket and opening the door, stepped into the house.

It was Amer who turned on the lights and telephoned to Jeannette in a voice that was almost inaudible. Then he went to the library where he found Craig slumped in a chair before his desk.

He put his hand on Craig's shoulder and was about to

suggest that they go to bed, but Craig shook his shoulder impatiently again without saying a word.

Amer drew back quietly and found a deep chair where he could sit and watch his friend in the dim light of the room.

After a long time he saw him lift a pencil and lean forward as if to write on a piece of paper that lay under his hand.

For fully half an hour the pencil moved jerkily, and yet with a regularity that was not writing. Then the pencil was laid aside and Amer got quietly to his feet and glanced over his friend's shoulder.

On the sheet of white paper were a number of small triangles—and in the centre, a large triangle the lines of which had been traced over and over till they were little more than a blur.

He moved back noiselessly to his chair and sat down.

And so the two friends sat till it was morning.

CHAPTER IV.

One

WHEN CRAIG ENTERED HIS OFFICE the next morning he was like a man in a strange dream. Some seventh sense told him that he was in his place and that some fifteen minutes were yet to spare before he must enter the trading room. He gathered his slips of paper together, thrust a half dozen trading cards into his pocket, and went into the corridors to make his early morning round of the firms for whom he had been doing business.

The first man he met was Sharples who hailed him from one end of the corridor as he stepped from his office.

"Fordyce is on the war-path this morning," he told Craig quietly. "I wouldn't be surprised to see his gang make a raid right now. We've got to stand up and take it if we're going to get out on the right side. Have you seen Charnley yet?"

"No."

"He'll be in for the opening," Sharples muttered to himself as he walked off.

A few minutes later Craig stood at the entrance to the board room and looked in at the gathering traders with a feeling as if he had come to a place he had never seen before. It was rather the feeling he had had on the morning after his return from France when he looked through the same doorway for the first time in four years. And as he watched his old associates hurrying past him and heard the voices of the messenger boys as they ran to and fro calling the names of the men they sought in the crowd, there came over him a vague feeling that he was looking on the scene for the last time.

He turned at the sound of a voice at his shoulder. It was Cade, Charnley's partner.

"Say, Magpie, are you carrying any barley for Claude Charnley?" Cade asked him.

The instinct of the trader served Craig when he replied.

"Ask Charnley."

Cade turned on his heel and strode through the doorway and across the trading floor to the farther side of the pit. A moment later Craig entered the room and took his position at the upper edge of the pit to await the sound of the gong.

Sharples' prediction concerning the Fordyce group showed signs of being fulfilled the moment the gong struck the signal for the opening. From every side the "shorts" crowded into the centre of the pit howling their offerings at an eighth, a quarter, three-eighths of a cent below the closing price of the previous day, which had been a dollar sixty-two and a quarter. Within a couple of minutes the first trade was made—at a dollar sixty-one and seven-eighths. Immediately more barley was offered at another eighth of a cent lower. The "bears" were fighting hard to control the market from the opening.

From his place at the upper edge of the pit, Craig watched carefully the men who were doing the trading. For some time he had been at pains to learn just who were in Fordyce's following. He knew them pretty well. He could see that none of the barley that had been thrown on the market at the opening had as yet been taken up by Cartwright or any of his men. Fordyce was offering barley through one broker and picking it up again through another in an attempt to depress the market.

"Pound 'er! Pound 'er!" Cartwright yelled above the voices in the pit.

For fully twenty minutes Fordyce and his followers pursued the tactics with which they had begun when the market opened. At the end of that time, probably not a thousand bushels of barley had actually changed hands although a score or more trades had been recorded at prices ranging downward to within an eighth of a cent of a dollar sixty. At that price Cartwright swept down and bought five thousand from a broker who he was convinced had been working for Fordyce. Immediately he bid an eighth of a cent more and got another five thousand. He raised the price another eighth of a cent and called for more barley. This time there was no response. Not another trade was made until the price had reached a dollar and sixty-one cents where it remained for an hour at the end of which the activity had died away and comparative quiet prevailed. Fordyce and his men had been repulsed.

Half an hour later, however, Craig sensed a new feeling in the air. Three or four times during the past few minutes he had been asked concerning Charnley's whereabouts.

Sharples came finally and led him quietly to one side, where they stood looking from a window with an air of idle curiosity at the smoke from a far-away locomotive rising against the clear sky of the morning.

"Listen, Magpie," Sharples said in a hoarse whisper, after he had talked for a few moments about the smoke, "something's gone wrong. Where's Charnley?"

"I haven't seen him," Craig replied.

"I got a story just now… never mind where… to the effect that he's through."

Craig stared at him. "Through?"

"He's quit! He's been carrying this stuff through half a dozen others—fellows we haven't known anything about. He may be long three or four million. If he's got cold feet…

by God, we're in for it! What's that?"

As he spoke the clamor in the pit rose suddenly to a deafening roar.

"Come on, Magpie—get under it and hold 'er!"

Men were hurrying across the floor from every direction. One after another, three young brokers rushed up to Craig as he approached the pit and asked the same question that Sharples had asked.

"Where's Charnley? Where's Charnley?"

But Craig was The Magpie once more. To all he turned an inscrutable face and growled in an undertone that conveyed no meaning to the men who had sought him out to give them the information they desired.

In his place once more at the top of the pit, Craig fought the bitterest fight of his life. Could it be true that Charnley had lost his nerve under the load he had been carrying and had decided to throw the burden on the men who had trusted him to make good his losses in the event of a reverse? The rumours that had gone the rounds were very evidently taken as true by the men on the floor.

At his elbow two traders spoke, their voices reaching Craig above the roar of the pit.

"Long three million... getting out of the country... report from Cade."

Three million bushels! Craig made a quick reckoning of the total amount of barley he carried for Charnley. A little less than half a million bushels. He glanced at the price recorded on the last trade. It had dropped to a dollar sixty. Already Charnley's loss on what Craig held in his name was a cent and a half a bushel—about seven thousand dollars. Craig had already given his check for seventy-five hundred dollars to cover losses on margins a couple of weeks before. A total loss to date of nearly fifteen thousand dollars if Charnley failed to make good the losses he had sustained. And for every additional cent the market dropped another five thousand dollars must be paid to the clearing-house!

The clamour in the pit had become deafening. One after another, the men who had been buying for Charnley threw their holdings into the market, preferring to take their present losses rather than risk complete bankruptcy by holding on in the hope of a recovery.

On the opposite side of the pit from Craig, Cartwright stood, his hands in his pocket, a grin of defiance on his face. He looked across at Craig now and then and smiled grimly as the price continued to drop, an eighth at a time, until it had finally reached a dollar fifty-nine.

When the next trade was made at a loss of another eighth of a cent, Sharples stepped up beside Craig and caught his arm.

"God, Magpie, if this thing goes on for another half hour, I'm broke! I'll not be able to put up the margins at the close. Two more cents and I'm done! That'll make the fourth time in my life that I've gone through the bottom— clean to hell!"

Craig seized Sharples and swung him about till the two men faced each other.

"You're not going yellow, are you?" he shouted above the din. "There are only three of us left—you and I and Cartwright. The rest have cold feet."

As he spoke, Cartwright came into the market once more and bought three lots, one after another in quick succession, in an attempt to change the sentiment a little. But his efforts were of little avail. Fordyce and his men were "pounding" the market with all their power. Fordyce would buy five thousand bushels and offer it immediately at an eighth of a cent lower. He would buy ten thousand and sell it again at a half a cent a bushel less than he paid for it.

And through it all Craig stood as he had stood in the old days when they had first called him The Magpie... unmovable... silent... his face grave and determined as he watched the churning mass about him like a hungry pack howling for the blood of their victim.

When the price finally touched a dollar and fifty-nine cents, Craig heard a new voice above the clamour. It was Sharples'. He had said a loss of two cents would make him bankrupt. One cent had melted away—he had only another cent to work on. Only good luck would make it possible for him to get rid of his load before the market broke below a dollar and fifty-seven.

Only two men were left to wage the fight against the Fordyce gang—Cartwright and The Magpie. And these two eyed each other across the scrambling traders as two men might regard each other across a placid pool of water lying under the sun.

When the price touched a dollar and fifty-seven, Sharples withdrew and left the floor. He had sold out his holdings and had gone back to his office a penniless man.

"Just about all one man could expect of another," Craig thought to himself as he saw Sharples disappear into the corridor.

He glanced at the clock. Only ten minutes were left before the gong should sound again for the close. Five minutes later, with the price at fifty-seven, Cartwright came into the market once more and bought everything that was offered him, in a last determined effort to turn back the enemy. Fordyce's men fell upon him in a mass, the din rose to a deafening climax, collars and ties were torn away by clutching fingers, men hurled themselves bodily into the thick of the conflict as if their lives depended upon the fortunes of the next few minutes—and then, clear across the tumult of cries came the note of the gong!

The market was closed!

The cries died down quickly, the men left the pit and scattered to all parts of the floor, the hum of voices was broken only by the sharp staccato of the telegraph keys, the crowd thinned until there were only a few stragglers left in the room, the recorders climbed down from their places and went off in twos and threes to where their coats and hats hung in the lobby, the doorkeeper spoke sharply to a half dozen lingerers and was chaffed for his officiousness, the janitors appeared with their brooms and brushes to mop up the fragments of paper that littered the floor, the doors were closed and only the faint echoes from the corridors floated back as a reminder of the struggle that was past.

As Craig left the building, Cartwright came up behind him and touched his shoulder.

"Magpie... by God, we could lick that whole gang ourselves if we had it to do. Did you go far behind?"

"Not far... but enough to do."

"Where in hell is Charnley? What happened to him?"

Craig shook his head. A fear had gripped his heart that made him afraid to speak of Charnley. Before leaving his office he had telephoned home. When he had received no reply, he had called Mrs. Nason, only to learn that Marion had gone out about noon and would not be back till five o'clock. Then he had called Charnley's apartment without getting any response.

Of course... a man must not knuckle under to fear... especially when there was only a suspicion.

Besides, he had to give his mind to other things for the

present... He had figured his losses following the close of the market. He had been forced to write a check for eighteen thousand, nine hundred dollars.

And his total credit in the bank was less than fifteen thousand dollars!

That afternoon was to remain forever a blank in the mind of Craig Forrester.

He had first gone home and searched through each room in turn for some trace of Marion.

From there he had gone to the Nason home and walked about the house without speaking to Mrs. Nason who followed him from place to place, asking him questions he did not hear.

He had gone to Charnley's apartment only to find the door locked and had waited for an interminable time, knocking and listening, waiting and knocking and listening again, only to turn away at last like one lost.

He had gone to Jeannette's place... knocked... waited... and listened. There was no response. Had the world, then, grown suddenly cold... was there no friend anywhere whose voice he might listen to for just a moment while he felt his way back again out of the darkness that was closing in about him?

Then he had remembered that Amer had gone with him to the office and had left him to attend a meeting of the strikers in the north end of the city.

He had driven to the Board of Trade Building where Martha had held her exhibit... How long ago it seemed! There he had found both Martha and Jeannette busy packing the exhibit to send it back to the Lane farm. He had watched them in silence for a long time. Then they had heard him mutter something about having to find Charnley... a loss in the market... had Marion come back? And after he had gone they realized that he had acted strangely.

From there he had driven over the city... up one street... down another... looking into the faces of everyone he met... seeking... seeking.

When it was dusk he had come back home and put his car in the garage at the back of the house. For a long time, then, he had wandered about the garage, tinkering at this and that... lifting something only to put it down again... wiping the dust from his car... going to the house for something only to forget what he wanted when he got there... returning to the garage and tinkering again...

Finally he had stood for a long time looking into the odds-and-ends box... vaguely wondering if what he sought might not be there...

Then he realized that it was something else he sought... not in the odds-and-ends box... but in the streets...

He left the garage and walked out into the street, found his way across the bridge in the deepening darkness, saw that there was a heavy fog settling on the river, but passed on without pausing to seek out the beauty he had once seen there.

And presently, when it had grown quite dark, he came again to the house where Charnley lived.

Two

When he knocked on the door, little hollow echoes awoke at the ends of the corridors.

Presently a step sounded lightly from within... the doorknob turned softly... the door opened uncertainly.

Marion's face appeared before him for a second, then vanished suddenly as the door was closed abruptly. A madness seized him. Stepping back a little he hurled the whole weight of his body against the door. There was a crash of splintering wood and a startled cry from within. He stepped back once more to break the barrier that still obstructed his path, but as he prepared to spring, Marion's face appeared once more and he stepped through the open doorway.

Closing the door behind him, he followed her into a large room where only the night before there had been merrymaking among Charnley's friends.

Marion sank into a chair and buried her face in her hands.

He looked at her unsteadily a moment, then took a step towards her.

"I want you... to come home," he said.

But she did not reply. He heard her sobbing softly and started forward to console her. Half way, he paused.

"No... no... not that," she said. "It always hurts me... that. I want him... Claude."

She continued to sob.

"Where is he?" he asked.

His voice was as gentle now as if he were speaking to a child. When she did not answer, he went to a chair on the opposite side of the room from her and sat down.

With his hands resting on the arms of the chair, he looked at her for a moment, then at the rich furnishings of the apartment, its curtains of fine velour, its polished table with a small wrack of books in the centre of it, its deeply upholstered couch, its tall lamp with shade of figured silk, its mirror and its pictures that adorned the walls, its piano with the white keys shining in the soft light.

Well... he had found her... he could rest a little before they went back home...

Back home? Were they going back home again?

The sharp click of a key in a lock caused him to turn his eyes toward the door that led into the hall. A door was opening somewhere... and was closing again. There was a sound of a footfall... and then... a voice.

"Marion!"

The voice had spoken very low, but it was the voice of Claude Charnley.

A sob broke from Marion and Charnley stepped quickly into the room.

From where he sat, Craig eyed him for some moments in silence. Then he got slowly to his feet, as if rising cost him a great effort. As he did so, Charnley came slowly across the floor and stood between him and Marion.

No word was spoken until Craig presently drew a deep breath and passed a hand over his eyes as if to clear his vision.

"They told me you were gone," he said. "We held them... the Fordyce crew... Cartwright and I held them..."

He laughed... a strained laugh... the laugh of a man whose senses have left him.

"We can do it... to-morrow... Charnley... with your help... your money... your hundred thousand. That was lucky, eh?"

Charnley spoke for the first time.

"I can't help you, old man. I didn't tell you, but I lost every cent in a flax deal a month ago. I can't help you with a dollar."

The man to whom he spoke looked dazed for a moment, then smiled. Then he began rocking slowly back and forth and rubbing the palms of his hands on his thighs. The muscles about his mouth grew tense, he sniffed a little, put his head on one side, and smiled again.

"Of course... lost... of course!"

His smile grew to a laugh as he stepped toward Charnley and lifted his hands slowly.

"Of course... lost! I don't care... not now. Now that I've found her... Money... huh! Well... come on... home!"

Charnley looked at him in terror.

"God—he's mad!" he whispered hoarsely.

As he spoke, Marion sprang up from where she had been sitting and with a cry seized Charnley's arm.

"Don't be afraid, Marion," said a voice that should have been Craig's, a voice so strange that she could never have recognized it. "I won't let him hurt you... I'll get him."

The words had no sooner left his lips than he sprang at Charnley and caught his two shoulders in his powerful hands. He lurched backward suddenly and turned. Charnley's feet left the floor and he shot bodily through the air and crashed to the floor at the farther end of the room. He gathered himself together and springing to his feet, made a rush for the door. But Craig was upon him again. Seizing him about the waist he lifted him clear of the floor and threw him back into the room where he fell scrambling at the feet of Marion.

In a moment he was on his feet again and with Marion behind him, was setting himself for a third assault. But none came.

Near the door, Craig stood breathing heavily from his exertions. His face had lost its tense expression. For the moment he looked as he had always looked, the glance from his clear eyes piercingly cold, his eyelids slightly closed, his head thrust forward.

"I know... I know," he said. "Both liars... and I ought to kill you... here... now... with my two hands. I ought to break you... like this..."

As he spoke he picked a vase from a stand beside him and crushed it between his hands.

"Like this..."

He lifted the table that held the books and reduced it to splinters on the floor at his feet.

He tore bric-a-brac from its place against the wall and crumpled it in his fingers.

He tore the curtains from the arch that led into the hall and ripped them to ribbons.

He seized the tall lamp that stood beside the piano, snapped the slender pedestal over his knee and sent the pieces crashing into the mirror against the wall.

Suddenly there was a thumping at the door and he turned toward it, a look of expectancy in his face.

"Amer!" he said. "Amer!"

He strode to the door and flung it open.

"Amer!"

But it was not Amer. The superintendent of the block had come to learn the cause of the disturbance.

He brushed the man aside and stepped into the hall.

"Amer! Amer, where are you? Amer! Amer!"

Presently he reached the street. Hatless he hurried off through the darkness.

"Amer!… Amer!… "

Three

Something led him northward along the main street of the city. It was there he had hoped to find Amer earlier in the day.

As he approached Market Square, the street was full of men and women who were hurrying in the same direction with him. No one seemed to pay any attention to the man who was running bare-headed along the street, crying unintelligible things as he picked his way in and out among the crowd. From somewhere ahead came the cries and clamour of a mob.

Directly in front of the City Hall, he came into the centre of the convulsed mob that filled the street from side to side.

He paused a moment and looked around at the faces made red by the glow of burning torches.

"Amer!... "

No response reached his ears. But above the heads of those nearest him he saw something that arrested his attention.

Somewhere in there he had caught sight of a face... a face that was familiar... he had seen it a moment and then it was gone...

He pushed his way through the crowd, his eyes fixed on the spot where he had last seen the face. Something was happening there... someone he knew was in trouble...

He did not see the blows that were being struck on either side of him... he did not hear the cries and curses that filled the air... he was searching...

There it was again... it was the pale, thin face of the boy he had known as Ivan...

Even as he looked the face disappeared once more... Ivan had been struck down...

Someone in that mob saw Craig leap forward into the thick of the struggling mass...

"God... there goes the Magpie! Look!"

The man who spoke saw Craig fight his way to the centre where lay the helpless body of the boy who had been struck down... saw him strike left and right at anyone who blocked his way... then saw him set upon by a half dozen at once. He threw them off him and cleared a space before him only to be set upon from another quarter by half a dozen more.

In the torchlight a heavy club rose suddenly behind him... and fell...

"He's down... The Magpie's down!... "

The man who spoke was Croker.

"Good God... he's up again!... "

And it was true. Lifting himself from the pavement, he stood above the body of the boy and fought with all the fury of a madman to turn back the unreasoning ones who crowded in to attack him. For a full minute he fought... then it was as if a great flame of fire had leaped suddenly in his brain... and after that... a great darkness...

CHAPTER V.

One

CRAIG'S FIRST IMPRESSION WAS OF A WORLD all white and strangely still... and then of white objects moving noiselessly about and casting no shadows...

Soon voices spoke... they seemed to be speaking to him... from a great distance...

Then he was aware of something touching his hand... ever so softly... and again a voice that spoke very close to him now...

"Craigie!"

He turned his head... slowly... painfully... then closed his eyes as the whole world about him began to turn dizzily... round and round...

Presently he opened his eyes again.

He could see clearly now, for a moment. He was lying on a white bed... in a white room. Someone was sitting beside him... looking down at him... touching his hand with her fingers...

"Marty!"

His voice was little more than a whisper and strangely unlike his own.

"Craigie! Don't move... don't talk."

Then, after a little while, he seemed to fall asleep again.

When he awoke, he was alone. A form clad all in white came to him and spoke very softly, then moved away. In a moment Martha Lane stepped noiselessly to the side of the bed and lifted his hand.

"Are you feeling better, Craigie?" she asked.

"Lots," he replied. "I'm... all right."

After a moment he tried once more to speak.

"But where's... where is..."

Martha leaned over him. "Don't talk, Craigie—not yet a while."

He began to realize that something terrible must have happened to him. The thought turned him sick. He closed his eyes again as if he would shut out the sight of something he did not wish to see.

And after a moment, he fell asleep once more.

There followed days, then, days during which he slept long hours away and awoke to find Martha coming towards him and presently to feel her fingers caress his brow and touch his hand.

And always he knew he must not talk, must not ask questions... especially, it seemed, he must not ask about Marion...

Then one day came Jeannette and with her, Amer, to stay for only a few minutes without much talking... and then to go away again just when he wanted to ask Amer some questions. The manner of their going made him wonder, too. Jeannette had kissed him with tears in her eyes and Amer had stood for a long time holding his hand and pressing his fingers softly, the tears streaming from his great dark eyes.

They thought he had not seen that... but he had... and he remembered.

Days after, he asked Martha why they didn't come, but she patted his hand gently and told him they would be back soon.

Something told him they would not come again...

Two

As the days passed and he grew stronger, he became more and more silent.

Then one day he was told he might sit up in bed with the pillows behind him for support. He smiled to himself at the efforts Martha and the nurse put forth to lift his shoulders so that they could get the pillows into position. He thought it funny that his arms were so nearly useless to help them.

But when he lay back against the pillows and looked at Martha standing beside him, he made up his mind to talk.

"Sit down, Marty," he said. "I want to talk to you."

She sat down close to the bedside.

"You have not told me anything," he said. "Lately I haven't asked... because I know. I don't know yet... just what happened. If it's bad for me to know it... I can wait. But I remember... something. I remember seeing her... and him that was with her... and I remember breaking something in my hands... I didn't harm them, did I?"

"No, no, Craigie."

"I'm glad... I remember something... a strange feeling about my temples... a feeling as if somewhere inside a rubber band had been stretched till it wouldn't go back again... And I remember a crowd somewhere and... what happened after that?"

"You were hurt," Martha told him, "and they brought you here."

"Then you came... and you've been with me ever since."

For a while he was silent.

"Don't sit up too long," she cautioned him. "If you feel tired you must let me know."

"Tired?" he smiled. "I'm as fit as a fiddle! Marty... you and I made a mistake when we..."

Though her heart was hungry for what he wanted to say, she got up quickly and leaned over him.

"Craig, dear, you mustn't talk any more. Let me take the pillows away."

He drew a deep sigh and let her have her way. Then he lay down on the bed and put his head on the cool pillow.

After all... it was very comfortable there... and he was tired... and yet... a great hunger had entered his heart...

Three

Days later, when he was permitted to leave his bed and sit in a chair by the window, he had a visit from Croker.

Martha left them alone together in the room and closed the door behind her as she went out.

They had cigarettes and a cup of hot tea while Croker chattered freely about all manner of things that had occurred since Craig had left the world.

The strike had been settled at last—as Amer had predicted it would be settled—with a victory for Blount. Tuttle still swayed the minds of his "people" and moved them with his fiery eloquence, but already his position was becoming a little uncertain. It seemed a new voice, as eloquent as his own, had made itself heard as a result of the failure of the strike, a failure for which many were disposed to hold Tuttle responsible. In the meantime, Blount was more secure than ever. Nason's men had returned to their work and Nason himself had hired an efficiency expert to reorganize his plant. In Europe, the time-honoured game of secret diplomacy was fast becoming the favourite sport of the governments.

Although Craig had been confined to his bed for less than three weeks, Croker told him the news as he might have told it to a man who had just returned from a year's sojourn in the northern wilds.

After a long silence, Craig spoke up at last.

"Of course, Croker," he said, "you haven't come in to tell me all this—though it's interesting—and I'm glad to hear you talk again. But they let you in because they knew you had the nerve to tell me what none of the others would mention. Well... tell me. Out with it!"

Croker lighted himself another cigarette.

"You're a good guesser, Magpie," he said. "I guess I needn't tell you about what happened on the market the next day. You've got that pretty well figured out here by yourself."

"I've got that figured out—just as you say. They'd have to sell me out. There won't be a thing left. But that's what a man may look for any time in life... and it really doesn't matter... a lot. But there'll be time to think of that later." He waited for Croker to go on.

"Well, since you must know... they have gone."

"Gone..." Craig repeated. "I feared as much... I believe I expected it... only I didn't let myself admit it. To tell you the truth, Croker... well, let's say no more about it just now. It's... it's ugly!"

"I have managed to keep it pretty well out of the papers," Croker remarked. "Of course a thing like that can't be kept—"

"I know... I know," Craig interrupted him. "That was good of you. And Amer... something has happened there, I know. I knew it when he came to see me the last time."

"Yes... Blount won out in handy style all round. Poor old Amer was arrested on a charge of having treasonable literature in his possession. He was given a quick trial by the authorities and was made an example of to the community. He's now on his way back to England... deported."

Craig was silent for a long time after Croker had ceased speaking. Finally he looked up.

"And Jeannette... of course... "

"Oh, she went with him. At least she followed on the next boat. He told me she had consented to marry him as soon as they arrived on the other side. And he was as pleased about it as a boy."

"And so the world goes on," Craig said slowly.

"And so the merry goes round," Croker added with a smile.

Four

When the month of October was drawing to a close in a glorious Indian summer, Craig stepped aboard a street car in the late afternoon.

For several days he had been going about the city in the pursuit of the ugly business he had still to do. There were lawyers and documents and sworn statements —and a host of other things that could not be avoided. He had come out of it all with only a few dollars in his pocket and without a foot of real estate in the city. His house was gone and his car, and he had surrendered his seat on the exchange to help meet his obligations. But when he was through, penniless as he was, he owed no man a dollar. He was free.

The car took him south from the city to a point where he found another awaiting him to carry him southward still through many miles of open country with quaint little French-Canadian settlements on either hand. He ate his supper at a little French house where he was known and paid them for a night's lodging.

And while the night was but half gone, he stole out under the stars and took the road that led into the east. When he had walked a couple of hours or more, the grey promise of a new day began to lift before him. From the side of the road came the sound of a waking bird. Presently the leaves that still clung to the branches of the trees began to take on colour, yellow and brown and crimson. And in the sky before him as he walked steadily on, the shafts of gold shot to the zenith, flooding the earth with the faint glow of early dawn. Then, suddenly, the woods were awake with flocking birds that rose from the ground in clouds and settled among the branches of the trees.

Finding a little slope all soft-carpeted with brown leaves, he threw himself upon the ground to rest a while before he went on. And as he lay with his body stretched at full length upon the earth, new strength seemed to come to him, the fresh new strength of the earth itself. And when the sun rose, he lifted himself from the ground and made his way still eastward with the new day on his face and brow.

Another hour brought him to a field he had known and had remembered often in his dreams. As he stood beside it and let his eyes cover its generous expanse, a team of dark horses entered the field at the farther end and stood while their driver hitched them to a plough. Presently there came a sound of the ploughman's voice and the horses strained forward in their traces. He watched them come down the full length of the field, leaving behind them a fresh new furrow through the stubble.

And when they were still some distance away, he clambered through the fence and waited till their heads were within reach of his hands.

Farmer Lane stepped from behind the plough and looked at him.

"Well, it's taken you a damn' long time to get back where you belong," said Farmer Lane.

Craig smiled. "I'm not there yet," he replied. "I want to get over on that place my dad left with you."

"If you think you're fit for it, after living like a tramp for the best part of your days."

For answer Craig took his position behind the plough and put the horses about. A moment later he had them headed toward the other end of the field, leaving behind them a furrow as true and straight as its mate.

"Well," Farmer Lane remarked, "you've not lost the knack. Maybe you'll do. You'd better go in and get some breakfast."

A short walk brought him to the gate at the end of the little path leading to an open doorway in which stood Martha Lane with the sun in her hair.

"I have come back," he said as he came before her and gave her his hands.

And together they went into the house and closed the door behind them.

The End

THE THROWBACK SERIES reintroduces public-domain books to contemporary readers, continuing the vital work of keeping Canadian stories alive and available. Our Throwback books also give back: a percentage of each book's sales will be donated to a designated Canadian cultural organization.

INVISIBLE PUBLISHING produces fine Canadian literature for those who enjoy such things. As an independent, not-for-profit publisher, our work includes building communities that sustain and encourage engaging, literary, and current writing.

Invisible Publishing has been in operation for over a decade. We released our first fiction titles in the spring of 2007, and our catalogue has come to include works of graphic fiction and nonfiction, pop culture biographies, experimental poetry, and prose.

We are committed to publishing diverse voices and experiences. In acknowledging historical and systemic barriers, and the limits of our existing catalogue, we strongly encourage LGBTQ2SIA+, Indigenous, and writers of colour to submit their work.

Invisible Publishing is also home to the Bibliophonic series of music books and the Throwback series of CanLit reissues.

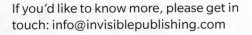 If you'd like to know more, please get in touch: info@invisiblepublishing.com

 Invisible